Other Works by Elias Anderson

Blood and Gasoline
15 Tales of Albert Fishman/Magic
The opiate Inside
Fire the Hand
Cookie Cutter Man

IN BLOOD AND BONE

THE DARK SEASON I

IN BLOOD AND BONE

ELIAS ANDERSON

First Printing: 2021

ISBN 978-1-7346486-4-5

Epic Publishing
www.epic-publishing.com

Special discounts are available on quantity purchases. For details, contact the publisher by email at publisher@epic-publishing.com or at the following address:

Epic Publishing
370 Castle Shannon Blvd., #10366
Pittsburgh, PA 15234

To Dayna, who gave me the best years of my life and whom I will never, ever stop trying to impress.

Also, to my son and daughter, two of the bravest, funniest, most amazing kids I ever could have hoped for.

I love the three of you more than I could ever explain.

CHAPTER
ONE

AJ looked up at the clock, not knowing in one minute he'd fall in love and, in three, he'd see his first dead body. It was 2:42 A.M.

A car pulled into the lot, the driver killing the engine and stepping out. AJ expected a night person: the paranoid, the destitute, or the stoned. Instead, it was a girl. Not a crackhead or a whore but a normal *girl*, and not many came in alone this time of night. This rare girl was not beautiful, or anything so mundane, but drop dead gorgeous, with blonde hair just past her shoulders, eyes the color of clover, and a smile that stopped his pulse.

"Hi," AJ said, feeling like a jackass.

"Hi." She headed to the refrigerated drink section, which glowed in the dingy gas station lighting as would the first star in a midnight sky, and with her, she took his heart. He saw a cockroach scurrying across the dirty tile floor and hoped she wouldn't notice.

She set a bottle of soda on the counter. "And can I

get a pack of smokes, please?"

"What's your poison?"

She smiled again. "Marlboro Lights."

AJ rang up her purchases, thinking he would sell his soul for a girl like this. "Six thirty-seven."

She swiped her card in the machine. "So, what's it like working here?" she asked. "Get a lot of weirdos?"

"Oh, yeah. You wouldn't *believe* the freaks that come in this time of night," AJ said.

"Oh, *really?*"

"Well, you know. Other than you, I mean." Red crept across AJ's face.

"How do you know?" she asked.

"How do I know what?"

"What kind of person I am. I mean, I could be Lizzie Borden, Tipper Gore. *Anybody.*"

"I've developed an eye for it working here. Now, if you'd come in twitching and talking to yourself, it'd be a different story."

She laughed and opened her cigarettes. "Do you mind if I smoke in here?"

"Nope," AJ said, flicking his Zippo open for her. "So, what's your name?"

"Clover."

Like her eyes, AJ thought. He felt himself blush and occupied himself by getting out a cigarette of his own to smoke with her. "I'm—"

She pointed to his name tag. "AJ. I know. I saw it when I came in."

"So. Clover. What brings you to Vito's Gas-N-Go at this time of ni…" AJ trailed off when a man walked into the store. He was a younger guy but had the old, wizened face of a drug addict. He wore an old, dirty trench coat, faded jeans, and a black, knitted hat.

He twitched.

"Can I help you?" AJ asked. The man in the doorway shuffled inside, the sound of his movements somehow empty.

"You okay?" AJ asked. "You need an ambulance or something?"

The man shook his head and tried to speak. His mouth moved, producing a gravelly whisper.

"What?" AJ's nose wrinkled as the guy got closer. It smelled like the guy had shit his pants.

"A-a..." The man cleared his throat and took another step forward, the only thing between them now was the counter.

His face was covered in acne, and even from where he stood, AJ could plainly see his teeth were for shit. The ones left in his head were either rotten or on their way. Meth, maybe? Smack? AJ didn't know what particular flavor the guy was killing himself with, only that it was one of them. Like he'd told Clover, he kinda had an eye for it.

"A..." the junkie said again.

"A what?" AJ asked, knowing the guy was high as shit.

"You...mmm...A...AJ?"

How in the... Oh. The name tag. "Yeah, that's me. Who are you?"

The man grinned, and then his hands, cold from the night air he'd been walking through, were around AJ's throat.

"Get off him!" Clover grabbed one of the junkie's arms, trying to pull him away. She got a backhand in the mouth that sent her to the floor.

AJ twisted free, ducking toward the counter, and pulling out a wooden baseball bat. It *whooshed* when he swung it, connecting solidly with the attacker's temple. The psycho blinked twice and shook his head to clear it, eyes narrowing.

"Oh, shit," AJ said, thinking, *PCP, maybe?*

The junkie's lips twisted into an ugly grin, and he punched AJ in the face.

AJ staggered back. He could already feel his eye swelling.

Clover was on her feet again. She grabbed a bottle of wine off the rack near the counter and swung for the fences, the bottle exploding against the back of the junkie's head. Cheap merlot and black glass spilled to the floor.

It was as if the man hadn't felt it. He turned, grabbed her by the face, and shoved her. She staggered back half a dozen steps and slammed into a display rack of pre-packaged pastries, knocking Hostess cakes and mini-donuts to the floor.

AJ adjusted his grip on the bat, flexing his hands, and taking an extra moment to square his feet like his dad taught him.

He took another swing.

He'd only played baseball up until his freshman year of high school and had been on the JV squad even then. Still, one fine spring morning, he'd managed to hit his only home run, and he still remembered it. He would some-times close his eyes and think of that moment because it had been a good one. A great one, really: the smell of the line chalk and freshly cut grass, the contrast on the deep, lush green of the outfield, and the clear, empty blue of the late April sky.

He remembered the sound the ball made when he connected with it and how he hadn't felt it. There had been a split second where he thought he'd given it the big whiff and struck out, but then the bench and the small crowd in the hometown stands exploded. The perfect white sphere of the ball shrank as it went over the centerfield fence, still on its upward trajectory.

This was like that, but it wasn't.

It was almost three in the morning, and it was cold out. Instead of the perfect, crisp light of the spring sun, there was the flickering of old fluorescent bulbs, the bodies of dozens of dead and ancient flies collected in the fixtures. The smell of dirt was there, but this was not the freshly turned and raked dirt of a baseball diamond. Rather, it was old and sour, with heavy undertones of feces.

The sound was different, too. A sound somehow both hard and wet, of something with a thick outer shell and a hollow center, a sound AJ would hear for the rest of life in the bad times, the dark times, the times he didn't want to be alone. The sound of the bat connecting with the guy's skull made his stomach turn.

Clover flinched at the wet crack, the junkie's eyes rolling back as he dropped to the floor.

AJ helped Clover steady herself as she stood amongst the fallen packages of snack cakes. A small rivulet of blood ran from her perfect lower lip, a smear of black dirt along her cheekbone from the man's hand on her face.

"You all right?" AJ asked, his voice shaking in time with his pulse hammering in his temples and the insides of his wrists.

"I think so. How's your eye?"

Eye, he thought. *What eye?*

The only eyes that mattered were hers. He held her chin and gently thumbed the blood away from her mouth. His face was reflected in those deep green pools and knew he could be happy forever if he could only see himself in them every day. For that glimmer in time, they were the only two people alive.

Then she spoke quietly, "We better call somebody."

AJ nodded and handed her the bat. "If he moves, hit him again."

Clover adjusted her hands for a better grip as AJ went to the phone.

* * *

The patrol car slowed near the intersection of 86th and Downing.

"I don't see a goddamn thing, do you?" Andrews asked, flipping on the spotlight and sweeping the sidewalk.

Fenster craned his head, looking at all four corners of the intersection.

"No, wait, I *do* see something," Andrews said. "I see a bum taking a dump behind that light pole about a block from here, but that doesn't seem like us, does it?"

"Call that one in for Animal Control," Fenster said, and the two of them chuckled. "I sure don't see no OD'ing dope-fiend, though."

Andrews grabbed the mic off the dash. "Dispatch, come back. Do you read, Dispatch? This is Four-Oh-Niner, come back?"

There was a crackle of static. "Copy 409. Dispatch reads you, over."

"We're out on eight-six and Downing, responding to that anonymous call-in? Supposed to be a man lying in the street, possible overdose? Can I get another read on that intersection?"

"That's correct, eight-six and Downing."

"Nothing to report here, Dispatch. He must have walked off."

"I'm sure he'll turn up in the morgue sooner or later," Fenster said, rolling his eyes. Goddamn needle-freaks always did.

"409, are you still in the vicinity? Come back?"

"Dispatch, 409 in the vicinity, over."

"409, we have another call, near your twenty."

"Go ahead," Andrews said.

"We have an assault at a Vito's Gas-N-Go, that's Victor India Tango Oscar—"

"I'm familiar, Dispatch. Off 75th?"

"Roger, 75th. Called in by an employee, suspect still on the scene, likely unconscious. Two civilians, including the caller."

"Now we're talking," Fenster said.

"Lighting 'em up, Dispatch. E.T.A. under five. Over."

"Roger that, 409. Report back at the scene. Over."

Andrews returned the mic and hit the switch.

"Make it scream," Fenster said.

"That's what she said," Andrews said, and they both laughed as he cranked the wheel and hit the gas.

* * *

AJ pulled the phone away from his mouth, holding it so the receiver was still tucked against his ear.

"You okay?"

"Fit as a fucking fiddle," Clover said, still holding the bat. She never took her eyes off the guy on the floor, her face a study in concentration. If that guy so much as farted she looked ready to break his spine. "You?"

"I'm on hold," AJ said.

Clover rolled her eyes. "This city's going to shit."

"Who you telling?" AJ said.

"Okay, AJ, are you still on the line?" the 911 operator asked.

"Yes, ma'am. I'm here."

"Okay, you're doing great. We have two officers just a couple blocks away. They'll be there in just a minute, okay?"

"I think I hear them coming," AJ said.

"Okay, good. When they pull into the lot, tell me. Is the person you hit with the bat still on the floor?"

"Yeah, he's not moving," AJ said. *Jesus Christ,* he thought. *He* really *isn't moving.*

"They should almost be there. Do you see them yet?" the operator asked.

"Not yet. I can definitely hear them, though. We need an ambulance, too. This guy, he needs help."

"We have an ambulance en route as well. It'll be there a few minutes after the officers, okay? The most important thing right now is your safety and that of your friend."

AJ opened his mouth to go on a rambling explanation that, while he certainly hoped he and this girl would be friends, it was still super early, and he didn't want to put a label on anything. He'd long resorted to humor under stress but, this time, he snapped his mouth shut with a click of his teeth.

"Do you see them yet?" the operator asked.

"No, I... Wait, yes, they're turning in."

"Okay, I need you and your friend to raise your hands and back up as far from the man on the floor as possible. You can hang up the phone now."

"Thank you." AJ put the receiver down as the cruiser ran through the last red light and turned into the parking lot.

"Put down the bat," AJ said, raising his hands.

"Fuck that," Clover said and, while she didn't drop the bat, she raised her hands over her head and backed with him toward the slushie machine, her eyes still locked on the man lying on the floor.

The two cops came in, their hands on the butts of their still-holstered guns.

"Clear!" one of them shouted, looking down at the man on the floor and back up to AJ. "Did you call this in?"

"Yes, sir, I—"

"Vacate," the other cop said, dropping to the floor and cuffing the man lying there. AJ tried to see what they were doing, but the first cop came forward, and Clover finally dropped the bat to the floor.

"Weapon here," the first cop said over his shoulder, ushering AJ and Clover toward the side door.

"I'll mark it," the second cop said.

"Do I need to put you in my car or can you both wait out front for me?" the cop asked. AJ looked at his nameplate, which read FENSTER.

"N-no, we'll wait out front," Clover said.

"Are you both okay?" Fenster asked. "An ambulance is on the way—"

"We're fine, man. Do what you gotta do," AJ said.

The cop nodded. "Again, straight out front. You run off, it's my ass."

"Right out front, we got it," Clover said.

Fenster nodded again and turned, trotting back toward the front of the store. AJ stared after him a moment.

"Come on," Clover said, tugging the sleeve of his hoodie.

They walked in silence toward the rear corner of the gas station, closely together, their shoulders brushing up against one another. They hit the corner and turned toward the parking lot, the alternating red-and-blue wash of the lights from the police cruiser jarring them out of their silence.

"The fuck?" AJ said.

"Right? I can't stop shaking," Clover said. Before he could take one of her hands, she stuffed them both deep into the pockets of her puffy, gray coat and huddled in on herself.

They stood on the sidewalk in front of the store, next to a trash can with an ashtray built into the top, smoking, and watching the police inside. Fenster spoke into his shoulder-mic, watching his partner, who knelt on the floor, checking their attacker's neck for a pulse.

AJ stared at the kneeling cop, willing him to find a pulse. Clover huddled closer to him, and AJ wanted to put his arm around her, but he didn't, and he didn't know why. Fenster switched places with his partner, kneeling on the floor while his partner spoke into *his* shoulder-mic. The warble of the coming ambulance rose, the scream of it swelling in the empty night.

Find it, AJ thought. *Fucking find it.*

Fenster kept checking it, putting his two fingers on the guy's neck, pausing, moving them, pausing, trying the wrist. Fenster looked up to his partner and shook his head. His partner spoke into the mic and removed the handcuffs he'd placed on the guy and, two minutes later, when the ambulance arrived, its siren no longer wailed.

CHAPTER TWO

In the parking lot sat Clover's Mazda, a squad car, an ambulance, and a rusted, green Ford. The Ford belonged to a plainclothes dick who made AJ nervous. That, and the lump the paramedics carried out of the store on a stretcher. Clover would tell the police what happened, and the security cameras inside would show it had been in self-defense but couldn't you do time for involuntary manslaughter or something?

The plainclothes dick thanked Clover and led her to the squad car, and AJ's pulse picked up a little. She wasn't cuffed, and the detective didn't put her in the car, just asked her to stay put. The paramedics had wrapped her in a thick blanket, which she had put over her head, swaddling herself up like a Russian babushka.

They made eye contact over the detective's shoulder and, though she didn't smile—looked too wiped out to smile—she gave AJ a slow nod that let him roll his shoulders and unclench his jaw and take a deep breath.

AJ took in the detective approaching him. He was heavyset, but not in a soft or flabby way, more like a chunk of rock jutting out of the earth. He wore a drab, brown trench coat and scuffed shoes. His name was John Lubbock.

"Those things'll kill ya, kid," John said as AJ lit up. The last three inches of a cigar were clamped in the detective's teeth.

"Yeah, well..."

"What's your name again?"

"AJ."

"Got a last name?"

"Oh, uh, yeah, sorry. Lancaster." He blew out a cloud of smoke, watching it dissipate in the eerie yellow of the parking lot lights. The detective nodded, and AJ shivered, zipping his hoodie up the last couple inches.

"Okay, kid," Lubbock said, "why don't you tell me what went down in there?"

AJ took a deep drag off his smoke and recounted the tale. He ended with, "...so, I told her to whack the bastard if he moved, and I called 911."

Lubbock thoughtfully chewed his cigar. "An' he didn't say nothin' to you?"

"Like I told you, he read my name tag, then he freaked."

"You get the impression he was there to rob you?"

"I mean, I guess he must've been, right? He didn't say like, 'gimme the money' or anything, just...freaked."

"An' you don't know him?" the detective asked, narrowing his eyes a little. "Maybe he's some regular customer. Comes in, has some kinda beef with you? Nothing?"

AJ shook his head. "I've never seen him before in my life."

John took off his hat long enough to scratch the back of his head. The ambulance left without turning on the lights or siren.

"So…" A lump formed in AJ's throat, stopping him from asking a question he already had the answer to.

John stared at him for a second. "Yeah?"

"Is, uh, is that guy, you know…dead?" AJ's voice cracked a little on that last syllable.

The detective's hard features softened for a moment, and he looked away while AJ wiped his eyes under the guise of scratching an itch. AJ sniffed and took another drag, huddling his arms into his sides for warmth.

Lubbock placed a blocky hand on AJ's shoulder and tossed his cigar into the gutter. "Yeah, kid. He was dead when we got here."

"I didn't, I mean, I never meant…"

The detective leaned in, giving AJ's shoulder a squeeze.

"Listen, you got no problem here. I mean, you did what *had* to be done," Lubbock said, speaking in a low, calming voice you wouldn't think the man possessed just by looking at him. He seemed to AJ to be the type of guy who would either yell, or yell really loud.

"But…I-I fuckin' *killed* him, right?"

"From what you said, and from what your girl told me, he woulda ganked you for sure, her too. You're the hero in this, junior. You ain't the bad guy."

"Yeah, well, I feel like I'm gonna puke," AJ said, taking a final drag and flicking the butt into the parking lot. "Big damn heroes, right? Why didn't he drop the first time I hit him?"

"PCP's my guess, but we know jack 'til the boys run a couple tests on him. I don't see how else he coulda stood up to that. You clubbed him pretty good, yeah?"

"Thought I was gonna knock his head off."

"Well, he was probably all junked up on some brand of shit or the other."

AJ nodded and looked at his watch. It was now a quarter after four. His replacement, a twenty-three-year-old coke hound, hadn't even made an appearance.

"So, can I go home now or what?" AJ was suddenly very tired.

"Naw. You and girlie there gotta come down and make a statement. But I'll see what I can do to speed things up for you. We contacted your boss, and—"

"There he is now."

A mint condition 1973 Coupe de Ville pulled into the parking lot. Vito Vincelli got out, a squat caricature of a Hollywood mobster, cheap suit and all. He knew how he looked and relished it, worked hard at the image. When *The Sopranos* came out, Vito started wearing track-suits and gold chains, the whole thing.

"My boy!" Vito grinned and slapped AJ on the back. "Johnny Law gave me a rough idea. You gonna give me some details?"

"Man, it was *fucked*," AJ said, tilting his head back and tapping the hand-shaped bruises on his throat.

Vito flinched. "Jesus, kid. He got you good."

"Yeah, I cracked him with that Louie, though," AJ said.

"Ain't you glad I kept it there?" Vito asked. "I *told* you that bat would come in handy."

"Hey, kid? That paperwork ain't doin' itself," John called over.

AJ turned to Vito. "I gotta go. I'll be here tomorrow night. I'll tell you then."

Vito nodded. "Hey, don't take any shit off no pig, you hear? You need one, we can get you a lawyer."

"Really?" AJ asked, relief washing through him. Despite what Lubbock had said, the idea of filed charges had been circling his head since the ambulance left.

"Of *course*," Vito said, slapping him on the back. "You got nothing to worry about, understand? Look, I'll see ya tomorrow. I'm goin' back to bed."

"Who's gonna watch the store?"

"What, Billy ain't here yet?"

"Nope."

Vito got red in the face. "It's four-fucking-thirty! That little cocksucker don't work here no more!"

"I'm sorry, man. I was gonna call you, but—"

"Go on, get outta here," Vito said, a vein standing up on his forehead. He pulled AJ in for a quick, one-armed hug, and then slapped him on the back, sending him back toward John and digging out a phone from his pocket.

By the time AJ got back to where the detective stood, Vito unloaded a string of profanities into Billy's voicemail.

"What's his name again?" John asked, watching with a cocked eyebrow as Vito gesticulated his fury, letting loose a verbal tapestry of slang and gutter English.

"He's a good guy," AJ said. "He helps me out a lot."

The detective gave Vito another slow look over, those X-ray cop eyes taking in everything, and AJ bet John was making an internal note to run a check on

Vito, just to see.

AJ knew it'd be a waste of time. He knew full well the impression Vito liked to give, and he was good at it, but the whole mobster image was for his own amusement more than anything. Sure, he owned a couple shitty little gas stations, but he also owned a few fast-food franchises, had a half-stake at a couple Starbucks, and owned a number of nice little dry-cleaning businesses. The only thing he laundered was other people's clothing.

Fuck it, though, AJ thought. *Let him look.*

AJ took a few steps toward the patrol car Clover now climbed into.

"Come on, kid, you ride with me," John said. AJ sighed and got in the detective's beat-down, old sedan, and they rode to the police station to give their statements.

***

For AJ, the next few hours were a long blur of bad coffee, and the same couple questions asked a few different ways. It was filling out paperwork and handing people his ID, and it was waiting. Mostly waiting.

He sat in a row of chairs bolted to the floor, like the kind you would find at a bus station, but somehow less comfortable. His eyes were grainy, and his stomach sour from the endless cups of awful Joe they kept bringing him.

He was exhausted, flat out. The first ninety minutes or so, he'd agonized over the man he'd killed. Did he have children who would wake up this morning and start the long process of being orphans? Was there a partner or a spouse suddenly and irrevocably alone?

What if he lived with only a dog or a cat now going to starve to death? Then there was the legality of it, and then the morality of it, and then the *reality* of it. Living the rest of his life knowing that, justified or not, he'd beaten a man to death with a Louisville Slugger.

All that agonizing had been forever ago it seemed. AJ shifted again so his ass wouldn't fall asleep and his back wouldn't cramp up.

I'd beat the fucker to death twice just for ten minutes in my own bed, he thought, surprising a snort of laughter out of himself. He felt bad for thinking it, and his stomach rolled again, but if he could make himself laugh after all this—

"What's so funny?" Clover asked, sitting down next to him, and making him jump.

"Where'd you come from?"

She leaned her head back against the wall with her eyes closed and pointed in one direction, then another. "I, hmmm, fuck it. Wherever, man. I don't know. You're next, though."

"I swear to God, if they ask me if I know that guy one more time, I'm hanging myself in the bathroom with my belt."

She held up a hand, pinkie extended. "Suicide pact?"

"Done and done," AJ said, twisting his pinkie into hers. She smiled, and he was free to take that smile in as her eyes were still closed.

"I can see you staring at me, psycho," Clover said, smiling a little.

AJ was too tired to be embarrassed or self-conscious and, instead, laughed. "Don't be a dick."

"Holy shit, this is the *worst* chair I've ever sat in," Clover said, sitting up and opening her eyes.

She sighed heavily, which turned to a yawn. She closed her eyes again and leaned her head on his shoulder, and it was the best part of his day. His week, maybe.

"They called my parents," Clover said. "This night is going to get so much worse for me."

"Why'd they call your parents?"

"I'm a minor."

"Oh, uh, huh. A minor."

"Yeah. Well, only *technically* a minor. I'll be eighteen in like, only four years."

"Get the fuck outta here," AJ said, laughing.

"I had you going, though, right?"

"What? No."

"*Oh, uh-huh, a minor,*" she said, dropping her voice a couple octaves and mocking him. "No, apparently my roommate woke up and kinda flipped that I wasn't home, and then that bitch called my parents, who have been looking for me ever since. My dad has been certain since the day I left home I was going to be murdered in an alley or something. So, of *course*, he's losing his mind. It's a whole thing."

"We could always go on the lam," AJ said, looking out the corner of his eyes at the top of her head, still leaning against his shoulder. Ten minutes ago, he would have given anything to be back home but now felt like he could sit there forever.

"Let's do it," she said. "We can hitch back to my car and just drive."

"We'll have to dump it eventually, steal something else."

"Oh, definitely. We could get a couple miles, though, switch the plates."

They sat in silence for a long moment, and then she spoke again.

"AJ?"

"Yeah?"

"Will you call me tomorrow?"

"Yeah," AJ said, smiling. "I'd like that."

"Me too," Clover said.

She sat up long enough to give him her number and settled against him again when a uniformed officer came to tell her that her parents were there, and that AJ was needed one last time.

She squeezed his hand, and they stood up together.

"Well," AJ said. "Good luck."

"I'm gonna need it, for sure," she said, turning to face him. "So, if they don't kill me, talk to you tomorrow?"

"Absolutely. If they lock me up, you'll be my one phone call."

She smiled, and it turned a light on in his heart.

Kiss her, you fucking nimrod, he thought.

Those few seconds slowed and stretched, and he was just about to lean in when the officer cleared his throat. Her smile faltered just that one little bit, and he could almost hear the window banging shut.

"Your parents are waiting," the cop said again, once more pointing toward the giant set of double doors.

"Got it. Thanks, man!" Clover said, her voice so full of gratitude and cheer there was no chance it was anything but sarcasm. AJ wondered if she had felt that moment of connection, too.

"Tomorrow then?" he asked.

"Tomorrow." She hit him with that smile again and walked off in the direction the officer pointed.

AJ stretched his back, which didn't really bother him as much anymore.

"Sorry for the holdup," the uni said.

"No worries," AJ said, looking once more toward the double doors Clover had walked through. "It's good. All good."

CHAPTER THREE

About seven hours before AJ dialed 911, and most of the way across the state from him, the battering-ram roar of a Harley Davidson shattered the quiet serenity of the countryside. The crumbling and pitted blacktop forced the bike to a crawl, the impatience of the driver evident in the way he gunned the engine.

Eventually, the busted and mostly forgotten road ended where a forest began, leaving two choices: turn right, or go back.

Here was the bright blue mailbox on a thick iron post the man on the Harley had been told to expect. He turned the bike, going across a cattle guard and up a road that, while unpaved, was well-packed and in better shape than the one he'd taken to get to it.

The bushes and trees had grown close enough to the little road to have scratched the paint of most anything wider than the Harley, but the bike passed untouched through their silent, reaching fingers. After about a quarter mile, the road curved, and the bushes and trees gave way to a large, well-manicured lawn.

In the center of the yard was a small white house in good repair, with a neat little porch out front.

The bike rolled to a stop in the driveway, and the man riding it gunned the engine once more, the sound of it rolling across the empty land like thunder. When he dropped the kickstand and shut down the bike, the silence seemed louder than the Harley. He dismounted the bike and walked up to the porch. To the left of the front door were two wicker chairs, a small glass-topped wicker table set between them.

Before he could reach the steps, the door opened, and out stepped the man he'd been sent to find. Short and of Asian descent, standing only five-five or so. He was thin and neatly dressed, wearing a light blue shirt buttoned all the way to the collar and tucked into dark blue slacks. His hair was cropped short and thinning in the front and on top, black, but heavily threaded with gray.

He had a neatly trimmed mustache that had not yet grayed as much as his hair. He somewhat awkwardly held a small package wrapped in plain brown paper and a white envelope tucked between his forearm and chest.

"Mr. Perish, yes?" he asked from his porch.

"That's correct," Mr. Perish said.

The man on the porch put his free hand out as though offering it to a dog to sniff, one perhaps already growling at him, and he opened his mouth to introduce himself.

"I know who you are, Jin," Perish said.

"Of course, you do, yes," Jin said, withdrawing his

hand with a clear expression of relief. "I was, ah, told to expect you, and to have this…ah, *artifact*, ready to give you? And the letter?"

Jin held out the box and envelope, his expression somehow both full of hope and regret. He was eager to be rid of them, but loathe to give either away.

"Let's sit first," Perish said. "Talk."

Jin hesitated, eyes flicking back toward his house, but he did as bade, taking the wicker chair nearest the door. Perish took the other one. Jin placed the parcel and envelope on the glass top of the table, setting them down slowly, carefully, then sliding them a bit closer to Perish, who ignored both.

In the front window of the house sat a red Abyssinian cat, perched on the ledge along the sill inside, its yellow eyes staring like lamps. It flicked its giant ears and meowed at them through the screen.

Perish sat there, staring at the owner of the cat and the neat little house, Jin sitting and staring back at his reflection in Perish's sunglasses.

"So, ah," Jin said, brushing nonexistent wrinkles out of the front of his shirt, then scratching his neck, "this will…conclude our business?"

Perish shook his head slowly back and forth, and something in the other man's face fell.

"There's something else coming, Detective—"

"I'm retired."

Perish took his glasses off, narrowing his gaze. Jin flinched back from it, if only a little, and shifted in his seat.

"We may still require your services, down the road," Perish said.

Jin looked down at his hands, folded in his lap. Perish noted the shaking in those hands. Perish exhaled deeply and set his sunglasses on the table, next to the parcel, the frames clicking against the glass top.

"This thing coming up, this is huge. Things are moving faster now," Perish said.

Jin swallowed hard. "I understand," he said in a low voice.

Perish leaned back in his chair, pointing at the envelope on the table. "Will this convince him?"

"John's a good man," Jin said. "He doesn't deserve this."

"But will this convince him?"

"He doesn't deserve this! Can't you find someone else? Can't they—"

"There *is* no one else," Perish snapped, leaning forward. "Not unless you want to come out of retirement. No? Okay. Then there's no one else. There are the two men in Bridgetown, but it's not their time yet, so John is who we have to work with, since you can't—won't—help us."

"I did help you!"

"But she got away, didn't she?" Perish asked.

Jin recoiled as though slapped and hung his head.

"Don't you worry, though," Perish said, standing up and collecting his glasses, placing them in a pocket inside his long black coat, "someone else will pick up after you."

"They got the governor involved! I took that case as far as humanly possible."

"Did you?" Perish asked.

"It cost me my career! Almost my *life*."

"*Oh. Well*, as long as *you* have *your* life, that's what

matters. Your nice little house, your cat. She's started killing again, Jin, did you know that? Sit and think about that, why don't you. People are already dying while you sit here, petting your cat and telling yourself you've retired."

"I *am* retired!" Jin snapped, his hands clenched into fists so tight the knuckles glowed white against his otherwise golden skin. "They *made* me retire!"

"If you're so fucking *retired*, how did you even *find* this?" Logan asked, finally picking up the small package. "This, and everything else you keep in that trunk full of secrets in the back of your closet?"

Jin flinched at the mention of his trunk. "How did you know—"

"You said it yourself, right? Cain knows everything." Perish picked up the parcel from the table and waggled it at the retired detective. "Pray to whatever god you believe in I'm able to bring this back to you,"

Inside, the cat meowed again. Crickets sang.

"You can't sit on the sidelines forever, son," Perish said, this to a man who by all physical appearances was ten or twenty years his senior. "Enjoy your *retirement*, for now. Sit out here and lick your wounds, put yourself back together. You've time enough for that, it seems. Let me suggest, though, if you have the opportunity to help down the road? You should. We're watching, Jin. Cain is always watching."

Jin nodded his head and sat silent, chastised.

Perish tucked the envelope into his coat, and then tore open the package, dropping the paper in the grass, and opening the black box it contained. Inside the box sat a glass ball, and it did something Jin had only seen a handful of times, glowing a soft, dark blue.

Jin was left sitting in his comfortable wicker chair on the porch of his nice little house, his mind already turning toward his agony and obsession, the contents of the trunk in his closet.

* * *

Clover let out a sigh of relief as she shut the door behind her parents. Dealing with them in any bad situation was tiresome, but this had been...*beyond*. Her father was appalled she had been awake at such an hour, let alone out wandering the streets. He acted like he hadn't known there was such a time as two in the morning.

"What were you doing out there, anyway?" he'd demanded.

"I went to get cigarettes." She mentally kicked herself in the ass. They hadn't known she smoked. After a lecture on the evils of tobacco that lasted an exhausting half hour, her father quoted scripture to her, saying how she'd never done anything like this when she lived at home, by golly.

"You don't know half of what I did at home," she snapped back. Another mistake. Her father yelled some more, her mother sobbed through the thick Valium and Percocet cocoon she spent most of her days.

Your wife's a drug addict, and you have the balls to lecture me, Clover thought. Mercifully, she'd kept that to herself.

But now, they were gone, and maybe she could get some peace. An hour ago, the prospect of sleep had seemed wonderful but, now, she wasn't even tired. Clover lay in bed, thinking of all that had transpired in the last couple of hours. She smiled. It hurt her lip, which was a little swollen and sort of purple, but the pain faded to almost a memory. Other than that, and a scrape on her back, she was fine.

Her mind kept turning to those few seconds that felt like an eternity when her eyes met AJ's, after he'd wiped the blood off her mouth. She thought of the tingle that had gone through her at his touch, seeming to erase the pain.

Clover Danning lay there in the gray light of dawn, thinking about AJ, and he was still on her mind when she drifted to sleep.

* * *

It was 7:23 A.M. Having worked the night shift for a few months, AJ was adjusted to being up at this hour. In fact, he never went to bed before nine in the morning or so. But sitting in that stale-smelling police station room, Clover an hour gone, he was drained.

His throat hurt from when he was choked, the coffee sucked, and he wanted to take a shower, maybe smoke a joint, and go to bed.

The door opened, and a cop stepped in. "You wanna go home now, or you wanna try for residency?"

"Thank Christ. What was the holdup, anyways?"

"Wheels o' justice, son," the cop said with a crooked smile, putting out his hand. "Officer Gomez."

AJ was much too tired to laugh, but he shook the man's hand. "AJ. Well, can we get outta here, or is this some clever façade to get my hopes up?"

The cop grinned. "Naw. Let's get you home."

AJ followed him to a police cruiser, and they left.

They didn't speak much. AJ had had enough of talking with the police for one night, even if it hadn't been this cop in particular. His mind was on two things: the man he killed, and the girl he met.

Mostly the girl.

A gray dawn washed over the city, slowly bringing it to life as they cruised through it. AJ watched as bakery trucks were filled for their morning deliveries, as a tired old man in a little pickup truck added a stack of morning papers into a street kiosk. There were people out walking their dogs and taking their morning jog, on their morning commute, their faces still a little puffed with sleep. As they got into his end of town, he saw men huddled around barrel fires, a car with all the windows busted out, and graffiti—the only real thing of beauty his end of town held, in his opinion—that seemed to be on every surface. He read the names he'd learned; Phloyd, one said. Another read Hero in a perfect, grimy Philly tall hand.

They were stopped five or six cars back from a light, and AJ looked out his window, up an alley, and watched an old bum lurch toward the mouth of it, his eyes blank, and his face twisted with anger. He seemed to be looking right at AJ, reaching one half-gloved and filthy hand out toward him as though he could stretch his arm another twenty feet and wring AJ's neck for being young, for having a place to sleep and food in his fridge.

The light changed, and the car rolled, and still the old man stared, his body turning after the cop car as it picked up speed. AJ wondered if maybe the old guy had needed help.

"Yeah, I saw him, too," Gomez said.

"You think he's all right?"

Gomez shook his head in a way that seemed both incredibly cynical and sad. AJ sighed and settled back into his seat, wondering if Clover had gotten home okay, if she had fake-numbered him, or if maybe, when she woke up, she would realize her end of the connection had been little more than adrenaline and high emotions. He wished he could shut off that loud, shitty part of his brain that had always been there, telling him he wasn't good enough.

"Left up here, yeah?" Gomez asked.

"Yup, that's me, second from the corner."

The car pulled to a stop, double-parked, but who the fuck was going to say anything? No one, not in his neighborhood.

"John—Detective Lubbock—told me what you went through tonight, man. I'm sorry this happened to you."

AJ smiled, touched in spite of himself. "Thank you."

Gomez nodded. "This city's a real piece a' shit sometimes, and I've seen the worst of it, but you know what? I see the best of it, too."

"Yeah? I could use some of that right now," AJ said, the sound of the baseball bat against a skull echoing in his head, again and again, thoughts of the pretty girl pushed far from the front of his mind for a moment.

"About a year back, right? About three in the morning, I'm on my beat, me and a partner, and this car blows through a red, right in front of us, doing like sixty, yeah?"

"Yeah?"

"So, we light 'em up, guy pulls over like right away, which we didn't expect. Then he jumps out of the car and waves his hands over his head. Turns out, the guy's wife is in the back, with their kid. Little boy, like two years old. Kid's not breathing, like, had an allergic reaction."

"Jesus," AJ said.

"No shit. That's what I said. We got a kit in the trunk, though. I grab the kit and just get in the back of the car with the mom and the kid and Mikey, my partner that night, he just looks at the dad, and he's like, follow me, and lights it up again. We're like sixteen blocks from Memorial, right? So, the dad has it fucking punched, and the mom's starting to lose it, and this kid's neck is like purple and all swole up.

"I open the kit and stab this kid with an EpiPen, and it's like letting the air out of a balloon, yeah? Like, you can see it help immediately, and I'm about to shit my pants I'm so goddamn happy this fuckin' pen thing is working, but the kid, he still isn't breathing. I start compressions, though, you know, resuscitation actions, all that. By the time we get to the ER drop-off for Memorial, this kid is sitting in his mom's lap, sucking his thumb. We saved that kid's life. *I* saved his life. Brought him back."

"Holy shit," AJ said.

"Yeah. Every couple of weeks or so, I stop by their place, you know, just kinda check in. I'm not supposed to do that, you know, but it's like…you know how plants will grow facing the sun?"

AJ nodded.

"This is like that, man. You gotta find the sunshine in all this, whatever it is, and just…face it. Every time I have a real shit day, you know, I think of that little kid. That family. Have a beer with the folks—off-clock, of course—and the kid makes me all these little drawings and stuff, like, recharges me, get it?"

"I do. Thank you," AJ said, stunned and repeating the advice to himself: *Find the sunshine and face it*, and was there anything he expected *less* to come from a cop?

"You did the right thing, from everything John says, and if John says it, that shit is like gospel 'round here, I promise you that. I don't know if you're worried about any kind of charges, accidental manslaughter or whatever the fuck, but I *promise* you, kid. John says you're good, so you're good."

AJ let out a long, slow breath. He'd been feeling better, figuring if they were going to charge him, they wouldn't have let him go, but he didn't really know how these things worked, and it was nice to hear.

"Thank you," AJ said. "Not just for the ride, but for…all of it."

"You're welcome. Remember that for me, huh? Find the sunshine and face it."

"I will, man," AJ said and put out his hand. Right then, it was not him and a cop, but just two guys, two people, and another bit of the weight he'd been carrying all night rolled off his chest. "Thanks again."

"No problem," Gomez said. "You gonna be around later today?"

"Until eight tonight. Then I gotta work. Why?"

"You may have to answer some follow-ups or talk to someone else if John moves to a different case."

"Shouldn't this be kind of an open-and-shut thing?"

Gomez shrugged. "As far as charges for you? Absolutely, that part is over. Anything else? You never know."

"Ain't *that* the fuckin' truth," AJ said. "Thanks for the ride, man."

Gomez tipped him a little two finger salute and dropped his car into gear. The black and white drove away, and AJ stood for a moment in front of his building, watching the taillights recede. He looked up at the morning sky, breathing deeply. There were a couple large birds circling overhead, and the slow sounds of light morning traffic, the hydraulic hiss of buses stopping, the rumble of a garbage truck a block over. Peaceful, in its own way.

AJ went upstairs, too tired to shower or roll a joint. He fell asleep thinking of the phone number now sitting on his dresser and when he could call it.

* * *

Detective John Lubbock sat in a darkened room in front of a television, which provided the only light. The footage was a little grainy but not horrible. For a traffic camera, it wasn't bad at all, really. They'd installed them all over the city the last few years. They were supposed to cut down on crime, make people feel safer. *It didn't do much of either,* John thought. They were occasionally useful for determining fault in a traffic accident, but he hadn't found much more use for them until tonight.

He checked the call log, and then the time stamp on the video. He'd listened to the call half a dozen times, didn't need to anymore. The panic in it was genuine. Whether it was panic for their friend or at the prospect of being caught or from their high being ruined, it was real.

In the tape, the car, nondescript, no license plates, probably stolen, swerved over to the curb and slammed to a stop near the corner of 86th and Downing. Two people in the front of the car got out. They ran around to the rear passenger door and opened it, then they both tried to climb in at once. The driver whacked his head on the car door, and it would have been funny if John didn't know that, in about five seconds, they were going to pull a man out of the car, each holding an arm.

They dropped the man on the sidewalk, arms still splayed above his head, ran back to the car, got in, and were gone.

Lubbock shifted in his seat, staring at the time stamp as the seconds rolled by.

One minute and nothing.

As the time stamp passed two minutes a small group of three crept up to the body. To John they looked like kids—late teens or early twenties—though with the quality of the footage he was dealing with, it was impossible to tell. His impression of their youth was more in their actions in any case. It was in the way all three of them kept looking over their shoulders instead of having one dedicated look out. It was in what appeared to be a short argument over who would rifle the pockets of the man on the sidewalk and in the way one of them actually jumped up and down upon finding the wallet, and the speed with which they all ran off.

Well, now we know what happened to his ID, John thought, taking a sip of his coffee. He grimaced a bit at the taste but relished it, too. It was like scratching a bug bite when you know it would only make it feel worse in the long run.

The time stamp on the video ran a little past three minutes and, on the screen, the man's foot twitched. John sat up a little straighter, leaning in a little toward the

TV. Three-and-a-half minutes in, and he goes into a full body seizure, then sits up like someone pulled his strings.

The man got to his feet, stumbled, rocked back and forth, and fell back to the ground. He lay there for a moment, rocking back and forth on his back, like a turtle stuck on its shell, and then managed to roll over to his hands and knees. He remained on all fours for a good ten seconds or so, and then his back hitched.

He vomited onto the sidewalk, and then struggled to his feet, swaying before gaining something a little closer to balance. He stood relatively still, then cocked his head to one side. He stayed that way for thirty seconds. Then he walked east on Downing.

The gas station. That's how you would get there from that intersection. He checked the time stamp when the man shambled around the corner of 86th and out of sight, by then, not much more than a gray-colored blob no bigger than an inch high on the screen.

John stopped the tape. 2:29 A.M.

AJ's 911 call had come in at 2:51.

Lubbock looked at the pictures Fenster and Andrews had taken at the scene. He knew it was the same guy. Same coat, same build, same fuckin' face.

Okay, John thought. *He shoots up with his buddies, takes a little more than he bargained for, gets a bad shot, whatever.* They were still waiting for the tox-screen to know what he was on for sure. His friends see him going over, put him in the car, call 911, drop him at an intersection. It was shitty, but it happened more in his city than he cared to think about. Lotta bad dope up there.

But let's say the guy isn't as fucked as his friends think he is. Just unconscious, as opposed to dead or dying. A few minutes goes by and he , and he gets up. He walks straight to the gas station, presumably to rob it, as they confirmed one thing: his pockets had been empty. No money, no dope, no weapon, still a little out of it from whatever his friends thought he OD'd on, loses his shit, goes after AJ and the girl.

Fine. Sure. A junky almost ODs, doesn't, then decides to hold a place up for some more dope money.

Open and shut, right?

"Right," Lubbock whispered. Only…lately, things *hadn't* so been open and shut. He sighed again and pushed those thoughts, those bad thoughts, those Todd Bowden thoughts, out of his brain and ejected the tape. He re-bagged it, put it in the evidence box, and stood, cracking his back, ready to walk the box back down to the boys in The Tombs so they could witness his return. He could sign for the contents when they checked it, and they would both sign when they re-sealed the box. Then it'd go back on the shelf, maybe forever.

Open and shut, John told himself. That's how the chief liked things, how the commissioner liked things, how the mayor and the *fucking governor* liked things. John thought of his old colleague Jin Makoto, who'd believed in working a fucking case, going where the evidence told him to go. Jin had been *police* through and fucking through.

Look at what that got him, though.

Forced retirement, a stack of gag orders and confidentiality agreements a foot high, a name that, while once synonymous with the kind of detective work any real cop dreams of doing, was now nothing more than a hushed whisper, like a curse. He was a fucking cautionary tale, and John's face burned a little with shame at the memory of standing by, helpless but to watch all that had befallen his old friend.t/

As a cautionary tale, though, the fall of Jin Makoto was nothing if not an effective one, so John swallowed his anger and doubts and the feeling in his guts he'd had in the months leading up to Jin's expulsion.

So, John thought, *open and shut.*

CHAPTER
FOUR

CHAPTER

FOUR

When AJ opened his eyes, he could tell by the light it
was well past noon. He lay in bed awhile. His mind went
back and forth between two things: the color of Clover's
eyes, and the sound the bat had made when it connected
with the guy's skull. Both thoughts followed him out of
bed, throughout his shower, and pounded in his head
while he sat on the couch. His apartment was small but
now seemed claustrophobic.

There was a window leading to the fire escape
between his bedroom wall and the kitchen. The window
was fucked and wouldn't stay up by itself, so when he
wanted it open to get some air, he had to prop it up. He
had a small table to the left of the window that currently
held only a hammer. He grabbed the hammer off the
table and opened the window, wedging the hammer in to
keep it open. A nice breeze blew in, but it didn't help as
much as he hoped it would.

He tried to read but found himself going over the

same paragraph again and again because he wasn't retaining or enjoying the prose. He tried to eat and couldn't, tried to watch TV and found himself restless, wanting to move.

Finally, he dug the scrap of paper out of his wallet and dialed the number.

Three rings. He was trying to think of what he would say to her answering machine when Clover picked up the phone. The sound of her voice pushed everything else out of his head, and he felt himself relaxing for the first time since rolling out of bed.

"Hello?"

"Hey," AJ said, the look of consternation on his face breaking into a smile.

"Hey yourself," Clover said. "Who's this?"

You can't expect her to recognize your voice right away, AJ reminded himself, though the disappointment he felt stayed where it was, like a hot little pebble lodged in one of the ventricles of his heart.

"It's AJ."

There was a long pause on the other end of the line, and just when he was starting to wonder if they'd been disconnected, she spoke.

"I'm sorry, *who*?"

Of all the responses he'd run through in his head, both good and bad, daydream and nightmare, he had not even considered this and, in his surprise, sputtered something unintelligible into the phone. That hot little pebble had become a good-sized rock.

"Oh, my God, I'm fucking with you!" Clover said. "I'm so sorry, that was *super* shitty, and I could almost *feel* a smile fall off your face from across town!"

Relief flooded through him, accompanied by something else, something warm and fresh.

I wanna marry this girl, AJ thought. Before he could say anything, they both laughed.

"Wooow!" AJ said. "That was good! Fuckin' cruel, but good."

"I know, I'm so sorry! How are you doing?"

"I'm okay, you?" he asked, walking around his apartment. He felt suddenly full of a crackling, jubilant energy. "How's your mouth? Your lip, I mean. Where you got hit?"

"Oh, it's not bad. My roommate had some Vicodin, so I took a couple of those," Clover said. "I feel a little stir crazy, though."

"Holy shit, *right?* Wanna meet for coffee, or something?"

"Ohhhh, my God, *yes!*" Clover said. "Where do you wanna go?"

"I could do with some breakfast, actually," AJ said, realizing as he said it his appetite was coming back.

"It's almost two, man," Clover said with a laugh.

"Oh, come on. You telling me you couldn't go for some waffles right now?"

"Actually, yeah, that sounds kinda great. There's this great little spot near me, they do breakfast all day, and it isn't an IHOP or anything."

"Let's do it, my treat."

* * *

After giving the name of the little café to AJ and agreeing to meet him an hour later, Clover swiped her phone closed and smiled. She took a long moment, closing her eyes and marking it in her memory. Right then, she was happy. While she knew very well she had a life that was inconceivably privileged and rich and easy by the standards of most of the world, it had been a far from perfect life. Growing up in the shadow of her parents' religion—their *mania*—had been a long and arduous task.

She recalled one afternoon in particular during her freshman year in high school, when her mother had beaten her for catching her wearing a different change of clothes than what she'd left the house in that morning.

The clothes her parents made her wear were all dull browns or boring dark blues, no hemline that stopped anywhere north of her knee, no sleeve not full-length. Though Clover had been there to try on nearly all the clothes her mother had purchased for her, and knew they were brand new, they still looked grotesquely old-fashioned and conservative which, Clover supposed, was probably the point.

Her parents would not allow her to do anything with her hair besides pull it back into a ponytail. She was not allowed to use product in it or even a curling iron. Forget makeup.

Clover had experienced many a tearful morning before school, staring at herself in the mirror and thinking she looked like a casting call reject from *Little House on the Prairie*.

Angie had been her savior. They'd lived down the street from one another as kids, and they were still roommates now. As early as third grade, when what you wore to school became suddenly and inexplicably important to the other kids and, almost overnight, it had seemed,

Angie had begun sneaking clothes to school for Clover in her backpack.

Freshman year went like this: Clover would walk down to Angie's house in the morning, where she would change into the clothes they had picked out the night before, and then Angie would help her with her hair and makeup—nothing much, usually just lip gloss and a little eye shadow or something. After that, they rode to school with Angie's older brother, Mark, who was a senior and who Clover once had the world's biggest crush.

Her freshman year had been perfect for this, as she'd had gym last period, so she was always able to hop in the shower and wash off her makeup and undo whatever Angie had done to her hair that day, change back into the clothes her mother had laid out for her that morning, and her folks were none the wiser.

This system worked like a charm until the first really perfect day of spring that final quarter of her ninth-grade year. Mid-May, this had been, the gloom and rain of April sticking around a little longer than anyone would have liked. The sun had been bright and strong in the cloudless sky that day, and she could tell it was going to be perfect.

And it would have been, if she'd been able to wear something not full-length or made of corduroy and wool. Clover had gotten uncomfortably warm on even the short morning walk to Angie's house.

At school that day, she'd changed into a cotton, V-neck T-shirt and a pair of shorts. Not even *booty shorts*, not short-shorts, and certainly not, as her parents had called them, hooker-shorts. They were even an inch past her fingertips when she stood with her arms to her side, as was required by the school dress code. She'd traded the thick, shin-high tube socks and penny loafers her parents made her wear for a pair of Angie's flip flops.

The problem was, she'd forgotten her geometry book and hadn't *realized* she had forgotten it.

Mom, though, Clover now thought. *Mom found it, going through my room.*

About halfway through second period, she was called to the office over the intercom. Clover had gotten a hall pass from her teacher and bopped happily down the hall, no inkling how wrong things were about to go.

She turned a corner and saw her mother standing there, textbook clutched to her chest. She looked at Clover, and her face twisted into that little moue of distaste she seemed to use so much.

She doesn't know it's me, Clover thought. *I still have time to—*

That was when her mother finally recognized her. And, oh, what a shock it must have been for her to realize the tramp in hooker-shorts oozing down the hall toward her was her own daughter. The little moue of distaste was gone, and it was replaced by something like fury.

Her mother dragged her out of school that afternoon by her ear as many of the upperclassmen and some kids from her own grade watched and laughed.

In the car, the screaming started.

Then they got home, and the screaming continued, her mother only taking a break to call her father at work and tell him what she'd discovered. Then the screaming resumed and, just before her father got home, her mother slapped her across the face.

It wasn't the first time her mother had hit her, but

it had been a *long* time since she'd done so, the last incident having been in sixth grade, when Clover made the mistake of saying church was stupid.

It turned out that time in freshman year had been the last time her mother had laid hands on her—her father, too, for that matter—but it had been the worst. The sound of the slap echoed off the walls of their living room, and her cheek had felt touched by fire, tears springing immediately into her eyes.

"You *can't* hit me!" Clover remembered screaming, and her mother had taken it as a challenge. She'd wound up and backhanded her, this time across the other side of the face.

"*I hate you!*"

"That's fine, sweetie," Mom said. "As long you know I'm doing this because I love you."

Her mother slapped her again, twice in fast succession, like an open-handed, one-two combo, the old left-right, and Clover hadn't heard her father walk in or come into the living room, hadn't known he stood behind her, already taking off his belt.

"FUCK YOU!" Clover screamed, her nose bleeding now.

She felt an explosion of pain as her father strapped her across the back with his belt, the sound like a gunshot. She staggered forward under the force of the whipping, and her mother greeted her by punching her—*fucking punching her*—in the stomach. She dropped to the ground, then to her hands and knees.

"Get used to that position, dressing like that," her father had said before bringing the belt down again, even harder this time, right across the small of her back, then once more across the shoulders. She'd been out of breath from the blow to stomach, and all she wanted to do was scream. It felt like she was going to explode somewhere in the middle. Between trying to suck air in and scream at the same time, something in her was going to give.

Her mother had stomped on one of her hands then, and when Clover heard one of the bones in her hand break, she thought, for a moment, they were going to beat her to death. She rolled onto her back and held her arms in front of her face, blood streaming from her nose, face covered in tears, her hand starting to swell like a cartoon hand.

Clover shook the memory from her head, that and all the others, of the church deacon they had taken her to—a man who had been an Army doctor during the war in Korea—to look at her hand because they knew he wouldn't report them to child services. She tried to forget the look in their eyes on that long, silent drive home, when she realized they knew they had gone too far, of the tearful reconciliation effort on her mother's part that had seemed genuine at first until she insisted they get on their knees and pray at the end of it, of the ever-widening gap growing between them that had still not closed.

Clover wiped a tear from her eye and took a deep breath and went to get ready for her breakfast date.

* * *

AJ walked the few blocks from the light rail station to the restaurant she had told him about, the exercise feeling good, like he was being cleaned out after the amount of time he'd spent in the last few days sitting in bad chairs and smoking in tiny rooms.

He stopped before going in as he spotted Clover, sitting at a small table near the big picture window in the front of the diner. She read a book and sipped a cup of coffee and, as he watched, tucked a stray lock of hair behind her ear. Her hair was like white fire in the beam of sunshine in which she sat, unassuming, unknowing at that second, right then, she was the most beautiful girl he'd ever seen. AJ shook his head a little, forcing himself out of his reveries, and walked into the diner.

She looked up from her book at the tinkling from the little bell above the door and, when she saw him, smiled. That smile bloomed like a rose of happiness inside his chest, his heart, his soul. Is there anything better for a young man in his early twenties than for a pretty girl to smile and be happy when she saw you? AJ wasn't sure what it could be, or how people would be able to stand it if there was.

She closed her book and stood to greet him when he approached the table. He was spared the awkward moment of not knowing how to greet her—handshake? kiss on the cheek?—when she leaned in and hugged him.

"How are you?" she asked, pulling back and motioning to his chair.

"I'm good. Tired more than anything. I didn't sleep much."

"Ugh, I know," Clover said, the two of them sitting across from one another. "It was brutal. I'm glad you suggested breakfast, though, I've been going a little stir crazy, sitting at home."

"Yeah, I know what you mean. It's been a weird day

so far, you know?"

Clover laughed. "Uh, yeah, man. Since midnight, I've been to the store for cigarettes, got assaulted, spent four hours in a police station, had a fight with my parents, and had to explain everything to my ADHD roommate."

AJ felt her foot against the side of his for just a moment.

"I also met a guy," she said, looking him in the eyes from over her cup of coffee.

"Oh, yeah? What's *he* like?"

"Wellll, he's a cop," Clover said, the two of them laughing.

"Zzzzing!" AJ said.

She smiled at that, too, but then the smile left her face, except her eyes, and she looked into his. "No, really, though, he seems nice. He's brave, and funny, has the same weird sense of humor as I do."

Her foot was against his again, under the table.

"I told you I'm married, right?" AJ asked as she took another sip of coffee. She laughed and almost spit her coffee back in the cup, kicking him in the shin under the table as she coughed and got herself under control.

"Fuck you," Clover said. "Ugh, that was *awful*."

"Hey, I wanted to tell you something, too," AJ said.

Clover leaned forward a little, and as AJ was about to continue, the waitress came and took their order.

"So," Clover said as the waitress walked off, "what were you saying?"

"I just wanted to tell you, when you hit that guy in the head, with the wine bottle? Like smashed it over his head?"

"Yeah?"

"That was just about the coolest fucking thing I ever saw someone do, like, outside of a movie, you know. In real life."

"Really?" Clover asked.

"*Hell* yeah! It was just… It was bad ass."

"Woulda been cooler if it had dropped him, though, huh?" Clover asked.

"It should have," AJ said. "That wasn't your fault, though. And, regardless, it was awesome, and I wanted you to know that."

"So, did the police find out what that guy was on?" Clover asked, thinking how sure she had been when she swung that bottle of wine it was going to end right there.

"Not that they told me," AJ said. "I know they ordered a tox-screen or something. Those probably take a couple days to get back."

She put her coffee cup down then and reached across the table, laying her hand in a warm and familiar way against his cheek. She put her hand under his chin and gently tilted his head back, grimacing a little at the bruises on his neck. She trailed her fingers down his throat and held two of them against his jugular where the bruise lay, as though she were taking his pulse. He looked at her split and swollen lip and, as he did, she turned her head a little so he could see the bruise on her cheekbone and under her eye.

"We're quite the pair, huh?" AJ asked.

"Is that what we are? A pair?" She took her hand away from the tender skin of his throat and rested it on the back of his other hand, which sat on the table.

AJ swallowed hard, not sure what to say. Instead of

speaking, he nodded his head, and she smiled again.

The waitress reappeared then with AJ's coffee and refilled Clover's. He watched her spoon sugar into hers.

"I don't believe you," AJ said. "You like a little coffee with your sugar or what?"

"Lee," she said, "I'm not satisfied until the spoon stands straight up."

AJ sat in stunned silence for a moment. "I can't believe you caught that."

Clover looked up from her coffee. "I almost didn't say anything. That's not exactly the most quoted line in the movie."

"Oh, there's so many, though."

She narrowed her eyes to slits. "Don't condescend me, man. I'll fuckin' kill you."

"Yes! Oh, man, that was one of Brad Pitt's finest moments right there."

"God, what a cast, though, right? Him, Christian Slater, Patricia Arquette, Dennis Hopper, Gandolfini, Walken—"

"Val Kilmer, fuckin' *Oldman*?" AJ asked. "He shoulda won an Oscar for that part. I watched that movie like four times before I realized *he* was Drexl."

"Oh, I know!" Clover said. "Dude's such a chameleon. From that to *Dracula* to *Fifth Element*? What was his name in that?"

"Jean-Baptiste. Emanuel. Zorg."

"*Zorg*!" she said, reaching across and squeezing his arm. "That's another great one."

"Yeah, it is. *True Romance* has to be just about my favorite movie, ever. Top three, at least."

"Oh, for sure," Clover said. "It's one of the few

absolutely perfect films ever made. I mean, what could you change? *Nothing*."

The waitress showed up then with their food, and they leaned back, AJ just then realizing her hand was still on his arm. He felt a rush of warmth and happiness spread through him as he looked into her eyes while the waitress unloaded her tray.

As they ate, AJ glanced out the window and across the street and saw a man in a trench coat and hat, leaning against a telephone pole. He seemed to be looking right at him and took a drink from a silver flask he pulled from inside his coat pocket. He replaced the flask in his coat, and then took out what seemed to be a pocket watch.

The waitress bumped AJ's coffee with a plate she set down.

"Oh, I'm sorry!" the waitress said. "Did that spill?"

"Nope, we're good. No worries," AJ said. He glanced back out the window, and then turned his head and took a longer look up the street as far as he could see in either direction. The man was gone.

"What's up?" Clover said.

"Nothing," AJ said.

"Getting paranoid?"

"No way, see?" AJ said, putting on the voice of a gangster from a movie in the forties or fifties with a little Cagney twist. "They'll never take me alive, see?"

Clover snorted a small laugh. "You're fuckin' nuts, man."

He smiled back, and they dug into their respective meals.

"So," AJ said after he finished his last bite of bacon, "any chance you want to hang out tonight? Maybe watch a movie or something?'"

"Ohhh, *or something*? I like the sound of that," Clover said. "I've always *dreamed* a guy would ask me to do... *something*."

"And you say *I'm* nuts."

"No, I would love to, but I can't tonight. Going away party for a friend of mine who's moving back home to Ithaca. Kind of a girls' night."

"*That* sounds made up," AJ said.

"I'm serious!" Clover said with a laugh. "What about tomorrow night, though? I'd love to come over and watch a movie with you."

"Yeah?"

"Yeah, I'd like that a lot."

"Me too," AJ said, feeling his face flush a little. "*True Romance*?"

"Yes," Clover said, again holding him in her eyes. "Please."

* * *

AJ sat on the train, leaning forward, elbows on his knees. He already missed her, and it ached, but it was a nice ache. His life had been a bit short on nice things as of late, but it went beyond the last twenty-four hours. The last few months had been hard ones, so this dull and pleasant throb in his center was a welcome respite.

The train slowed as they neared his stop, the last one the train made before heading back the other way. The train hissed, and the doors opened. It was relatively empty of people for this time of day, but AJ hung back and let a crowd of teens get off before he stood and made for the exit.

He walked through the platform to the stairs on the other side that went up, over another set of tracks, and then back down the other side.

AJ whistled a little song to himself, thinking of the way Clover had made sure the syrup was in every square of her top waffle before cutting into it, something he used to do as a kid he guessed some people never grew out of.

He stood in the middle of the walkway for a moment, looking down the train tracks and back toward downtown, same as he always did. It'd been foggy lately, as the year advanced toward winter, but today was clear, and the sunset was brilliant, golds and oranges and reds slowly spreading across the horizon.

The walkway was encased in hard, clear plastic. It was a hamster-tube for people. AJ had always liked the look of it because it seemed like something out of a movie from the fifties about what the eighties would be like, oddly quaint and somehow almost futuristic at the same time.

Every time he took the light rail, he'd spend a few minutes in the middle of the walkway, which was about ten feet wide, so he didn't have to feel self-conscious about being in anyone's way. His eyes followed the golden, glowing clouds until he looked nearly straight up. There was some kind of giant bird, wheeling in the sky, circling slowly, wings spread widely, riding whatever atmospheric drift that allowed it to hover up there endlessly.

The bird then folded its wings and dropped like a stone.

The fuck? AJ thought, wondering if he'd just witnessed the avian version of a massive coronary, only mid-air. The bird then spread its wings, and he chuckled to himself. The bird was diving after food, that was all. It wasn't a hawk, the neck looked out of proportion to the rest of the body, but it was still diving, getting closer.

AJ looked around to see if anyone else was watching this, if there was perhaps an ornithologist in the crowd that could offer a timely explanation.

No such luck. He was the only one on the walkway. He took a few steps toward the other set of stairs, and then stopped. The bird was still diving, closing in rapidly.

AJ stood, mesmerized, watching as what had once just been a black dot in the sky growing larger, and with alarming speed.

It came right at him, still diving, its massive wings pumping and increasing the speed.

"Shit!" AJ said and took a step back from the curved, plastic wall. The bird slammed into it at an incredibly high speed with a deafening *thump* and a *crack*, and if the wall hadn't been there, it would have hit him right in the face. The *thunk* of the impact reverberated through the tube. AJ realized the crack had been the sound of the bird's neck, maybe even more of its hollow bird bones shattering on impact.

There was nothing but a red smear slowly running down the side of the curved walkway wall. AJ took a couple steps to the side and leaned forward, his forehead pressed against the smooth, cool surface, looking down. He could see the lifeless body of the bird lying between the tracks, a few black feathers still see-sawing toward the ground.

He looked around again. Surely *someone* had to have seen this.

He didn't know vultures lived near the city.

Still, there was no one. AJ shook his head, zipped his hoodie up the rest of the way against the chill in the air, and headed down the other set of stairs.

As he neared the bottom, he heard something, a graveled voice that may or may not have been forming words. AJ turned and looked behind him and jumped back—his heart already pounding from the kamikaze vulture—at the man who was nearly on top of him.

"Hey, man, sorry I didn't see you," AJ said, taking a few more steps backward as the old vagrant advanced.

His nostrils flared with the stench of the man, a smell of shit and dirt and disease. The man's eyes were clouded and red, his nose a red knob of skin, crooked, and with a massive patchwork of busted capillaries from years of booze.

The man wore an old, dirty watch cap, and what was left of his thin, white hair was greasy and unwashed. He held his cracked red hands out and took another slow step forward.

AJ made a show of patting his pockets, though he knew he had no cash on him. The man took another step forward, and AJ retreated again.

"Sorry, man, I got nothing on me. Take, uh, take care, though."

The man kept coming forward. AJ turned and walked off, quickly, casting an eye back over his shoulder at the man still stumbling after him, his face a rictus of anger.

"I'm sorry!" AJ said. "I got nothing."

The man kept coming, so AJ put his head down and walked faster. He did his best to ignore the unintelligible nonsense being shouted at him. It could have been the truth about the aliens or who shot JFK. Maybe he was telling AJ to go fuck himself, or maybe it was nothing but a guttural caveman expulsion of nonsense syllables.

The wind and sounds of another train washed away whatever meaning, if any, the words might have had. Relieved, AJ spotted a cab, held his hand up to hail it, and jogged forward.

I am definitely running toward the cab, AJ told himself when the cabbie nodded at him and switched off his light. AJ climbed in and rattled off his address. He tried not to think about what percentage of his bank account this little cab ride, a trip he always made by foot, was going to cost him.

"Sure thing, buddy," the driver said, and the cab pulled away from the curb.

AJ turned and looked back. The homeless man still lurched after him, arms outstretched. AJ glanced upward, and in the reddening sky, he saw another two vultures, circling, circling.

* * *

AJ sat on his couch, rolling a joint, his eyes checking the clock on the wall, making sure he had enough time to smoke, and then relax a bit before going to work. He knew he should call his parents, too, but after what had already happened, he wasn't in the mood for it.

Down the hall, he heard a door creak open. He waited for the sound of it slamming shut.

He finished twisting the joint and ran it through his mouth to seal it, then held it out, gently turning it between his fingers, admiring the symmetry of it. There were a couple slow footsteps in the hall, and he set the joint in a small tray on the coffee table and grabbed his remote control off the arm of the couch and flipped on the TV.

Talk show, skip, talk show, skip, infomercial, skip, *Dr. Phil*, skip, another couple clumping footsteps in the hall, and then he settled on the weather forecast. The forecast was just ending, though, and the weatherman tossed it back to the anchorwoman, with her perfect smile and tanned skin even at the end of fall in the Pacific Northwest, the result of a tanning bed and a few hours in a makeup chair for sure.

She cautioned any parents watching with children in the room that the next story might be upsetting and gave these hypothetical parents time to scoot their hypothetical kids out of the room.

"New developments tonight in a series of strange and morbid thefts involving the bodies of the recently deceased in the greater metro area," the anchorwoman said. "The county morgue reported the disappearance of a body awaiting autopsy to determine cause of death, which we have been told was of a suspicious and possibly criminal nature. There has been another instance of that same crime today, this time from a city hospital. When asked if he believes the crimes to be related, the official police spokesperson chose not to comment—"

What the fuck, AJ thought, clicking the TV off. He wanted to move, to go, but at the same time didn't know what to do or have a destination to head to. He wanted to talk to Clover, but he'd just seen her this afternoon, and he didn't want to come on too strong. He didn't really believe in the three-day rule or whatever the fuck it was. If he liked a girl, he called her. She'd told him at breakfast she was busy this evening, though, and he didn't want to interrupt her time with her friends.

AJ sighed and picked the joint back up.

There were a few more clumping steps in the hall and, this time, he heard a kind of groan and someone scratching at his door. His heart sped up in his chest at the surprise. He put the joint back down and went to the door, looking through the peephole.

He recognized the woman on the other side after a moment. He didn't really know her, but she lived down the hall from him. He'd sometimes hold the door open for her when she was bringing in a load of groceries, or they would exchange polite nods and awkward smiles when they checked their mail at the same time.

It took him longer to recognize her than it should have but, then again, he'd never seen her naked, soaking wet, and covered with blood.

"Holy shit," AJ said, scrambling to unlock his door. He opened it, and she stood there, covered in blood like an extra in a horror film, her hair in wet tangles, her skin pale.

"Oh, my God, are you okay? It's Karen, right? Are you—"

Then her hands were up, and she came for him. The cold, somehow fishy feel of her fingers scrambling around his neck and glancing off his cheek as he turned his head made his flesh crawl. He took a couple steps back and almost fell over the coffee table, and she came into his apartment, her mouth hanging slack.

She barked out a single syllable, her voice thick and gurgling, like she was speaking around a throat full of infected phlegm. It sounded like she said, *"Book."* She held her hands up again and came for him. Her hands gripped his shirt, and one of her cold fingers hooked into his mouth. He gagged and resisted the urge to bite only because he didn't want the taste of her flesh and blood in his mouth.

Instead, he grabbed one of her wrists and twisted it away, looking down at it and seeing for the first time that a wide, black mouth opened on her inner forearm. Inside that dark, meaty cavern, there were tendons, and he could see the insides of her wrist, layers of skin, and a thin layer of yellow fat and red muscle, slit almost down to the bone. He screamed, and she turned her hand, the skin around the wound somehow loose, slippery with blood and water, and he lost his grip.

His hand slid down her wrist, and his thumb went *inside her arm*. It was cold and gristly, like when he would help his mom as a kid by reaching inside the half-thawed Thanksgiving turkey to get the giblets and neck out.

She lurched forward another step, once more groping for his throat. He put his hands up to block her seeking fingers and those black, gaping rings on *both* her wrists. She clutched him for purchase, hugging him close like a lover, her blood-covered breasts pressed against him, wetting his shirt, sticking to his skin. They tottered a few steps across his living room in some obscene parody of a slow dance.

AJ surged forward and used his weight against her, finally knocking her back. Her bare, white feet slipped in the pink mixture of water and blood on the floor, and she turned enough for him to see her back. It looked like one giant bruise, not just on her back, but the back of her arms, legs, her ass. He came forward again and shoved her out into the hall, slamming and locking the door behind her.

"Oh, what the fuck?" he said, his voice high and keening. He grabbed the phone and dialed 911.

"911, what's your emergency?"

"Hi, yes," he said, out of breath and panting. "I was… I'm being attacked, this woman, I don't know, she's covered in blood and—"

"Sir, is your call coming from 1524 Clarkson, Apartment 3B?"

"What? Yes, yes, it is."

"Okay, Mr. Lancaster, we have an officer on the scene—"

"You what?"

"I'm sending him in now. Is the intruder still in your home?"

"No, I shoved her out into the hall."

"Lock the door and wait for the officer to knock, it's Officer Fenster, he'll identify himself. Do *not* open the door for anyone but Officer Fenster, do you understand?"

There was a pounding on the door, and his name being screamed.

"Oh, shit," AJ said.

"Is your door locked?"

"It is."

"Okay, the officer is entering your building now—"

AJ dropped the phone with numb fingers and

collapsed back onto the couch. He heard footsteps running up the stairs and a surprised cry of disgust.

Another howl of his name came from the hall.

"Ma'am, put your hands above your head and— Back! Get back!" Officer Fenster screamed in the hall. *"Back or I'll shoot!"*

There were two more dragging footsteps, and then a gunshot.

AJ covered his ears, though it was too late. They were already ringing, and he just sat there for a while. He didn't know how long Fenster had been pounding on the door to be let in when he finally stood from the couch. AJ only knew Fenster was now threatening to break the door down.

AJ unlocked it, his hand dropping from the lock to his side with a clap. He didn't have the energy for this. He turned the knob and pulled the door open a little, and this seemed a monumental feat. It drained him. His throat ached with thirst and from being throttled for the second time in two days. He ignored Fenster's questions and padded slowly, like an injured old man, into his kitchen for a glass of water.

Ten minutes later, he sat in the back of a police car, watching the city roll past around him, headed once more for the police station uptown. The neighborhood he'd come to call home rolled past, meaning nothing. The landmarks through which he'd navigated the last few years of his life were no more to him than stock footage in the background of an old movie.

He hadn't grabbed a jacket when he left, and his shirt was still damp, and with what? Water? Blood? He didn't know, and he didn't care enough to look down at himself to see. The cold seemed to revive him a little, bringing him out of his stupor, and it was only then he started to wonder why there had been a cop already at his building, deciding it would be the first—well, maybe not the *first*—question he would ask.

* * *

John stood in the apartment of Karen Rosenthal, the woman who had attacked AJ in his home, the woman Officer Fenster had shot.

There had been blood on the kid, and in his apartment, on the floor, a long trail of light spatter leading from his place up the hall to Karen's apartment.

John had followed that trail, the hallway now completely taped off, the floor of the building evacuated for the night, the lower men on the police totem pole had been given the unsavory duty of going to door to door, every apartment on the floor, and asking people to pack up their stuff for a night and hit the bricks.

More blood had led from Karen's front door to her bathroom, where John now stood.

The tub was an old one, and most of the bath Karen had drawn to sit in while she slit her wrists open had drained. Some of the blood was still wet and red, but most of it, especially along the sides of the tub, had dried to a black crust.

John sat on the closed lid of the toilet and scratched his head, trying to put it together.

Okay, he thought. *She draws the bath, gets in, cuts her wrists, bleeds a lot, then climbs out, walks down the hall, wet, naked, and covered in blood, and attacks AJ, who says they'd never passed anything but a friendly word now and again?*

He wanted to think the kid was still keyed up from the other attack, that maybe the neighbor had come over, panicked when she felt the life really start to rush out of her, and had been looking for help…but the circle of bruises on the kid's throat, and the way he croaked when he talked didn't jibe with that, nor the way she had come after Fenster.

This was nothing, though. All these things were just noise when he thought of her body, lying in the hall, face down on the old, gray carpet worn through to the padding in most places. Her back, ass, calves, the backs of her thighs and arms, had looked dark. Bruised.

Not possible, Lubbock told himself. There had to be an explanation other than what he was thinking because what he was thinking was fucking crazy.

He once more pushed thoughts of Todd Bowden and Jin Makoto out of his head. He sighed deeply and carefully picked his way out of the bathroom, making sure he didn't step in any of the blood splatter on the floor.

* * *

Vito was pissed. He'd called everyone who worked for him, excluding AJ, and the earliest anyone would come in was midnight. That left him with a couple hours to kill before they showed. He sat behind the counter, thinking of all the things he could be doing instead of being here. Like kicking the shit out of that junkie, Billy. The little prick hadn't even bothered to call.

The bell above the door dinged, and Vito looked up.

In walked a man dressed in black: trench coat, pants, and boots. His white hair was pulled back in a long ponytail that ended between his shoulders. Vito stared at himself in the mirrored shades, wondering if the man was half-blind. There was a nasty scar running from his forehead to just above his upper lip. It looked like it went right through the middle of his eye.

"Can I, uh, help you?" Vito asked, not really caring if he could or not. In his experience, the customer was never right and was usually an asshole.

The guy shook his head slightly and grunted a negative. He looked around the store, then quite noticeably sniffed the air. He looked around some more. He knelt and picked up a piece of dirt off the floor and sniffed it. Then he crumbled it between his fingers and stood.

"What is this?" Vito asked. "Fuckin' health inspection?"

Finally, the other man spoke. "Can you answer a couple questions for me?"

"That depends on who the hell you are and what the hell you ask me."

"I'm Detective Quidman. I just got transferred over to work this case. You know, what happened last night?"

Vito stared at him, running everything through his Bullshit-O-Meter, picking his teeth absently with the ever-present toothpick. This guy didn't look like no cop to him.

"You, uh, got a badge there, *Detective*?"

He pulled his coat to the side. Vito saw the unmistakable gold shield attached to his belt. Maybe the guy was vice.

"Whatcha want?"

"The kid who was attacked, how well do you know him?"

Vito shrugged. "All right, I guess. Why? He in some kinda trouble?"

Quidman muttered something that sounded like, *I hope not.*

"Excuse me?" Vito asked.

"I said no, no trouble." Quidman shook his head.

"Anything else you want?"

"Yes, what was his last name?"

"You boys don't talk amongst yourselves much downtown, do you?"

Quidman just stared across the counter, his face a total blank.

What the fuck is this? Vito asked himself. *What kinda cop doesn't know the name of the victim in a case he's working?*

Vito sighed and rolled his eyes. "Fine," he said. "Lancaster."

Quidman's eyebrows hopped up a little. "His name isn't Munroe?"

"What is this shit? I didn't say Munroe, did I? Jesus."

"Do you have the tapes from those cameras up there? With what happened on them?"

"*Tapes?*" Vito asked, snorting. "Where you think we are? 1986?"

Quidman stared at him for a long moment, his head cocked to the side a little. Vito shifted from one foot to the other.

"DVDs, then?" Quidman asked.

"Yeah, I got 'em. Why?"

"Give them to me."

"What for? I already gave 'em to the guy last night,"

Vito said. "Officer whoever the fuck. Andrews?"

"We need another copy. The one you gave us was scratched."

"And they sent a *detective* all the way back here for one? You must be *really* lighting up the force to have them trust you with such an important job."

"Get me the discs, *sir*, or I'll run you in on obstruction charges," Quidman said.

Vito held his hands up in acquiescence. "Oh, hey, no need for all that, friend. Never let it be said I was the cause of a wagon such as yours to be unhitched from so bright a shining star. I'm nothing if not a friend to my fellow working man. Please, allow me a moment."

Vito turned, and then went into the office to get the discs. He'd already burned an extra for the cops the night of the attack and had made another besides, and why not? He would need one for the insurance company likely as not and, in the back of his mind, he'd probably known the pigs would manage to fuck it up.

As he unlocked the cabinet in his office where the discs were kept, Vito wondered again if the kid needed a lawyer. Left to the devices of these shit-heels, he'd probably end up getting the fuckin' lethal injection for having the *cogliones* to defend himself.

Vito grabbed the DVD the *stronzo* pig was after and went back to the counter, handing it over.

Quidman took it from him without a word and left.

"You're welcome, Detective Fuckbag," Vito mumbled as the guy walked out the door.

* * *

The man who wasn't Detective Quidman tucked the DVD in one of the many pockets inside his coat as he walked around the corner of the gas station and hopped on his Harley, riding back to his motel.

Lancaster? Could that be right? The kid had to be a Munroe. He'd never heard of the wrong person being attacked before, not even this early in.

Back at his seedy motel, he popped the disc into the player that had probably only been used for porn flicks up until now. He used the fast forward until he found what he was looking for. He only needed to watch the entire scene once but replayed it over and over. Though he recognized something of the kid's lineage in his face—something in the nose, perhaps—this was of small consolation.

It didn't matter if it was on video, he could spot one of *them* anywhere, and this man—this *thing*—walking through the doors of the gas station, attacking the kid, was one of them.

"Damn," he said. "It's happening again."

* * *

John walked to the break room and poured himself a cup of the road mud that passed for coffee around the station house. He wanted a donut, but there was nothing left in the box but crumbs.

"Buncha animals," he muttered. He didn't know how some people could be so damn inconsiderate.

He took a sip from his cup of Hi-Test and turned his mind to other things, mainly to AJ. He seemed like a good kid, especially compared to most of the smart-ass degenerate punks he came across in a day's work.

John frowned, thinking of how shell-shocked the kid had seemed when he'd been brought into the station again tonight, this time over the woman who had attacked him.

What John's mind kept turning to, though, was the way AJ's face had collapsed when he heard the guy who had attacked him was DOA. But John could relate. In his fifteen years on the police force, he'd only fired his gun twice on duty. He killed a man with one of those bullets. Sure, the guy was a junkie and a murderer, but John had lost a lot of sleep after that incident.

Had that been remorse, though, or disgust? The mess had been horrible. A .44 will make a skid mark of the human head from six feet away.

John tried to shake the memory of that shaved head exploding like a rotten melon and took a sip of coffee. He wondered how the kid would sleep tonight. AJ had looked exhausted when John had seen him out to another squad car so he could be driven home, and the kid had mentioned having something at home to help him sleep. John hoped the kid had taken it and gotten some rest.

John checked his watch. 7:36 A.M. As he turned to head out of the break room, a rookie patrolman hurried around the corner and ran into him, spilling the last half of John's coffee.

"Ah son of a bitch!" John chucked his crumpled paper cup at the recruit.

"Sorry, sir!" The recruit scrambled to pick the cup up off the floor.

"Why dontcha pull your head outta your ass and watch where you're going?" John asked, wiping the coffee off his hand onto his overcoat.

"I was told to come and find you, sir, high priority."

"Who wants me?"

"The guy from the coroner's office needs to see you."

"Which one?" Irritation burned in John's mind as the coffee burnt his arm.

"Huh?"

"*Which office?* The headquarters or the temp unit next door?"

"Oh. N-next door," the uni said.

Something sank inside Lubbock's chest, and he struggled to shake the heaviness that stole over him.

"We didn't lose another fuckin' body, did we?" John asked, his voice a low rumble.

The uni ran his hand over his face. "Isn't that a shit-show? Thank *God* that happened to County and not us. But no, no, sir. He didn't say anything about a body. You hear the hospital morgue had one taken?"

"Yeah, I heard that," John said. But then, with what had happened at the end of the Bowden case, John had to wonder...

"Some shit I don't think I'll ever understand," the uni said. "This is one of them."

"Yeah, sure is," John said. "Look, be more careful, huh?"

"Yes, sir. Sorry about the coffee."

"Yeah? Good. You can clean it up." John headed next door, finding each step a little harder to take than the last.

Open and shut, remember? John thought. *Open and fucking shut.*

By the time he got next door, the coffee had cooled

and left his sleeve cold and soggy.

John walked through the door and saw Paul Diamond, head of the temp unit. He was a short, round man with a balding head and thin rimless glasses. He possessed a certain instinct that would have made him a great detective, but why he chose to spend his entire working life in the company of dead people, John didn't know.

John forced a smile he absolutely did not feel to his face.

"Ay, Paulie!"

Paul squinted through his glasses. "Hello, John. How are you?"

"Ah, good, Paulie. How's things?"

"Well, I've run across something very, very odd. Of course, it could be some kind of clerical error, which is most likely the case. But in the event it's not—"

"Whoa, whoa, Paulie. Take it easy, huh? I wanna get outta this coat and into a shot of Wild Turkey."

"Ah, yes, how…hard boiled of you. Come here." They went to a table where a body lay, covered by a black, plastic sheet. Paul pulled it down to the stiff's waist. "Do you know this fellow?"

"Yeah, I know him. He's the guy who got whacked at the gas station yesterday morning. Busted with a ball bat."

Paul frowned. "Very peculiar."

"What? What's the problem here?"

"Well," Paul said, pushing his glasses up again. "This is the guy you thought was on PCP, meth, something? Said he withstood getting hit in the head with a wine bottle, and once with a bat, before finally dropping after being struck with the bat a *second* time, right?"

"Right," John said. "You get the tox-screen back on him yet?"

"So, I *know* this guy took some damage," Paulie said, ignoring John's question. "His skull is fractured in three different places. Come here."

John stooped closer over the body as Paulie lifted the head, turning it as he spoke.

"This here, along the back, you can feel a hairline fracture, I even did an X-ray to be sure. This is from the wine bottle. There were still bits of glass in his hair, and the skin had split open. No blood, though. Weird, right?"

John was about to object, but then stopped. That *was* strange. Normally, a head wound would absolutely gush.

"Again, here," Paulie said, indicating the side of the corpse's head, "the second fracture, this being from the first strike the kid— What's his name?"

"AJ," Lubbock said, his voice papery and thin.

"This is where AJ hit him the first time with the bat. You can see his skull is dented here, even. Then we have the coup de grâce, the kill shot. Again, split the head open. Split his fucking *skull* open, a little. No blood."

Lubbock felt the world gray out a bit before the color swam back in. He had missed this. *How* had he missed this? All of them, him and the cops at the scene. The EMTs hadn't said anything, either.

Did you miss it, though? John asked himself. *Did you miss it, or did you* ignore *it?*

"Then we have the tox-screen," Paulie said.

"Y-yeah?" John asked. "What'd that look like?"

"Heroin. *Only* heroin. No meth, PCP, bath salts,

not even a fucking Adderall. Absolutely nothing that's an upper, nothing explaining how this guy could sustain three blows to the head that were hard enough to fracture his skull, and nothing to explain why those wounds didn't bleed, either. We're not talking a little heroin, either. A lot. Even considering the guy's tolerance, what he had in him was enough to kill him twice, maybe three times over."

John thought of that traffic camera footage: three minutes of motionlessness, followed by a giant seizure, then sitting up as though he were being pulled by strings.

"And this isn't even all of it," Paulie said. "Come here."

John followed Paulie to another table, where Karen Rosenthal was laid out.

"Similar situation with her," Paulie said. "Gunshot through the lungs, right? No blood."

"She was covered in blood," John said, though to him his own voice sounded far away.

"Sure, all from her wrists. Nothing in the wound, no blood in her lung. Not to mention the lividity, John. You said when you got there, she was face down, yes? No one had moved her?"

Lubbock didn't answer verbally, didn't seem capable of it. He shook his head.

"Lividity starts thirty minutes *after* de—"

"I know fuckin' lividity, Paulie!"

"Of course, right. Sorry. But to get to *this* point…I mean, after six hours or so, the blood vessels begin breaking down, but any time before then it would have been altered, at least a little, by the position you found her in."

"What the hell you sayin' here, Paulie?"

Paul sounded exasperated when he spoke, the way a teacher might sound after a day of explaining an extremely simple lesson to an equally simple child.

"I'm saying she'd been dead for *at least* six hours before she was shot, John. Probably closer to ten."

No way, John thought. *All these stiffs finally drove Paulie right outta his skull.*

And yet, he knew the same things about lividity Paulie knew. Not the intricacies, of course, but the basics.

John's head swam, and he was glad there had been no donuts left earlier. He wasn't entirely sure they would stay where they were supposed to right about then had he eaten any.

"Sweet Son of Mary, Paul. What the hell is going on?" John looked down at the woman on the table, a body that had walked into AJ's apartment and tried to choke him out, and all this *at least* six hours after bleeding to death in her tub, according to Paulie.

Not just according to Paulie, Lubbock thought. *You knew this shit the first time you saw her.*

John leaned in a little closer, looking Karen Rosenthal in the face. Her skin was pale, nose a perfectly straight line.

Then her eyes popped open.

"Oh, what the f—"

Her hand shot up and stopped the words in John's throat.

"Holy shit!" Paul yelled. He backed away quickly, falling when his feet tangled together.

Both cold hands clamped around John's throat and squeezed with an unbelievable strength, the fingers digging into his flesh. "AJ Mmmm…Munroe," her dead voice spoke. Then it laughed.

John reached into his shoulder holster and pulled out his gun as he gagged, pushing the barrel into the eye of this thing that should not be, and pulled the trigger.

The sound was deafening in the small, tiled room. It echoed again and again, although neither man could hear it above the high-pitched buzz that invaded their ears.

Dry chunks of dead scalp and skull scattered on the table and across the floor, but there was no blood. Not a single drop. The hands around John's throat tightened ever so slightly before the corpse thumped back down onto the table, lifeless once again.

* * *

John sat in a chair outside Chief Don Harris's office, a cup of coffee in his shaking hands. His throat hurt, his voice scratchy when he talked.

It couldn't happen, he told himself.

It just did, asshole, he argued inside his head.

It was now almost 8:00 A.M., and John was bone-weary. All he wanted was to drink a shot of whiskey or four and go to bed. Was that really so much to ask? He looked around the station house. Utter chaos. No one really knew what had happened, or what to believe, except for John, Paul, and Don Harris, the Chief of Police. Everyone else was told some half-crocked story the woman had been unconscious when they brought her in and came up on them during the examination.

No one could be told anything unless John and Chief Harris both had the highest confidence in their abilities and discretion. There was to be absolutely no press. Harris had said if anyone leaked, he would have their badge and their balls or tits on his desk within the hour they spoke. This was understood and accepted.

All this was bad enough for John, but there was still something worse. Not so much that a corpse had laughed at him, but what it said.

Munroe.

AJ Munroe,

What was all that about? As far as he knew, the kid's name was Lancaster not Munroe. Had he heard right? Or was the kid a liar? John supposed it was possible, but he didn't believe it. Besides, what purpose could possibly be served by lying to the police about his last name? He had to know they'd find it out.

Could AJ's involvement in all this be a case of mistaken identity? He hoped so, for the kid's sake.

Just then, Terrance Wills, a young black man who'd turned detective about a year ago, came out of Harris's office. John liked him, respected his abilities. "Hey, Wills."

Terrance looked around, finally spotting John, who waved him over.

"This is some kind of shit, man," Terrance said.

The chief had filled Terrance in on what had really went down, upon John's request. If he needed help on this, it was damn sure gonna be with whom he wanted to work. Wills didn't look well, looked a lot like John felt, in fact, like his whole world had been blown into some entirely different orbit.

"Yeah, it is. You willing to work with us on this?" John asked.

The young detective swallowed hard, and a new gleam came into his eyes. "Whatcha need?"

Wills pulled a leather-bound notebook from his back pocket and flipped it open.

"Good man. Okay, you know that kid involved in this, the one we brought in earlier?"

Terrance nodded, and John continued. "Good. Dig up everything about him. Check his driver's license, his social, run a check on his prints, everything. And one other thing."

"Yeah?" Wills asked, looking up from his notes.

"Find out the connection between him and the last name of Munroe. I'm not sure of the spelling, so check 'em all. If there's a link, you find it."

John watched as Terrance wrote the name in his book, underlining it three times.

"Yes, sir," Wills said. "I'm all over this one. I'll have what you want before I go home, or I don't go home."

John slapped him on the back. "Thanks, T. This is why you were my number one pick."

Terrance smiled at the compliment and hurried off. John watched him until he turned a corner and was gone, and then leaned forward, his elbows on his knees, covering his face with his hands. He trembled and tried not to vomit, doing everything he could to hold it together just a little longer.

He thought of Jin Makoto and Todd Bowden. He thought of where Jin was now, exiled to some little house in the middle of nowhere. His name had been scrubbed from the Bowden case, which was *illegal* for one thing, and just fucking *wrong* for another, and all because he hadn't been able to let things go. What bothered John Lubbock was that he was that same kind of cop. Until Jin, that tenaciousness had seemed like an asset. Now?

After Jin, and with what had happened?

More and more it was seeming like a fucking liability.

* * *

The phone rang. AJ sat up and looked around, still halfway asleep. The phone rang again. He rubbed his eyes and coughed to clear his throat, picked up the phone, and pressed the TALK button.

"Hello," he said, hoping it was Clover.

"Is this AJ Lancaster?" It wasn't Clover.

"Who wants to know?"

"Detective Quidman. I've been transferred to your case, and I was hoping you could answer a few questions for me."

"Oh. Well, yeah. What do you need?"

"The name Munroe mean anything to you?"

AJ hadn't heard that name in a long time and was sort of stunned to hear it now. "Munroe? Uh, why?"

"Well, something came up, and I wanted to check it out with you."

"What came up?"

There was a brief pause. "The man from the gas station? That name, Munroe, was on a list in the attacker's pocket, along with several others. All the rest had been crossed off, and that one was at the bottom."

"Well, it does mean something, actually. I'm adopted. That was my birth name, Munroe."

"Have you had any contact with your birth parents lately?"

"Not fucking likely. They died when I was six months old." AJ knew all this was on record. He knew the police could look it up any time they wanted and was a little pissed at being woken up for this.

"Okay, I appreciate your time."

"Wait a minute—" he started to say, but the line went dead. He looked at the phone and hung it up. It seemed like an odd way for a cop to operate.

The clock on the wall read 2:30 in the afternoon. He decided he might as well get up and shower when there was a knock on the door.

"Hold up," he called and put on a pair of pants and a shirt that didn't stink. He walked back into the front room and opened the door.

"Detective Lubbock?"

"Yeah, so, listen, kid—"

"Why didn't you tell me about this list?" AJ asked, a slow anger starting to build in his chest.

"List? What list?"

"The detective I just talked to on the phone said the guy who came after me at work was carrying a list with—"

"Whoa, whoa, whoa, kid. *Who'd* you talk to?"

"Detective Quidman?"

"*Quidman?* Doesn't ring a bell," John said. "What'd he want?"

"Asked me about a name," AJ said.

John closed his eyes for a long moment and looked to AJ as if he were fighting off a sudden bit of vertigo. AJ was about to ask if he was okay when John finally opened his eyes.

"What name?"

"Munroe," AJ said.

"Sit down, kid. We gotta talk."

"Lemme put some coffee on first. You want some?"

After he poured two mugs full and handed one to the detective, AJ sat on the couch and recounted the phone conversation. He could sense the detective knew something big he wasn't quite ready to give up yet. Maybe something huge.

"First of all, kid, I'm positive there's no Detective Quidman on the force, and I know for a fact the guy who attacked you wasn't carrying around any such list. The name of the corpse is James Bradley. Ring a bell?"

AJ thought about the name for a second, and then shook his head. "No. Who is he?"

"I didn't think so. It's not important. What, uh, what I really wanted to talk to you about was your neighbor."

"Yeah?"

AJ's hand crept toward the circle of bruises on his throat.

"Well, this ain't gonna to be easy to tell you, and it'll be a helluva lot harder for you to hear, but bear with me, all right?"

"Okay," AJ said with a feeling like a rising tidal wave welling up inside him.

"Kid, she's dead."

The wave of anticipation broke, leaving nothing but the crusted seafoam of disappointment in its wake. "Yeah, I was here, remember?"

"Kid, stay with me here. We think, no, we *know*, we have forensic evidence, in fact, that before she came to your door, she'd cut her wrists in the tub—"

"Come on!" AJ said. "My fucking *finger* went *inside her arm*, remember? I *told* you that. I *know* she slit her wrists."

"Okay," John said, seizing on this. "I remember you telling me that. Remember what you said? How you told me it felt when your finger went in there?"

"Yeah."

"You said it was cold, right? Like putting your hand in a turkey thawing a couple hours?"

"Right."

"Okay," John said. "Think about that. Now listen, kid, and holy fuck, do *not* interrupt me again because I don't know if I have the energy for this. I been up for close to thirty-six hours now, and I still have a ton of shit to do, so just listen to me, okay?"

AJ nodded.

"Okay, kid, she slit her wrists and bled out. She had been dead for maybe six hours before coming to your door."

"What is this?"

"I'm not done, kid."

"What is this shit, Detective? Some sick fucking joke down at the station?" In his heart, AJ knew otherwise.

"Oh, I wish it was, son," John said. "But you better calm down, and you better listen because, well, just... just look."

At that, John bared his neck, showing AJ the nasty red marks that hadn't been there last night when they'd talked at the station about what happened with Karen. John began the story, with the coroner telling him Karen Rosenthal had been dead for close to six hours and ended with the shooting. He told AJ the name she had said prior to being shot in the head.

AJ took it all surprisingly well. He sat there on his end of the couch, shell-shocked and silent, staring blankly at a TV that wasn't on, trying to let all this new and hideously twisted information be either accepted by his brain or rejected.

There was a loud knock, startling AJ out of his daze and bringing John to his feet. The detective's gun was out, and he stepped to the door, peering through the peephole. He breathed a sigh of relief, putting his gun back in the holster. John unlocked the door and opened it, letting in a uniformed officer.

"What's the word?" John asked.

"You're supposed to come back to HQ," the younger man said, then jerked a thumb at AJ. "Bring him, too."

John nodded and closed the door as the other man left. The fact they were leaving pulled AJ out of the daze John's news had left him in, if only a little. Moving helped. He walked back and forth through his apartment, putting on a jacket, grabbing his keys and cigarettes and a lighter, each step bringing him slowly back into himself. Finally, the two of them walked outside and got in John's Ford.

AJ wished he'd never woken up that morning, that he'd slept through until all this crazy shit was over with. But no. Here he was, riding in an unmarked police car that stank of old fast food and cigar smoke.

No way. No way in hell, AJ thought. *All this, it's impossible.*

Yet, John assured him it was true. John didn't strike AJ as the sort of guy who ran around believing tabloid trash like this, but he was apparently a strong believer in...well, in whatever this was.

The overwhelming idea he'd somehow been grossly misinformed about the natural order of things wouldn't go away. People would change their religions over this. Hell, they'd drop everything and invent new ones.

If it happened last night, would it happen again? And had it happened before?

I can't believe I'm putting stock in this horseshit, AJ thought again and again as they drove through the city. But there was a part of him that hadn't been there before, a part that *wanted* it to be true. It was like a long-dormant instinct awakening, shaking the years of hibernation from its mane and getting ready for war.

A short while later, he sat in a room with three plain-clothes detectives and the chief of police himself, Don Harris. The chief was a huge, square-jawed man with features that looked as though they'd been poorly carved from a block of granite. His black hair was shorn close, Marine style, and he had a case of serious cauliflower ear.

Then there was Terrance Wills, and next to him was a redhead named Steve Nielsen.

John made the introductions.

"Why don't we start by telling us about the name Munroe," John said.

All the eyes swiveled to AJ, and his mind threw up an image of a firing squad taking aim. AJ cleared his throat, not sure if he would be able to speak until he did. "My parents died when I was six months old."

Of course, he remembered none of the story he began to tell. It was what he had gleaned from other sources, facts people told him and an old newspaper clipping he still carried in his wallet. It had been the middle of December. the family was going Christmas shopping. The three of them got into the car, AJ in a baby seat in the back, his parents in the front. The roads were icy, and snow was falling.

Their station wagon had been hit head-on by a van less than a block and a half from home. The only survivors had been the man driving the van, who was piss-drunk at nine in the morning, and AJ. He was told his dad lived for two days in the hospital. Being so young, and having no other relatives to speak of, AJ was adopted quickly by Hal and Gina Lancaster, who had legally changed his last name to theirs.

Finally, Don Harris leaned back in his chair. It groaned briefly in protest of the man's size. He was six-foot-six and built solid as a brick.

"Well, son," the giant of a cop said, "we need to find out who else knows you're a Munroe."

"There isn't anybody else except my parents," AJ said.

"We still haven't been able to get a hold of them, even though I've had a guy calling every half hour since this situation developed," Harris continued. "Do you know if they were planning on going out of town for a while, perhaps even here to the city?"

"No, they should be there. My dad teaches at the college in town, and classes just started up again last month."

Harris nodded. He decided to call the boys upstate, where the Lancasters lived, and have them check in. There was a knock on the door, and the desk sergeant popped his head in.

"Guy out here, boss. Claims he owns the gas station—"

Vito squirmed around the sergeant and into the room.

"Can I help you?" Harris asked, not knowing who Vito was and being unaccustomed to people barging in on him.

"Very doubtful, Gigantor, but I think I can help you." Vito seated himself and spoke, recounting the story of his visit from a Detective Quidman. John had looked into it. There wasn't a cop named Quidman in the entire *state*, let alone in their house.

"...and so, I says to the guy, I says, why should I, you know? And this prick fuck tries layin' obstruction on me!"

"Did you give him the DVD?" John asked.

"Yeah, I gave 'em to him! He said he was a cop for chrissakes! He had a *badge!*"

"And you're positive he mentioned the name Munroe?" Terrance asked.

Vito gave him a look he reserved solely for people he found dangerously close to complete and total idiocy "No, it's a ruse, my dear Watson. Yes, I'm fucking sure! It's what I said, ain't it?"

"Mr. Vincelli, can you give us a description of this man?" Don Harris asked.

"Why don't I show you?" Vito slid a jewel case down the table to Steve, who popped it into the DVD player. The six of them watched in silence, rewound it, and watched again.

John sat back and crossed his arms on his chest. "Whoever this jack-off is, I'm willing to bet he's a major part in this. You ever seen him before, kid?"

At first, it was as though AJ hadn't heard.

"Kid?"

AJ snapped out of it, giving his head a quick shake,

and blinking his eyes. "Huh?"

"You ever seen that guy before?"

"No," AJ said quietly. "No, I've never seen him before."

AJ felt like he was coming down from a bad acid trip. Before, he hadn't given much thought about who was responsible for all this, but someone had to be, right? And this happy fuck sat right at the top of the list.

AJ leaned back, sighed heavily, and checked his watch. It was now 4:20 P.M.

"Hey, can I go home? Unless there's something else you need from me." AJ looked around the table hopefully, his tired eyes setting upon each of the separate but equally tired faces in the room. He knew John had gotten maybe five hours of sleep in the last twenty-four hours, and he didn't think Don Harris had gotten any. Not from the look of him, anyway.

"We're going to have to send someone with you. We need a full guard on you until we get this sorted out," Don told him.

"I'll get someone to cover your shifts," Vito said.

AJ could live with that. Fifteen minutes later, he was in a patrol car, *again*, and on his way back home.

* * *

John Lubbock was about to start going over the statements Steve had collected when one of Don's impossibly huge hands rested upon his shoulder. He looked up at his chief.

"John, you need to get home. You look like shit."

"Gee, thanks, Don. You should have been a motivational speaker. You missed your calling."

"I'm serious. You can't help this kid by running yourself into the ground."

The detective sighed, the sigh turning into a deep yawn.

Harris gave him his *see what I mean?* look. Lubbock nodded and stood, taking a cigar out of his pocket, and biting off the end.

"I'll be back by midnight."

"If I find out you were here before six tomorrow morning, I'll suspend your ass. And that's a promise, old friend." Harris looked as though he was serious, so John didn't press the issue. Instead, he nodded, put on his coat, and left.

A short while later, John walked into the only place he ever really went to drink, unless it was back at home. The thought of his small, empty apartment was more than he could bear tonight, and after everything he'd seen, he wanted nothing more than to have a small slice of something normal and sane in his life.

This is why he went to McNulty's when he went anywhere. It was a third-generation cop bar run by the same family of hotheaded, fuckin' asshole Irish since about 1910. It was the only bar that had stayed open throughout Prohibition, as John had heard the owner, or his son or grandson, tell it. It had been a cop bar then, too, and had flourished.

Evidence of the prosperity in decades past was still there. It was in the fine leather of the booths, though most of it was faded and cracked. It was there in the brass fixtures, though they were tarnished, dusty, forgotten. That prosperity was in the top of the bar itself, thirty-five feet of single-piece mahogany. It was topped in glass, and the glass was coated in grease from the food they served, and the hands that touched it, with crumbs and ashes and spilt drinks, spilt stories, spilt time.

If you cared to look through that skin of grime, or if you were around for last call the night before St. Paddy's Day, when they always polished that glass until it gleamed, you would see the old-world craftsmanship and grandeur in that bar top. Not many people cared to look anymore, John found, and had noticed that even he had, lately, stopped looking.

Here, though, nothing really changed. You would always find the same men, even when they were different. There would be a couple unis, patrolmen for the most part, every now, and then a motorcycle cop or a statie. There would be a few of the younger detectives, out to listen to the old timers, and there would be the old timers themselves.

Not all of them would be swapping stories with the new kids, many of them would be tucked into corners in pairs or threes, drinking heavily and speaking of heavy things. A lot of them came in to drink alone, too.

John didn't want to drink alone, not tonight, and his spirits lifted a little when he saw who was at the bar.

The three men were old-school, the very definition of it. They had close to fifty years on the job between the three of them: Kurtz, Sully, and Rick Polaski. Kurtz still carried a set of brass knuckles and was always looking for a reason to use them, Sully was about as crooked a cop as you could find, and Polaski was a full-blown alcoholic.

There had been plenty of times John had carried

Polaski out of the bar and stuffed him into a cab, and plenty more where Polaski wouldn't let him. On his off days, he would be found on that same stool, open to close, pounding them back. On the days he was on, he spent his lunches here, usually, and was in just about every night after he clocked out.

"Jesus Christ, it's like a bad joke in here," John said, winking at Jimmy the 3rd, who was behind the bar, then turning back to the three on his side of the mahogany. "A German, an Irishman, and a fuckin Polack go into a bar…"

"Johnny, how you doin'?" Jimmy the 3rd asked, already tipping John's drink into the glass: three-quarters full of Wild Turkey and a single ice cube.

"Good, kid, how's the old man?"

"Fuckin' miserable," the 3rd said back, laughing.

"He'll settle this," Polaski said, reaching out to John's arm.

"Settle what?" John asked.

"We're talking about guys who were just solid *police*, through and through," Polaski said.

Any night you walked in and Kurtz, Sully, and Polaski were holding down their stools, there was better than even odds they were having this same conversation, talking about cops they had known who had been real cops, good cops, had been solid *police*, likely hoping someone would apply that label to them.

Sully slid down to make room for John, who eased onto the bar stool and felt the weight leave his heart as it left his feet.

"This Jew-fuck has the balls to tell me Sammy was better'n *Parkins*," Sully said.

"For the last time, I'm *Catholic*, you stupid Irish fuck," Polaski said, signaling to the 3rd for another round.

"Sammy?" John asked. "You mean Molina?"

"Yeah, Molina," Kurtz said. "Lost his shit and did himself. You remember that, dontcha, John? You worked that with him a little, didn't you?"

"Sammy's last case, the writer's wife," John said. "I didn't really *work* it. I worked with him, though, at the time."

"Whatta you think?" Polaski asked. "I said Sammy lost the plot."

John nodded, dropping a tenner on the bar for Jimmy the 3rd, and then taking his glass. He held it up to the light a little, as he always did, turning it in his hand as he thought, allowing the heat from his hand to slowly melt the single ice cube. Only when it was gone would he tilt the glass to his lips, and then would down the glass in three long swallows. Every time he drank, no matter how many drinks he had, that was how he drank it.

Just one tonight, though, John told himself.

"Sam...Sam was solid police," John said. "The fact he killed himself don't take that from him. I expect you three to know that."

"That's what I said!" Sully said, slapping John on the back.

"Parkins was solid, though," Polaski said, nursing everything except his drink.

"Sure, he was solid," John said, nodding. "Park was solid, absolutely. He wasn't fit to sit in the same squad room with the likes a' Sammy, though."

"Here's to Sammy," Polaski said, raising his glass. The others raised their glasses. John raised his glass but didn't drink, not yet, though he had rather liked Sammy and had taken his suicide hard. Given that Sam had descended into a cloud of alcohol fumes he carried into the office with him at ten in the morning the month before he took his own life, John wasn't sure drinking to him was a great way to remember the guy.

"Speaking a' fuckin' crazy," Sully said. "That old partner a' yours, down Bridgetown?"

"Who?" John asked, snapping his head around.

"The fuckin', whatsit, the fella with that thing makes you count shit over and over? Your fucking *partner*."

"OCD," Polaski said.

"You mean William Coe?" John asked.

"Yeah, Coe, that's it. Jesus, I heard stories a' that guy. Fuckin' freak, yeah?"

"Whatever else he is, that man is the single finest detective I ever worked with, *bar none*," John said. "He has the highest homicide close rate in the country right now, if you care to look it up."

"Yeah, no, I know," Sully said. "I just mean, you gotta have some stories about the guy, right?"

John just looked at Sully for a long moment, then back at his drink. The ice cube was about half gone. Polaski called for another, as did Sully and Kurtz. John thought about his old friend, all the time they'd been partnered together, the cases they'd solved, the guys they'd put away, the night Coe had saved his life.

Yes, Bill Coe had been nothing *but* solid police, side to side and straight through the middle. More cop than these three would ever be, old-school or not, fifty years on the job or not. John felt a stab of shame, thinking of what Bill would say if he knew John was in here, having to force himself to only have one drink. No, he wouldn't talk about his old friend and his condition. *Conditions*. Not here. Not with them.

"You know who was fucking *solid* police?" John asked. "Another fella I used to work with, down in BPD. Harry fucking Mitchell."

"Yeah?" Kurtz asked. "The guy with the kid got took, yeah?"

"Yes," John said, staring at the ice cube, willing it to melt. He didn't say how after four years, little Alice Mitchell's body had finally been found. Bill had called and told him this just last week, and John had arranged for flowers to be sent. The thought of Harry having to put his little girl in the ground was almost enough to get John to raise the glass to his lips, but he stayed his hand.

"Jesus Christ, the poor bastard," Sully said.

Polaski shook his head and took another drink. "This fuckin' world."

"Harry left the force after his daughter was taken," John said. "He had a nose for bullshit like no other, though, like a fucking human polygraph. Brutal, too."

"Brutal, huh?" Kurtz asked.

"*Brutal*," John said and shook his head. "I seen him beat a confession out of a guy once. It was a thing of beauty. Guy came in hard as a coffin nail…lifetime in the system, rap sheet you couldn't fit on this bar, nothing but beat on as a kid, in and out of foster homes, hit juvie on a murder rap. Fifteen years old when he stabbed that little boy to death."

"Why, Detective, those juvenile records are supposed to be sealed," Kurtz said, smiling.

"Yeah, sealed," Polaski said.

"And a judge'd never hear me say otherwise," John said. "Anyway, this guy, he walked out a' juvie the day he turned adult. Learned to work the system, just the kinda perp that ain't ever gonna crack on his own, you know? The kind that you gotta crack yourself."

"Fuckin-a'," Polaski said, taking a long drink.

"You need a guy broken, you called Harry. Another little boy was missing. This guy, he'd fallen *twice* on pedo charges as an adult, one of them a fucking three-year-old. Getting worse. We knew the guy had him, the little boy. We *knew it*. I knew it, Coe knew it. Just fuckin'. *Knew. It.* We just couldn't get the place out of him, where the kid was. So, we called in Harry and turned off the camera. Harry beat this guy *to death*, understand me? I mean literally. Resuscitated him right there in the fuckin' grill-room, still cuffed to the table."

"I heard about that," Sully said, his voice soft.

"He was like a fuckin' scientist of hurting people, Harry was. He knew how to beat a guy unconscious without even leaving a mark. This guy, though, *he* was marked. Harry took his time, no rush. Just step by step by step until the perp cracked. His eyes were swollen so bad we had to cut 'em like they used to in boxing, so he could sign the confession when Harry was done with him."

Melt, John thought, staring at his drink. *Fucking melt.*

"Was the kid okay?" Polaski asked.

"No," John said. "He was alive, though."

Kurtz let out a low whistle.

"What about up here?" Sully asked.

"Eh?" John asked, looking up from his ice cube, which was really more of a sliver now. Almost.

Just one drink, John thought again. *Just this one.*

"Who's the best guy you worked with up here?"

"Oh, that's no contest," John said. "Jin."

"Who?" Sully asked.

"I gotta call it a night, boys," Kurtz said, slamming back the last of his drink and dropping a twenty on the bar.

"Yeah, have a good night, Frank," John said, then turned back to Sully. "You fuckin' gone soft on me, Sully? *Jin.*"

Sully pulled a face and just shook his head, looking down at his glass.

"Oh, the *fuck* you don't know Jin," John said. "Makoto? Fucking come on, Sully, you *rode* with the guy for, like, six months!"

"Don't ring a bell, John, sorry."

"Worked the Bowden murd—"

"Night, John," Sully said, setting his empty glass on the bar and dropping a bill for Jimmy the 3rd to pick up. "Have a good night, Jimmy! Pole, I'll see you tomorrow."

Polaski nodded.

John looked back in his glass. Almost gone now. He held the drink in both hands, willing it to melt.

"I can't believe fuckin' Sully," John said. "How many he put back tonight, make him forget Jin like that? You know who I mean, right, Pole? Worked the Bowden case, got... Well, fuck it, the brass ain't here. Got pushed out after that, remember? Ended up with the commissioner involved, a senator or some damn thing. *Christ,* that case, though! I ne—"

John looked up and found with a start the chair next to him was empty, the stool slowly spinning. He looked up as the door closed, and Polaski was gone. John looked back to the spot the Pole had recently vacated and stared at the half-full drink still sitting on the bar.

Rick Polaski never left a drink unfinished in his life, John thought.

Jimmy the 3rd came by, picking up the cash and stacking the glasses. "You can't talk about him in here, John," the 3rd said. "Even I know that."

John opened his mouth to speak and snapped it shut again. He looked down at the drink in his hand, and the ice was finally gone.

To Sammy, he thought. *Sammy and Jin.*

He tilted it up to his mouth and drained the glass in three long swallows, the Turkey burning going down and lighting up like napalm when it hit, but God it was good. Too good, really.

John set his empty glass on the bar, said goodnight, and left.

About twenty minutes later, John walked into his small, one-bedroom apartment and shut the door behind him. He shrugged out of his trench coat and flung it onto the back of his chair and hung his fedora on the doorknob.

He stood staring at the bottle of Wild Turkey on his kitchen counter, telling himself how he'd said *one* drink earlier. Only one. After a moment that was longer than he would have admitted—longer than he realized—he turned away and sat in his favorite chair with his feet up, to think. Not about anything in particular for something is always overlooked, but the case in general.

Right now, it was obvious this kid had a part in something he had no knowledge of. Someone was trying to grab hold of him and pull him into it, kicking and screaming. The alleged Detective Quidman was the only suspect right now, but John had long ago learned to never close his mind to other possibilities.

And where could AJ's birth name of Munroe fit in? John was sure the kid was safe now, but he had no idea what they were up against. None of them did. He thought again of Jin, and how after looking into it long enough, the pieces of the Bowden case had stopped adding up. It had seemed like an open-and-shut thing: nasty to be sure, a serial murderer of women?

Of *course*, it was nasty. But Jin had caught the first body that was found and had ran with it. He'd had all the help he could ask for at first, guys putting in hours even when they knew they weren't getting OT, doing goddamn *police work* because there was a guy out there, killing women, and they all wanted it to stop.

And it did, finally. When Jin walked Todd Bowden into one of the interview rooms, head hung, hands in cuffs, Jin was looked at like a rockstar, like a kind of *god*, and the relief that had been in the station house had been palpable. It had been thick and real, a physical thing. It was over, people kept saying. It's over. Finally over.

But for Jin, that was when it really started. Between the shit Bowden started talking in his confession, and the thing, later, with his wife's body, there was too much that didn't quite add up. Jin was too good of a cop to let these things go, and the more he dug, the worse it got.

John was deeply ashamed of how he'd turned his back and let it go when he'd been ordered to.

Fuckin complicit, he thought now, that old shame burning fresh and hot on the back of his neck and in his guts. In his heart. *You are an accessory. Aiding in the total destruction of one of the finest men he'd ever worked with.*

He didn't know what all Jin had found, if anything. The way the brass had gotten involved, and not just the brass but worse, the *politicians,* John had always figured it to be some kind of massive conspiracy involving someone rich and powerful. Someone connected with those at the top, or even someone *at* the top.

Could it have been more, though? Something like this?

Good God, could it have been *something like this?*

Detective John Lubbock sat back down in his chair, surprised to find he'd gotten up while in his reveries and poured himself a glass of Wild Turkey, three-quarters full and with a single ice cube floating in it.

Fuck it, he decided, seeing Karen Rosenthal's eyes open again and again, staring up at him from the coroner's table. If this wasn't a two-drink night, there never was one.

It was a long time before he was able to sleep.

CHAPTER

FIVE

I can't believe they're having this asshole guard me, AJ thought.

He'd been given some bullshit cover story for being on protection. The higher-ups had wisely chosen to keep this numb fuck out of the loop. Officer Gomez had driven him home last night, and that had been fine. Gomez was a good guy. But when his shift ended, he was replaced by…this.

Upon greeting Gomez, Officer Aaron Burrell remarked on what a shitty section of town they were in. AJ stared out the window, watching the vultures as they circled above.

Gomez shook AJ's hand, and AJ thanked him, and Gomez left. AJ gave Burrell the tour, such as it was.

"Man," Burrell said. "This place is *tiny*! It would drive me nuts living here. How do you do it?"

"Happily, until now." AJ poured himself a cup of coffee, got another pack of Red Apples out his carton in the freezer, and sat on the couch.

"Jeez, kid. You smoke, too?"

"Only when I'm real fucking annoyed."

Burrell nodded. Not only was he rude, but he was stupid, too. This was somehow worse, that he couldn't understand when he was being insulted.

The following six hours had been the longest AJ had spent in recent memory, and this included that endless first night in the police station after James Bradley first attacked him.

AJ had been in the bathroom when he heard his phone ring. He washed his hands as he heard his answering machine kick on.

"Oh, my God, you have an *answering machine*?" Clover's voice filled the apartment, making AJ smile as he headed for the phone. "That's so cool! I didn't know your apartment was in 1995."

"Ooooh! A ladies' man, eh?" Burrell said.

AJ tried to ignore him, he really did, and picked up the phone.

"Hey!" he said into the cordless, walking into the other room. "Sorry about that. Little slow to get to the phone."

"Or to the modern era," Clover said, laughing. "I think the only person I know who still has a landline is my Gramma. In her nursing home."

"Yeah, yeah, I get it. You're *hilarious*. Comedy Central call you yet about your own stand-up special?"

"Aww, you know about Comedy Central?" Clover asked. "Okay, I'm done."

"Get that out of your system, did you?"

"I did!" Clover said. "So, we still on for tonight?"

"Of course!" AJ said. He'd talked to Gomez a bit about it, and Gomez had assured him it wouldn't be a problem. He hadn't yet figured out how to tell her he was on police protection yet, but he supposed he could cross that bridge when she got there.

"Cool! I'm about to grab something to eat, and I'll be over."

AJ gave her his address and directions. He was a bit embarrassed by where he lived because Burrell was right, the neighborhood *was* kinda shitty. It didn't faze her, though.

"Oh, I know where this is. There's a great old theater near there, right? The Esquire?"

"Yeah!" AJ said. "I love that place. They just played *Josey Wales* last month."

"Shit, I *went* to that!" Clover said. "It was just the weekend, right? When'd you go?"

"High Noon Matinee, on Saturday."

"I was gonna catch that! I had a flat tire on the way over, though, and had to hit the three o'clock instead."

There was a long moment where AJ thought about it, how they were very nearly at the same movie at the same time.

"So close," Clover said, her voice a little far away, as though she were speaking to herself. "Anyway, *weird* right?"

"Yeah, it really is."

"Well, I'll see you soon, okay?"

"More than okay," AJ said. He pressed the END button on the receiver and stood there a moment, wishing she hadn't gotten that flat tire, or that he had went to the three o'clock show, that maybe they would have met each other in the lobby, or—

"Who's that? Some sweet little piece you got lined out for later?" Burrell asked.

AJ jumped a little and turned to see the cop standing in his doorway, leaning against the frame. Burrell wiggled his eyebrows lecherously.

And I can't stand no more, AJ thought. "What are you, fourteen?"

Burrell stared at him blankly for a second, a stupefied look permanently attached to his face. "What do you mean?"

"I mean you're a grown man, and you act like I did when I was fourteen. And I was *immature* for a fourteen-year-old."

"Calm down, junior," Burrell said, finally taking offense to something. "I didn't know you were such a fun guy."

"Yeah, and you're a real barrel of fucking monkeys yourself," AJ muttered.

"Huh?"

AJ hated to stoop to this, but he thought there might be only one way to pull it off. He had to drop to Burrell's level. Antagonizing the guy wasn't going to get him anywhere, and the last thing he wanted was to have this asshole chaperoning them.

"Look, that girl I got off the phone with? She's coming over around seven-thirty, and it might get a bit... odd...if you were in here. *If* you know what I mean..." AJ tipped him the heavily suggestive conspirator's wink he hadn't used since his ninth-grade year.

"Ohhhh. I getcha." Burrell's eyebrows hopped up and down again, and he favored AJ with a perverted grin he could have done without. "I don't see what I can do, though. I mean, the chief said—"

AJ cut him off. "For you to guard me. Right. But couldn't you do it even better from the hall? I have a chair I use at my computer you could take out there."

"Is it comfortable?" Burrell asked, a note of child-like suspicion in his voice.

AJ showed him the large, padded chair, which happened to be very comfortable indeed. Plus, it had wheels, which he figured would be enough for someone of Burrell's obvious intelligence. A mental picture of the large, dull-eyed man racing up and down the halls in his chair popped into AJ's head, and he barely stifled the laughter.

"I've got a lot of books, too, if you wanted to read," he offered without much hope.

"Well, the chair is good, but I'm not much of one for reading, you know?"

"Well, I've also got this," AJ hunted around the coffee table for a moment before finding what he was looking for.

"Oh, hey! I love these things!" Burrell's eyes lit up when AJ gave him a little electronic poker game. He sat on the couch and started playing immediately.

"So, you'll help me out here?"

"Huh?" Burrell looked up from the game of five-card draw he'd instantly become immersed in.

"Will you help me out with this?"

"Oh, sure. No problem."

AJ breathed a sigh of relief, and Burrell cursed as he lost a hand.

* * *

The man who wasn't Detective Quidman opened his eyes. Not that he really needed to sleep, but old habits die hard. His name was Logan, or at least it had been for so long it didn't really matter one way or the other. There were a lot of things that didn't matter, and even more he didn't want to remember.

But, right now, there were some serious issues at hand that needed his undivided attention. Things looked bad. It hadn't seemed this bleak since the first time, all those years ago. Life had been simpler then. There were no TVs or radios, not even a morning newspaper. The world had moved on, becoming an endless barrage of information. Besides, people had been more superstitious back then, and they wouldn't buy this now. It simply wouldn't be accepted the way it used to be.

Logan just had to hope *He* hadn't found the book yet. It was unlikely, but it was still a possibility that couldn't be ignored. But he didn't think The Next had it either, and that could be nearly as bad.

Logan knew the police would probably try and stop him from getting to the boy, but any efforts they could make to prevent him would be to no avail. He loaded his guns: a Taurus .357 he'd just picked up with a seven-chamber cylinder, an automatic .45 with a laser sight, and a shotgun he'd made himself. It was double barreled, except the barrels were stacked instead of being side by side and fired any standard 12-gauge ammo. It was semi-automatic, pump action, and mean.

He put the .45 in his side holster, the .357 in the back, and then put on the shoulder sling he had devised for the shotgun. He checked the sheath strapped to his right thigh, and the knife with the foot-long blade that was within it. Atop it all went his trench coat, which served as concealment for the weapons.

He took a small, round object about the size of a billiard ball from the pocket of his coat. The brown paper wrapping he'd picked it up in was still crumpled and stuffed in the bathroom trashcan. The object let off a pulsing, blue glow.

It was time to make contact.

***

The intercom next to the door buzzed. AJ stepped over the coffee table and thumbed the TALK button. "Hello?"

"It's me," said the voice on the other end.

"Who?"

"Clover."

"I'm afraid you have the wrong apartment. There's no one here by the name of Clover."

"Let me in, dick," she said and laughed. AJ pressed the button and checked himself in the bathroom mirror one more time, making sure there was nothing in his teeth. Then he opened the door and leaned out to Burrell to say, "Hey, you need anything, man? Take a piss, drink of water?"

Burrell responded with a negative grunt, never even taking his eyes off the game. At the end of the hall, the door opened, and Clover walked through it and once again into his heart.

"Come on in," he said as she neared and held the

door open for her. "Welcome to my humble abode."

"Thank you." She smiled at him and walked through the door. The cop didn't give her a second glance as she passed him. She turned to AJ once the door was shut. "Why is there a cop here?"

"Well, after what happened—"

"You mean at the gas station?" *That doesn't seem like something one would need police protection for,* she thought.

"No, after that. After you left, actually. Someone kept calling the station and threatening me, saying they knew what I did. So, they thought it might be best to keep an eye on me for a while." AJ felt a terrible pang lying to her, but what was the alternative, really? She'd think he was insane if he told her the things John had laid on him.

She was shocked. "Why didn't you tell me earlier?"

He shrugged. "I dunno. I didn't want you to get all worried or anything. Besides, it's probably nothing anyway."

She couldn't think of anything to say after that. A short but uncomfortable silence ensued. "So, why don't you give me the tour?"

"Delighted!" AJ did his best Robin Leach impression and held his arm out with a flourish. She giggled and took it, following him into the other room. AJ showed her his ludicrously small apartment, feeling like a jackass as he pointed out the bedroom. They soon came to the kitchen.

"This is my hammer," AJ said, motioning toward the little table to the left of the window. "I use it to prop my window open because my landlord is a dick and won't replace anything."

"*Very* nice," Clover said.

"This is where I try and keep food," he said as he opened the fridge. "Want something to drink?"

"Please. What do you have?" She leaned over to look in the fridge so she could put her hand on his shoulder.

"Water, beer, and, uh, beer."

"Wow. Can I have a minute to think this over?"

"Nope," he said, shutting the fridge. "Time's up. No beverage for you."

She smiled and rolled her eyes at him. "A beer would be great. As long as it's not Coors."

AJ opened two bottles of Honey Brown, and they sat on the couch. She took a bottle and looked him in the eyes. AJ was too helpless to do much but stare back. It was only for a moment, a flicker in time, but those few seconds seemed to go on for eternity, and he would have been just as happy if it had.

He stared into her deep, green eyes, eyes the color of clover, and was forever lost in them, drowning in the kindness and hope they held. This visceral instant slowly came to an end as she raised her beer, the almost surreal quality of it all fading as softly as the light dies from the day when the sun drops below the horizon.

"What should we drink to?" she murmured.

Us, he thought, and she nodded like she'd heard him. The bottles clinked, and they drank. AJ blinked several times, clearing his head.

"So," he said, trying to clear his throat, "wanna start the movie?"

AJ put his copy of *True Romance* in the DVD player, and they sat on the couch. As the movie played out, they didn't talk much, but the silence was comfortable this time, almost necessary.

Clover finished her beer, AJ's empty bottle sat on the coffee table. She set hers next to it and walked into the kitchen, returning with another bottle for each of them. She sat close enough their hips touched, and she leaned against him in a familiar way. He slipped his arm around her, and there it rested, as if it had always been there, until the screams began in the hall.

* * *

Officer Aaron Burrell sat in his chair. He was hooked on this little game and had finally started to win. He smiled with a childlike look of pleasure on his face as the electronic victory song played from above the screen.

He was distracted by footsteps. The man walking slowly down the hall wore a nice suit, as if he'd just come from somewhere important.

If he can afford a suit like that, why does he live in a dump like this? Burrell asked himself, then did the mental equivalent of a shrug. He hit the DEAL button and went back to his hand.

The guy in the nice suit stopped directly in front of him. Burrell looked up at the pale skin and glazed, sunken eyes, and what little police instinct he possessed lifted its head like a drugged rhinoceros.

What is this guy? A drug addict? That's it…maybe a needle freak.

"Can I help you?" Burrell was answered with silence. He stared up into the sallow face for a moment, then set the poker game on the floor next to the chair. He stood up, taking full advantage of his six-foot-three frame.

"I asked you a question. Now, is there something I can help you with or isn't there?"

"Izzn derrrr," the junkie said in a thick, gravelly voice, grinning widely.

This guy's fucking trashed! Burrell thought, thinking further he would love to crack this junkie one in the head. His hand rested on the nightstick, fingers drumming on the dark, oily wood. He had to focus, though, as he wasn't here to crack some junkie's skull open. Still…

"Funny, huh? Well, you best move along really quick, else I'm afraid all the fun is gonna run outta this situation in a hurry."

The other man leaned in closer and spoke one word, clear and unmistakable: "Munroe."

Then he jammed his graying middle finger into Burrell's left eye, all the way past the second knuckle.

The pain was immediate and totally debilitating. Burrell felt the finger wiggle around inside his skull, and a tortured gurgle escaped his lips. It was all he could manage. There was no way he could speak, not as bloody tears ran lethargically down his face. All sound was gone except for the manic buzzing of agony that began in his eye and resonated throughout his entire body.

The finger slowly pulled out, followed by a rush of crimson. The officer's tongue finally came to life when his eye slid out of his head and onto his cheek.

He screamed.

* * *

AJ jumped off the couch as if bitten by it, his initial

statement of shock lost within the wail coming from the hall.

"What was *that*?" Clover asked.

How does she sound so calm, AJ thought, shaking his head, the only answer he could give. He set his beer on the table and went to the door, peering through the peephole.

The peephole was filled by Aaron Burrell's bloody, screaming face, his eyeball dangling at the end of the optic nerve, the empty socket staring into infinity and weeping gore.

AJ saw a hand reach around the back of Burrell's screaming head, and then the head came rushing toward him. He jumped back from the door as the face slammed into it, letting out a small scream of his own.

Thunk.

The door shook in its frame, and the screaming in the hall went on.

"Oh...fuck...call the police," he said weakly.

"What is it?" Clover asked, and again he marveled at how much more *steady* her voice sounded compared to his own.

"Call the police!"

Thunk!

Clover picked up the phone and dialed 911.

THUNK!

The screaming suddenly cut off, ending with a ragged, choking sound.

THUNK!

A long, black crack ran up the center of the door as the old wood finally began to give.

"Yes, we need assistance," Clover said into the

phone. She sounded like she was ordering a pizza as she rattled off his address while his door was bludgeoned from outside. He heard more screams and shouts throughout the building.

"Yes, that's correct," Clover said into the phone. "Look, lady…get someone here right fucking now because some asshole's trying to break the door down!" She turned off the phone and threw it onto the couch.

There was an inhuman cry of rage and hate from the hall, not a nonsensical roar but an actual word, a name being screamed. The sound of it followed AJ for the rest of his life, echoing through his nightmares and into the darkness during the small hours of the morning, when the world is the deadest, the blackest, the coldest.

"MUUUUNROOOOE!"

It was followed by a crash, and a large chunk of his front door finally gave, busting out in a cloud of splinters. Clover screamed. AJ turned to face what was coming for him, and it was the very face of death.

Heeeere's Johnny! Jack Nicholson laughed in his head. He then thought of the fire escape. He'd forgotten about it until now, and the sick, omen-like feeling he'd doomed them cast a trembling shadow upon his heart.

The walking corpse kicked the rest of the door in and took its first step into the apartment. AJ looked around frantically for a weapon, trying to back Clover toward the last bit of potential safety.

"Go open the kitchen window, get on the fire escape." AJ grabbed two of the empty beer bottles off the coffee table, the only weapons to be found.

"You have to come," she said, backing up and trying to pull him with her.

He turned back to the monster advancing slowly into the living room. There was a murderous, predatory gleam in its eyes.

"Munroe," it said in the voice of decay.

"What do you want from me?" AJ's voice cracked at the end. Sirens were in the night, far away, as if an echo from a dream the mind faintly recalls. Too far away to do him any good.

All right then, he thought. *Kill me if you can, you macabre son of a bitch.* AJ wound up like a major league pitcher and threw a bottle hard as he could. It flew eight feet, the mouth of it letting out a low whistle before it struck his attacker's forehead and exploded. Glass rained to the floor, sounding like a nice spring shower in the land of perdition.

The monster laughed.

I'm fucked, AJ thought simply. He turned to Clover. "Go!"

They ran the short distance to the kitchen. She struggled to get the window open as he felt a cold, familiar hand grip the back of his neck from behind. AJ tried to turn but was lifted off the ground and slammed face-first into the wall.

The window went up with a screech of rusted metal, and Clover was about to climb out when she stopped and stared at what was coming toward her from the fire escape. It resembled nothing she had ever seen, even in a nightmare. Most of the flesh was gone, rotted away to expose maggot-ridden muscle and yellowing bone. The stench that accompanied it was nearly enough to make her vomit.

It wore a long, black coat, and a beaten Yankees

baseball cap pulled low over its ruined brow. It lunged forward, grabbing at her. She pulled away just in time, eluding its grasp, but not entirely avoiding it. Its cold, slimy hand brushed her wrist and left a graying smear of rotted flesh and three fat, white, squirming maggots on her skin. She screamed again and frantically wiped her arm against her pants.

Clover backed away and bumped into the counter. She jumped, and then turned around. Her mind cleared as the light glinted off the long, steel blade of the knife that lay in the sink. Her panic melted, and her survival instinct took over. She picked it up and turned back toward the window, feeling nothing. Her eyes darkened from the bright green of promise to the deeper color of a jungle predator.

AJ collapsed to the floor and saw what was coming through the window like a cat burglar from Hell.

The one that had grabbed him walked forward, AJ drove his foot into the monster's kneecap; AJ heard it snap before the monster reared its head back and screamed in pain.

The evil grin widened, and the eyes burned with hate. It kneeled, hands locking around AJ's throat, lifting him to his feet. He was slammed against the wall again, the back of his head knocking painfully against it.

The Yankees fan was now in his house. It turned away from Clover and walked toward him.

Clover gripped the knife tightly and lunged forward, jamming it through the side of the Yankees fan's neck. It slid in easily and popped out through its throat, the blade jutting out the windpipe and nothing but the hilt visible from the back.

Again, Clover fought the urge to vomit as it turned on her.

It made thick, choking noises, and clawed at the knife, then staggered another step to the side, ending up in front of the window. Clover saw her chance and charged kamikaze style.

The Yankee fan's head slammed into the top half of the window, and the glass shattered. Clover had one shining second to think it'd worked, when she was pulled through the window onto the fire escape.

AJ watched as Clover, and the other corpse went out the window. He was quickly running out of air. The world swam and grayed in and out before him. He let go of the monster's hands, for he knew he wasn't strong enough to contend. He had one chance, and maybe thirty seconds, until he passed out. Aaron Burrell's screaming face came to mind.

Eye for an eye, you fuck, AJ thought, and jammed both his thumbs into the eyes of the thing that was killing him. He held onto its head for dear life, fighting away unconsciousness and driving his thumbs in further, shaking it back and forth to do as much damage as possible. His head was filled with its screams.

AJ pushed away from it, his thumbs pulling out of the sockets with a sickly double *pop.* One cold, jelly-like eye clung to his left hand, and he shook it off like a giant booger. The eye flew from his thumb and struck the fridge with a liquid *flup,* sliding down the faded yellow of the metal door.

AJ wiped the slime from his hands, eyes never leaving his blind and reeling attacker. Its blank sockets gaped widely as the creature screamed and lurched around the room. AJ felt cold inside and acted on it. Clover would have understood.

He grabbed his hammer from the little table he'd set it on when closing his window for the night, turned, and swung. He struck the gray skull, splitting its flesh and crushing bone. The force of the blow combined with the busted knee dropped the fiend to the faded linoleum. It immediately pushed itself back up.

A darkness in AJ ignited, turning from the need to survive into the dull, red haze of rage. AJ lost contact with his rational mind, striking again and again with the hammer, bludgeoning the monster's head into a smear of poisoned black sludge on the floor.

He always wondered how long he would've continued the crazed and relentless beating if the sound of a gunshot and Clover's scream hadn't stopped him.

* * *

Clover bit her lips against a cry of pain as the glass came free. She dropped it and bled freely, not realizing how close she'd come to impaling herself on the filth-covered blade still jutting from the monster's throat.

It rolled forward and took hold of her wrist.

"Let…go…of…me!" She put every ounce of her strength into pulling away. Her wrist slipped free of the icy grip, and she scrambled back, standing up near the window, her back to the wall. It stood and came for her.

KA-BLAM!

She'd been looking in its eyes, but now the head was gone. Her face and neck were covered in cold, vile gore. Maggots writhed on her skin. The monster collapsed to the fire escape, the ruined remains of its head sticking to Clover and the wall directly to her left.

She cleared the gunk away from her eyes and mouth, looking to the alley below. She saw a man standing there, his long, white hair blowing in the wind. He was dressed in black and holding a gun. Then AJ was beside her, after having carefully climbed out of the window. He held her and whispered something and

cold

asked if she was all right

cold

and it's all dark and cold and

out

* * *

For a horrible second, AJ thought Clover had been shot. He saw she was still breathing as she passed out, and he lowered her to the fire escape floor. She was bleeding badly from a cut on her arm but, other than that, seemed—

"Hey!" came a shout from below.

AJ stood up, stepping on the headless corpse, and nearly falling. He regained his balance and looked down.

He recognized the man from the surveillance tapes; the hair was a dead giveaway. It was the man claiming to be Detective Quidman.

The man below stowed his gun, the hulking weapon disappearing within the empty blackness of his trench coat. The sirens were louder now, nearby. In one hand, he held something, some small object, AJ couldn't tell what, but it emitted a soft, blue light. The man looked at the object as the light faded, and then stuffed it into one of his coat pockets.

"There's not much time!" the man called up, backing toward a Harley parked against another building.

"Who are you?"

"I can't let the police interfere with me, but I'm here to help you."

"What do you want from me?" AJ asked for the second time that night.

"You are The Next. I can't stop this without you... no one can!" The stranger swung one leg over his motorcycle as a police car skidded to a halt in the mouth of the alley.

The bike came to life.

"I'll find you again!" the man upon the chopper called, and then was gone, roaring into the night on the back of a black-and-chrome American dream. Cops spilled out of the car. AJ stared after him for a long moment, and then pulled off his shirt and sat down next to Clover, wrapping it around the cut on her arm.

"What the hell am I into?" AJ asked himself aloud, and then squeezed his eyes shut against the world.

CHAPTER SIX

AJ rode in the back of the police cruiser in silence, thinking of Clover. She had been taken to the hospital to be treated for shock and to get her arm sewn shut. She was still in the dark about the whole living-dead thing, and he wasn't sure she'd want to be enlightened. regardless of the outcome, though, he'd have to try.

He'd seen the monster she'd faced on the fire escape, how far decomposed it had been, and wondered if, after that, he'd really have to try that hard to convince her.

The cruiser turned into the station house and parked. AJ waited in the same room he'd been in before. It was past midnight. That was something, at least: he'd managed to live to see another day.

AJ was still sitting there, numb and waiting, unaware of how much time had passed and perhaps in shock himself. Finally, the door opened and in came Terrance Wills.

"Hey, man, where you guys been?" AJ asked, shaking the young man's hand. "Where's John?"

"At home, where I wish I was. But that don't matter. Follow me." The two left one cramped and stinking interrogation room for another. "I just brought your girl back from the hospital." Wills cocked an eyebrow at the end of his statement. "She was my top priority, being as she don't know shit about this. I imagine you want to fill her in?"

"We kinda have to, don't we? And after what she saw?"

The detective seemed to take the question as rhetorical.

They stopped in front of a room, and AJ pushed the door open. Clover sat at the table, wrapped in a blanket, and smoking a cigarette. The black thread holding the pale flesh of her forearm together stood out like a broken promise, peeking from under one end of the bandage.

Terrance said, "I'll leave you here until I get word from Harris." Then he left.

Clover looked up and smiled as AJ sat down across from her.

"You all right?"

Her smile, thin to begin with, strained a little. "Why does this keep happening to us?"

AJ took a deep breath and began. He told of Karen Rosenthal's suicide and return. He told her about Lubbock being attacked in the morgue, and he told her about being adopted.

"I'm positive the things that attacked us tonight were the same way. Undead, I guess, is what you'd call it…" He cleared his throat and trailed away at the end.

She won't believe me, he thought. *She'll say I'm fucking crazy, or I smoke crack, and she'll leave, and I'll never see—*

"So, how do we stop them?" Clover asked.

He looked back at her, his head cocked to the side. "You believe me?"

"That *thing* I fought with wasn't, well, *normal.* I mean, I could see part of his *skull.* And I don't see why you'd lie, so what else is there?" She just sat there, same as before, her face calm. But her eyes glowed like round, green fires, and she bore a smile of trust and belonging.

At that moment, she was the essence of everything innocent and beautiful in a life that seemed immersed in death and chaos. She didn't have to be a part of this. *She* didn't have dead people dropping by her work or following her home at night, wasn't seeing vultures everywhere she went. She'd simply been thrown into the mix by the busy hands of fate and was still there. She wouldn't desert him or think him mad.

She had helped him.

AJ knew right then he could die for this girl.

* * *

Clover didn't know where she was. It seemed like a tunnel, underground somewhere. The dirty, gray cobbles of the floor were slick with what could only be blood. Her arms and legs were bound, chained to a wall. Out of the darkness across this terrible room came a man, his face obscured by shadows that should not have been.

He stank of madness and torture, and he came closer all the time. He leaned in, telling her things that made her cry, touching her and making her wish she could crawl right out of her skin. Leaning forward, his pale, ghostlike face moved like a brutal moon crashing to Earth. He raped her mouth with his, kissing her and forcing between her lips a long, black tongue that was really a snake. It thrashed and slithered down her throat, and she awoke, a scream held silent on her lips.

She hadn't had a nightmare in years.

It was now 4:24 A.M. according to the digital clock on the bedside table. Clover lay shaking in a bed that wasn't hers, in a room where she was the stranger.

The police had moved them to a safe house, a two-bedroom suite in a hotel. AJ was in the room next door. There were two cops in the front, another outside, with rotations to be made every four hours.

It was odd, though, being guarded. It didn't make her feel safe. It reminded her that something she didn't understand was coming for them. Clover shut her eyes and ran her hand along the cool sheets on the other side of the bed, picturing AJ lying there asleep. She felt a little better, thought of how he'd looked at her in the police station. And it wasn't just that he'd looked *at* her, he looked *inside* her.

When he'd reached across the table and took her hands, a warm current flew between them. It had only lasted one long, wonderful moment before Terrance opened the door to take them to the hotel. She felt a little of that same current return when she thought of him.

She shook her head to clear it, the nightmare already fading, although she would be forced to remember it much later. But, for now, her fear abated, first growing ragged along the edges, and finally unraveling into the nothingness from whence it came. Clover lay quietly with her eyes closed, but it was quite some time before sleep found her again.

* * *

"Why wasn't I called?" John shouted into the phone. It was exactly 5:30 in the morning. He managed to stay home that long, but there was too much cop in him not to call to make sure nothing had happened.

Inside, he believed nothing *had* happened because it was *his* fucking case, and someone would have called him. *He* was the one who had stayed up for God knows how many hours. *He* was the one who put a bullet in that…thing that was once a woman named Karen.

"No one thought to—" the voice on the other end tried to explain.

"You're damn right no one thought! I'm gonna walk through those doors in exactly twenty minutes, you hear me? I want a full report of every single thing that's happened since I left, not so much as a fucking *fart* unaccounted for!" John slammed the phone down and grabbed his trench coat, cramming the fedora on his head on the way out the door.

As he drove, John tallied everything up in his head, thinking for a second he should be grateful the white-haired stranger had shown up last night. Word was that he'd saved the two kids. Or had he? In his head, John repeated his mantra: *Never close the mind off to other possibilities.*

It was closer to forty minutes before he stormed into the station house. The rain slowed traffic, and he got soaked walking in from his car.

He did, however, have his report. It was hastily complied but complete. John scanned the prelims as he walked toward Don's office, his eyes snagging on a particular name: Terrance Wills.

Could that be right? John had worked with Wills a few times in the past, once on a particularly nasty homicide, and the younger man had never failed to report anything of even minor significance to him. His attention to the absolute minutia of all aspects of a case, from the crime scene to the witness statements and everything between, was the main reason John had wanted him aboard.

Terrence not giving him a call the *minute* he found out AJ had been caught up in something else disappointed him more than anything. John sighed and kept walking. A bitch of a headache was coming, pain slowly building between his eyes. All this bullshit, and it was only a quarter after six.

Outside, a brilliant stroke of lightning tore the blackness in two. The thunder came, and it rained even harder.

John knocked on Don's door and walked in, not waiting for a response.

"You look like you died an hour ago," John said in a pleasant, conversational tone.

Harris looked up at him from his desk, red-eyed and haggard. He'd probably been up for the last thirty-six hours or so.

"I was about to go get a bite to eat. Care to join me?" Harris stood and grabbed his leather coat off the back of his chair.

"We need to talk," John responded, not giving second thought to the invite.

"Don't start. I've been in here and on the phone for the past hour, chewing a variety of asses on your behalf."

"Good. From now on, I want to know what happens when it happens." *This is CNN* ran through his head in James Earl Jones's voice.

Harris nodded and took a sip of coffee, grimacing at the taste. "You will."

"So, where are you keeping them, anyway? Benny's?"

"At the hour they went in? Huh-uh. They got enough to deal with. They're at the Fireside, off Horizon."

John whistled. Most people put on protection were lucky enough to be crammed into a Super 8. "Why the luxury?"

"Manager owes me a favor," Harris said and shrugged. "Besides, I like the hell outta that kid, you know?"

John nodded. "Too bad this shit had to happen to him."

Harris agreed and eventually coaxed John across the street for a breakfast you couldn't fit in a little metal flask. He'd resisted at first, wanting to get up to the Fireside, but Harris made a good point: they wouldn't be up yet anyway.

* * *

AJ opened his eyes and looked around the unfamiliar room, wondered vaguely if Clover was awake and somehow knew she wasn't. His watch said it was after 8:30 A.M. He yawned and shook his head, then got up, and dressed, realizing he hadn't eaten since he'd shared a pizza with Burrell.

With a dead man, he thought. AJ joined the others in the front room where John Lubbock sat on the couch, talking shop with Officer Gomez, who'd given him a ride home on that long first night.

"Hey, kid. How'd you sleep?"

Like the dead almost came out, but AJ thought that might be in poor taste. "I slept great, but it's weird to be awake in the morning. This is when I usually go to bed."

"You been through a lot of shit lately. Your body knows when to adjust."

"What do we have as far as breakfast goes?" AJ asked, looking back and forth between the cops.

"There's a room service menu up there," Gomez said, pointing to a little table by the window.

"Eat up, kid. Taxpayers' treat," John said, and Gomez laughed. AJ didn't find it all that amusing, so he assumed it was a department joke. He kept quiet and perused the menu.

He could eat pretty much anything, so long as it wasn't eggs, but what he was really looking for was something for Clover.

He ended up ordering the breakfast platter for her, which was an array of bagels, fruit, and muffins, with a side of hash browns and bacon. For himself, he ordered French toast, home fries, bacon, and biscuits and gravy. He also had a couple pots of coffee and a tray of pastries sent to the room. There were cops there, after all.

"Oh, and uh, could you see if you can't score me a pack of smokes? I'm about out," he said to the desk attendant.

"Sir?"

"Smokes. I need some cigarettes."

"Oh. Well, of course. Is there any particular brand you favor?" The attendant had a slight British accent, as AJ imagined all desk attendants at good hotels did.

"Pack a' Red Apples, with a filter if you have 'em."

"Very good, sir."

He hung up the phone and joined the others, sitting in a large, high-backed chair.

"So, what are you thinkin' about this *Detective Quidman?*" John asked him, using finger-quotes when he said the name.

"Well, I get the feeling he's actually dealt with this before. He has a thing about cops, though," AJ said, saying the last part almost apologetically.

"From what I hear, he's got a thing about guns, too," John said. "But you trust him?"

"Definitely."

"Okay. If you trust him, we trust him, long as he's willing to sit down and tell me exactly what the hell's been going down these past couple days."

"I don't know. He took off pretty quick when your boys showed up last night." AJ remembered how the blue-and-red flashers had gleamed off the chrome of the chopper.

"Damn right, he took off quick. He ain't exactly operating within the normal means of the law here, kid."

AJ shrugged it off. "Hey, man, we need all the help we can get."

A few minutes later, the guard in the hall pushed in the room service cart, stacked with food.

"Jesus, kid, you eat much this week?" John asked.

"Well, I ordered the pastries for you guys, and the

coffee, too." AJ set the tray of donuts and pastries on the table, along with a pot of coffee, then pushed the cart into Clover's room.

* * *

Clover thought of her parents, especially her father with his strict, Bible-thumping ways, and wondered what they would make of all this. She believed they would throw her into a psych ward if she ever spoke a word of it around them.

Just then, the door opened slowly, and AJ stepped in. Whenever she thought of him after that, this image, this moment, was the one she wished would come into her mind first, him standing there with that irresistible grin on his face, perfectly framed in the doorway, bringing her breakfast in bed.

As Clover finished eating, she had to fight off her feelings of shame and gluttony, a holdover from childhood, the result of her mother's incessant reminders for her to watch her figure. She had been lucky to escape with misplaced guilt instead of a severe eating disorder.

She stifled a burp with the back of her hand and laughed.

"Ugh, excuse me!"

"Nice," AJ said, and she was happy to see he laughed instead of being grossed out.

"I hate to tell you this," Clover said, "but you have to leave now so I can get dressed."

"The ol' Burp and Boot, eh? Sad to say, I've received this treatment before."

She laughed, and then beckoned him closer with her

finger. "Come here. I have to tell you something."

He leaned forward, and she put one hand on each of his shoulders and put her mouth next to his ear.

"Thank you," she whispered, and before she knew she was going to do it, she kissed him.

It began as a quick peck, but blossomed, and when their lips finally parted, he looked into her eyes and kissed her between them.

"I'll be in the front room," he said and smiled. She smiled back, and then shooed him out. She sat there for a moment, her whole body warm and tingling. She wouldn't say it out loud, or even let herself think about it, but she knew what was starting to happen.

* * *

AJ tried to wipe the grin off his face, but he must have missed some of it because Gomez took one look at him and gave him a knowing wink.

"How was breakfast?"

"A hell of a lot better than dinner." AJ watched the rain through the window. "So, what's the plan for today, anyway?"

"Well, we figured *you* would stay here, and we would guard you," John said.

"Then, after that, we thought maybe we would guard you while you stayed here," added Gomez. He waggled his eyebrows and stuffed most of a donut in his mouth at once, more for AJ's amusement than to eat it.

AJ grinned and shook his head. "Well, since the itinerary is so full, we better get busy." It wouldn't be the most exciting day he ever had, but considering what was passing for excitement lately, he thought he would manage fine. If shit went down, it went down, and they'd do their best to deal with it. Giving himself an ulcer over it wouldn't help.

"AJ? Could you come here for a minute?" Clover called from her room. He nearly dropped his cigarette when he walked in. The guy from the alley and the security tapes, the one who most definitely was *not* Detective Quidman, was perched on Clover's windowsill like a gargoyle.

"You…uh, wanna come in?" AJ asked.

The stranger shook his head. "I don't have a lot of time here, so we need to hurry this up. Now, do you have a book—"

"I have lots of books," AJ interrupted.

"It's not a normal one. Did your real father leave you anything after he died?"

"Just a trust fund I can't get at until I'm twenty-six."

"But no book?"

"I don't know. Why?"

"Call your family. If we don't have the book, it's gonna make this all a lot harder to do."

"Make *what* a lot harder to do?" AJ asked calmly but wanted to scream.

"I don't have time to explain. Just get a hold of them and—"

"You want me to call them up and ask if my dead parents left me a book twenty-some years ago?"

"Yes. It's dark red, old, very thick. It has a big lock and a symbol on the front of it. Find it."

"Everything all right back there?" John called from the front room.

"Yeah, no problem," Clover yelled back.

"That the cop working on this? The main one, I mean? Detective Lubbock?"

"Why?" AJ asked.

"Give him this," the man perched in the window said, reaching into his long black coat and pulling out an envelope.

AJ took the envelope and looked down at it. It was made of the thick, soft paper you knew was expensive. On the front it said *Det. John Lubbock*, printed in a neat, careful hand.

'Wait, what is this?" AJ asked.

"Just give it to him. I've got to go. I'll be in touch."

"Wait! What's your name?"

"Logan." And then with a liquid smoothness, he reached in and pulled the drapes shut in front of him. When AJ opened them back up again, he was gone. They were on the fifth floor, but there was no sign of him.

AJ stared out the window until Clover brought him back to reality with a hug.

"What have I gotten into?" He hugged back and rested his head on her shoulder.

"Not you. *We.*"

* * *

AJ had been calling his parents house periodically since the day after he was first attacked, and had yet to reach anyone. It scared him. Although there was nothing rational to base these fears upon he didn't feel like the most rational of people at the time. If Logan thought of going to his parents for this book, wasn't it possible someone else would think of it, too?

Logan had been gone about ten minutes ago, and AJ now sat on the bed, pressing the phone against his ear so hard it hurt. A hard lump had formed in his throat by the second ring and he was holding his breath by the fifth.

"Hello?"

"Mom?" He breathed a deep sigh of relief.

"Hey, you! What's up?" She sounded as chipper as ever.

"Where have you guys been since, like, Thursday?" AJ asked, ashamed to realize he had almost given her up for dead.

"Well, we turned off the phone and finally went through the attic," she said, a note of near triumph in her voice.

"You guys did the attic?" As long as he could remember, his parents had been threatening to go through the attic to clean it out and separate the crap from the keepsakes.

"Yuppers. Oh, hey, that reminds me. We found something up there we should have given you a long time ago."

AJ could almost feel his heart stop in his chest. "What is it?"

A book, he thought.

"A book," she said.

"What kind of book?" His mouth went dry. Inside, he already knew. He felt it, like a giant gear slipping slowly into place, like great, invisible wheels beginning to turn in concert with one another.

"Well, it was one the orphanage gave us. It was in your birth father's will, along with the trust fund." She sounded a bit ashamed of it all, of forgetting a dead man's wish for over twenty years.

"What's it look like?" he asked, thinking red, old, thick.

"Old. It's damn thick, too."

"Were you planning on actually giving it to me someday or what?"

"I'm sorry, sweetie. We were saving it for when you were old enough to take care of it. It's just that we—"

"Put it in the attic," AJ finished for her. "Okay, well, I'm gonna be up there within the next couple of days to get it, so don't let anything happen to it."

"Don't worry, sweetie. We'll take care of it. So. How's things?"

He opened his mouth, and then clapped it shut again, thinking of everything that had been happening.

Great, Ma, he thought. *Beat a dead guy* back *to death with a bat, another with a hammer. I'm under police protection but, on the upside, I met a girl!*

"Good, Ma," he said. "Things are good."

"*What* is happening in that city of yours?" she asked. She always said it like that. Anything bad that ever happened that made it on the news, she asked him about it like he was the cause of it.

"What do you mean?"

"All these bodies going missing. Don't tell me you haven't seen this on TV. People stealing bodies from hospitals, morgues, ringing a bell?"

"Oh, yeah, I heard about that. Just the two, though?"

"It *started* with two. On the news, they said four more in the last twenty-four hours, and that it might even be higher than that, and people aren't reporting it. Afraid of lawsuits from the families, they said."

"Who said that?"

"The woman on the news," she said and sighed. "I told you that city was bad, Amon," she added, using the name she reserved for times of worry or stages of high piss-off.

"Ma, I'm fine," he said. He felt bad about lying to her, but considering the alternative dampened the effect.

"I wish you'd let us help you move into a better part of town, that's all. There's nothing wrong with taking money from your parents."

"Ma…"

"I know, son. I'm sorry. But wait till you have kids someday, and I guess then you'll understand."

The title of an old Credence Clearwater Revival song, *Someday Never Comes.* hit him and sent a shiver up his spine like a bent coat hanger.

"Promise me you'll reconsider? About the money?"

He promised her, and they talked for a while longer: how was he eating, how was work? He asked how his dad's classes were going, said he had to go, and reminded her he'd be up to get the book.

"Okay, hon, I'll see you soon. Love you."

"Love you, too, Ma. Bye." AJ hung up the phone and turned as Clover walked into the room. "They have the book."

"Get *out*!"

"Yeah. They finally went through the attic yesterday, and it's been up there for all my life, I guess."

"Your mom found it yesterday?" Clover asked.

AJ nodded.

"That's pretty…convenient."

"Extremely," AJ said.

"You know how we were almost at the same showing of *Josey Wales?*"

"Yeah."

"And I never really told you why I came into the store the night we met, did I?"

"For cigarettes?"

"Sure, for cigarettes. It didn't strike you odd I drove halfway across town to buy them, though?"

AJ stopped and thought for a moment. "Actually, no. I hadn't thought about it."

"It was almost three in the morning when I got there, you remember that?"

"Of course."

"I was asleep up until about midnight. Then I snapped up, wide awake. Like I'd been shot up with coke or something while I was asleep. I got this urge to be up, out. I walked around my living room for a while, just... pacing, like you see on bad sitcoms. I smoked my last smoke and decided I *had* to have more. So, I got in my car, and started to drive. There's a 7-11 like five minutes from my apartment, but I didn't want to wait for the light to change, coming out of my complex, so I took a right instead of a left. It felt nice, being out, driving around. I felt *better.*"

'So, you kept driving," AJ said.

"Yup. Now, I've been to that neighborhood a ton of times. That neighborhood the theater is in? I love it, all the old shops and stuff. I wasn't consciously driving over there, though. If a light was green, I kept going, if it was red, I turned right so I didn't have to wait."

"And there you were," AJ said.

"There I was. I've been thinking about that a lot these last few days. When they were stitching my arm up is when I started *really* considering things. I bet if we sat down and told each other about the last six months, there would be a ton of times we were at the same place at the same time and didn't know it. Then, one night, I wake up and go for a drive at two in the morning, something I've *never* done, following the traffic lights. I walk into Vito's, what was it, three minutes ahead of the other guy?"

"About that, yeah."

"We're told everything might hinge on a book you're supposed to have but have never seen. You call your mom, and she just *happened* to have dug it out of deep storage in your attic yesterday?"

"Yes," he said, his voice a whisper.

"I don't know what's happening," Clover said, "but it's meant to happen. *We* were meant to happen."

She stepped closer to him, setting one hand on his chest, looking up into his eyes. She opened her mouth to speak but didn't. Instead, she stepped forward, laying her head on his shoulder, and hugged him tightly and, for a long moment, they were quiet, and together, and happy, though perhaps a little afraid.

"When this is over, though, you have to take me on a *real* date," Clover said, and the two of them laughed. "Breakfast at two in the afternoon? You gotta step your game up, man."

"Deal," AJ said and pulled her to him again.

Outside, the rain continued to pour.

* * *

Logan peeled off his drenched trench coat and set it on a chair near the electric fireplace he'd turned on, hoping to dry it. After he visited AJ and the girl, whose name he *still* didn't know, he had simply gone back to his room. He'd managed to procure it last night. There hadn't been any vacancies, but he'd found a middle-aged man about to check in and had given them twice what they paid for the room. He took his .45 out of the shoulder holster to make sure it wasn't wet and to dry it off if it was.

All this was done slowly, in a detached sort of way. His mind and all his senses were trained on the boy upstairs. Being who he was, AJ sent out a kind of mental signal very few people could pick up. It was like there was a homing device in his head.

Part of his thoughts also returned to the book as it was pivotal to their cause. He had lied to AJ and the girl, said it would be much more difficult without the book. But if the other got His hands on it…well, they were all fucked. Not just *them*, but everyone, everything.

His assessment of the situation was a grim one. Everything hinged on the foresight AJ's real father had with regard to who *he* was and who his son would someday be. The Next.

He was at least a little confident the late Mr. Munroe had taken some sort of measure to ensure his son would get the book. Not once since this all began centuries ago had the book, and the knowledge in it, failed to be passed down.

Of course, he also had to take into consideration the fact the late Mr. Munroe's life had been cut unexpectedly short by a car accident.

Then there was the letter. He had to hope what was contained in it was enough.

But, right now, it all looked so damn bleak, as if the day's falling rain managed to bleach all the hope from his soul. But no matter how bad, how hopeless the situation might be, he had no choice but to fight with every fiber of his being. To step aside or to bow his head in defeat to an evil such as this would be perhaps a far worse sin than what he was fighting against. Logan sat back in his chair and waited. It was all he could do.

* * *

AJ had no idea how to get in touch with Logan. He had no idea why they had to have the book or what to do once they did, although, he assumed reading it would be a large part of it. He didn't know how much time they had but, nonetheless, felt an unexplainable urgency. With each tick of the second hand, time ran away from him, pulling some final apocalyptic event nearer and nearer, like a guillotine blade suspended over his head.

"We have to get our asses in gear. I've got to tell them about the book," AJ said to Clover. Hand in hand, they walked out into the living room.

"What's up, kid?" John asked.

"Well, there's a couple things I guess we need to talk about."

"Just you and I, or is this an all hands on deck situation?"

"I, uh, I guess everyone outta hear," AJ said.

"OK, one sec," John said. He took a walkie-talkie off the table next to him and double-tapped one of the buttons. A moment later the door to the hall opened and the guard let in Steve Nielsen.

"Sit down, Steve. We need you to hear this, too. It'll save me the pain in the ass of telling you later," John said. Steve pulled a chair over and sat. He looked around the room at them and then , and then AJ began to speak.

John listened with an open mind. He believed what the kid said about the book, at least the fact that said book *did* exist. But what to make of it? He had assumed they could simply shoot the shit out of these things, these creepers, until they stopped coming after the kid, but this made more sense. They were dealing with something supernatural—a word John hated to use but hadn't been able to find a better one—so they would need something supernatural to stop it.

AJ finished his story, telling how his parents had recently unearthed the book while dredging through the attic.

"Well, we can send someone up there ASAP—" Steve began to suggest. John shook his head as AJ vocalized the objection.

"I have to go," he said simply. "Do you want to tell my parents why a book needs a police escort? I'm sure if you told them, it could be the key to defeating the living dead, they'd understand."

John rubbed the fading bruises on his neck and chewed his cigar. The kid had a point. They couldn't run around telling everyone, not unless they wanted to get locked up where they made you write letters home in crayon because they were afraid of what you'd do with a pointed object.

"We won't send you up there alone."

"Good! I'm not too keen on the idea of a solo road trip right now."

John turned to Steve. "How long you think to get clearance on this from Don? Hour? Two?"

Steve exhaled deeply and stared at the ceiling, ticking things off on his fingers to himself before looking back to John. "I'd say two, tops. We'd want a couple unis in tow, yeah?"

"Yeah, at least. We could be there by what then? ten tonight?"

"Closer to eleven, depending on traffic," Steve said.

"That's no good," John said. "We brought 'em here to protect em, yeah? I don't like the idea of driving around in the middle of the night, not when we don't really know what we're up against."

"If I showed up tonight there's no *way* my parents would let me leave before the morning, either," AJ said. "Not without a *whole* lot of explaining. So…tomorrow?"

"Yeah. Tomorrow," John said. "Quick question, though. How'd you come to find out about this book, and that we needed it? Don't tell me you just kinda forgot about until now, kid. I hope you respect me too much for that."

"Uh…" AJ rubbed the back of his neck and looked to Clover.

"Give it to him," Clover said.

"Gimme what?" John asked.

AJ reached under his shirt and pulled the envelope from the back pocket of his jeans and held it out.

"He was here, wasn't he?" John asked.

"Who?" Gomez asked.

John stared the kid down and lost a little respect

for him when AJ was unable to look him in the eyes. He took half a step and gestured toward John with the envelope. Clover sighed and stepped forward, snatching the envelope out of AJ's hands.

"He just left," she said, holding the envelope out to John, staring up at him with an intensity that made him blink and fall back a step.

"Who just left?" Gomez asked. "Ain't nobody other than Steve and the room service guy been in or outta that door all day."

"Gentlemen," John said, clearing his throat and taking the envelope from Clover. "I believe we've been visited by... What's he calling himself now? Not *Detective Quidman* still, I hope?"

"His name is Logan," AJ said.

"He came through the window," Clover said.

"What the fuck?" Gomez asked. "Your window? Your *fifth story* window?"

"Hang on," John said, reaching out and touching Gomez's shoulder.

John stared down at the envelope, given to the kid by a man who impersonated a cop and had shown up not only at two of the crime scenes this case had so far created—the gas station, and the kid's apartment—but also here, through the fifth story window of a hotel room where no one but the people inside that room and maybe four others knew where they were. These things were strange enough, but these were not the considerations that had John feeling like he'd been kicked in the back of the head.

No, what was getting to him was that his name was written on the envelope, and even more so, it was written in a hand he recognized.

Jin, Lubbock thought, his mouth dry, his eyes seeming to burn.

John looked from the envelope, to AJ, and back to the envelope again.

"The fuck is this?" John asked.

"I don't know. He said to give it to you is all," AJ said, taking a step back.

John pulled a less-than-regulation knife out of his pocket and flicked the short but brutal blade open and used it to cut through the envelope. Inside was a single folded sheet of thick, cream-colored stationery. John removed it from the envelope and opened it.

In the top left-hand corner, where he knew it would be, was a single square with the initials JM inside it, embossed into the stationary.

"What's it say?" Steve asked.

Lubbock ignored him, swallowing hard as he read the letter.

John-
Hello, old friend. First, please know I tried to keep you out of this as long as I could. I don't know what the man who delivered this to you has done so far, only that, during the normal course of things, I myself would likely have arrested him for them. Those rules no longer apply. This will go against every instinct you have, but you have to trust him.

I know you remember my last case, and though I'm sure what you are now involved in is different in its own horrible way, I know it must be the same in ways that are even worse, or I wouldn't be writing this. This is beyond law and order and chain of command and everything about life as you've come to know it.

I don't blame you for turning away toward the end of the Bowden case; it wasn't your time. It was my *time. This, John, now, this is your time, and you must not turn away. I know the man who delivered this letter only as Mr. Perish, but regardless of what he calls himself, or has called himself in the past, trust him, John. You need him. If you ever trusted me, and I know you did,* trust him.

Right now, you are staring down the impossible. I know from personal experience how hard this is, how it seems the world is falling down around you like the backdrop on an old stage, but I ask you again, do not turn aside. Above all else, trust him. *Godspeed, my friend, and good luck.*

JM

John carefully folded the letter and put it back inside the envelope. He rubbed his eyes, and then walked to the fireplace. He stared down at his name, written in his old friend's hand, and then carefully fed the envelope and the letter to the fire.

"John?" Gomez said.

"What'd it say?" AJ asked.

John walked back across the room and sat on the couch, then looked up at all of them in turn.

"Tomorrow morning then," John said.

Steve opened his mouth to speak but stopped when John held his hand up, shaking his head once. John leaned back on the couch and chewed his cigar. Clover got a cigarette from AJ, and Terrance Wills poured himself a cup of coffee.

Somewhere downstairs was a rattle of gunfire, sounding almost small and distant. The radios the uniformed cops had on their shoulders came to life, a distorted cacophony of static, screams, and gunfire.

John was on his feet immediately, his pistol in his hand. He shot a quick glance to Steve, who was also on his feet. Gomez had drawn his piece and backed AJ and Clover away from the door, toward the master bedroom.

The two guards in the hall came in, and all eyes turned to John for guidance. He had one moment of raw panic when he hated all of them for putting this weight on him, for so easily putting their lives in his pocket. It seemed he could feel the extraordinary weight of each of those lives on his chest, packed so tightly within him it left no room for his heart to beat or his lungs to breathe. The fire crackled, and John recalled a line from the letter Jin had written him; *This, John, now,* this *is your time, and you must not turn away.*

"Okay," he said, drawing in a deep and shuddering breath, the cop in him taking over. "AJ, Clover; back bedroom, and *now.* Do not *open that door* until you hear *my* voice."

"Got you," AJ said."

"Can we have a gun?" Clover asked.

Everyone turned toward her and John looked like he'd had a bucket of ice water thrown in his face."

"Ah...no. These two are all the gun you'll need, I promise you," John said, pointing to two of the uniformed officers.

Clover was about to reply to that but John pushed through, talking over her.

"Steve, Gomez, you come with me." He turned and looked at the two guards. "One of you stay in the hall, one of you stay in here and, if anything, I mean *any fucking thing,* happens to either of those kids, you'll have a lot more to worry about than you do right now. Understand?"

The two uniformed officers nodded.

"Then let's move." John led his men out into the hall.

* * *

Logan was on his feet before the first blast sounded down the hall. He slung his shotgun into the shoulder harness and grabbed his pistol. There was another blast, and he heard screams. His first instinct was to head toward the trouble, to stop it if he could. But not now, not here. His number one priority had to be The Next.

He threw on his coat and went into the hall. He still had to go toward the lobby to get to the stairs, and he passed a crowd in the hall fleeing the opposite direction. He got to the stairwell door and peered quickly around the corner. What started as a glance turned into a stare.

There were members of the dead, two of them. He watched them tear a lobby security guard's arm completely off his body. A red splash hit the wall, and the guard was thrown to the floor, screaming and thrashing, blood spraying from the ragged stump. His arm dropped to the floor next to him, the hand still opening and closing spasmodically. Logan entered the stairwell and ascended to the fifth floor.

* * *

The elevator dinged, and the door slid open. The

three police officers were backed to the sides, away from the open door. John peered out cautiously. He saw two undead about fifteen yards from the elevators, busy killing a hotel security guard. They watched in a horrid fascination as one of the guard's arms was pulled off like a chicken wing. John led the others out of the elevator, securing cover behind two large, marble pillars on either side of the elevator.

"This is the police!" John yelled, peeking around the pillar at the nearest creeper. There was no way anyone could even pretend this creature was alive. There was almost no skin on his face, just rotted muscle and exposed skull.

Lubbock looked to Steve. "We may have a serious problem here."

* * *

Officer Nick Black stood in the hall, as per Detective John Lubbock's direct order, his back to the door and his gun drawn. He had been told in confidence what the situation was, that somehow the dead were up and walking. But he didn't really believe it, did he? Shit no. There had to be a mistake of some kind, maybe even an explanation, because that shit didn't happen.

He thought it was possible for someone to maybe *look* dead, sure. Crack addicts weren't exactly the picture of good health. And there were people with diseases, too. Like leprosy (that was still around, right?) and that Ebola thing. That could make someone look dead. But for someone to actually be dead, *physically dead*, and get up, causing problems? Nope.

At least, that was he kept telling himself until he saw what came lurching around the corner. It was shaped like a man, kind of, and had at some point been one, but now it was nothing short of a nightmare with legs and Freddy Krueger's complexion. There were patches of flesh missing, with some flaps of dead skin hanging off the face. Long, stringy hair hung off what little scalp was left.

As it drew nearer, Officer Nick Black realized it had not once been a man but a woman. It wore the last remnant of a burial dress, and he could see the sagging lumps of skin above the stomach that had to have been breasts.

For the first time since he was nine years old, Nick Black was afraid in a real, visceral sense. This was not the fear of missing a car payment, or when he'd started shitting blood last year and had been sure what turned out to be hemorrhoids had meant he had colon cancer—which had killed his grandfather—and that he was dying.

No, this was the sort of fear that gripped your heart and your guts and your *fucking soul* in one cold, black fist and squeezed. It paralyzed the body and threatened to snap the mind. It rendered you unable to think, to move, to breathe, to scream. This was the fear of the nameless beast of fangs and claws and glowing, red eyes under the bed or hiding in the closet, waiting for the lights to be turned off.

Even worse than that, this was that fear *realized,* it was the thing that was strictly confined to the most horrific childhood nightmares and to the darkest corners and crawl spaces, finally stepping out of the blackness and into the full light of day.

When the monster staggered toward him and howled, Nick Black knew he was going to die.

* * *

Logan sprinted up the stairs two at a time, with only two more floors to go until the fifth. He rounded the banister and began his way up the fourth flight, then stopped, staring at what stood at the top.

Two of them, two totems of his oldest enemy. It didn't matter they had been so recently brought to this grotesque and rotting perversion of life. Each one of them represented *all* of them in Logan's eyes.

The three of them stood that way for a moment, two opposing factions that knew they must kill the other, poised to strike.

Logan raised his .45 at the same time the creeper on the left took a flying leap down the stairs at him. He pulled off a shot and caught the creeper in the chest, but it wasn't enough. The monster slammed into him, sending him crashing into the wall, thumping his head. His knees buckled with the impact, and he slid halfway down the wall. His vision blurred, and he hung onto consciousness through sheer force of will.

He dropped his gun, and it lay on the floor about six feet away, having come to a stop about half a foot shy of falling down the flight of stairs he'd just ascended. There was no time to go for the pistol or to grab the shotgun on its sling around his back. The bastard that had jumped on him was quicker to regain its feet and once more came for him.

It lunged for his throat, jaws open wide. Logan

brought his left arm up and, instead of his throat, the teeth sunk into his forearm. The arm of his coat grew a darker shade of black as blood soaked it, the creeper's cold fingers reaching for his throat, his eyes, his face.

"Mother*fucker*!" Logan drew his knife with his right hand and, with a grunt of pain and effort, slammed it into the side of creeper's head, right through the soft spot at the temple.

It went into a kind of seizure, the jaw clamping down even harder. The filmed eyes rolled back in its head, and it fell against him. He pulled his knife out with a squeal of blade against bone and a spurt of thick, gray fluid, but the teeth remained stuck in his arm.

Fucker locked up! Logan thought, and then the second creeper, having taken a slower, more shambling pace down the stairs, reached the landing, shuffling toward him.

Logan slid his back down the wall, dragging the first creeper along with him, putting as much distance between himself and the second one as possible. It wasn't much. The landing was maybe ten feet side to side. He reached the corner and tried to force the jaws open with the blade of his knife, but the angle was wrong, and he couldn't get the kind of leverage he needed. When these fuckers went lockjaw, they locked on *good*.

The second creeper was within his range, so he pivoted, slamming the body of the one latched onto him against the wall and using it for balance. He kicked the second creeper square in the chest, sending it crashing to the floor and buying himself a little more time.

He intended to use it.

He raised his left forearm as high as he could, letting

out a low scream of pain as its teeth sank deeper into him, and he tilted its head back. He slammed his knife into the spine through the side of its neck, again, a third time, and a fourth, sparing a look over his shoulder. The second creeper slowly pulled itself back up, using the stair railing.

"Come on!" Logan's blade found its spine a fifth time, and there was the crack of an old, rotten branch letting go.

He sawed through the rest of the neck, the integrity of the muscle and bone weakened by death and re-animation. With a final grunt of effort, he tore the head loose, stepping back as the body collapsed to the floor. Greasy streamers of blackened gore clung to his fist and knife. Logan turned, the rotting, severed head still stuck to his arm, blood from the wounds running into the mouth and out the ragged, severed esophagus, splattering the tiles of the landing.

The other creeper came for him.

A strange thought occurred to him then, and he could never determine whether it was one of his own or if it came from his subconscious, perhaps something he had read or overheard.

—and opened wide there came a long, dark doorway, and on the other side of it was death.

A sudden calm ran over his body, silencing his pain and clearing his buzzing thoughts. All that was left was to react.

In one fluid motion, he tossed the knife in the air, flipping it backward, and catching it by the blade even as he drew his arm back, and then brought it forward as hard as he could.

There was a low, harmonic sound as the knife flew six or seven feet, turning over once mid-air, and then it was buried to the hilt and quivering, right between the second creeper's eyes. It took one final step forward, and then dropped, the *thud* of it echoing up and down the stairwell.

Logan took in a deep breath and picked up his .45 and started back up the stairs, cradling the severed head still locked onto his arm against his chest as he ran like some grisly prize.

* * *

Screams of death rang in John's ears, echoing off the polished stone and marble of the lobby. There was a split second of space in the mass of running people and that was all he needed. He leaned out and took aim, firing off one shot. He hit the target, and the dead man's jaw blew apart. Letting out a mangled scream, it staggered toward him.

John glanced over at Gomez and Steve. Their words were lost in the sounds of terrible violence, but John could read Gomez's lips: *I'm going.*

"No, wait!" Steve followed Gomez out into the open.

A uniformed officer stepped from behind the pillar and emptied his service pistol into the jawless zombie, its dead body stiffly jerking with the entrance and exit of each bullet, dusty flesh popping out of its back in tatters. It fell to the ground, but another advanced, taking two shambling steps amidst the hail of bullets and fell upon Gomez, who appeared frozen in shock.

John watched as Gomez's throat was torn out,

watched the other man, the friend, the colleague, collapse to the lushly carpeted lobby floor. Gomez lay there, a silent scream on his face, his body twitching, with arterial blood so dark it was almost black, gushing out of the ragged hole where his Adam's apple used to be. John fired twice into the thing's head, and it fell to the ground, still once more.

Gomez weakly slapped at his own throat, the blood pumping through his fingers and pooling next to him on the floor. John stared at the man trying in vain to hold his life inside him. His body shuddered, and his eyes rolled back, and he stilled. John turned away from the glazing eyes, the blood. There was so much he could *smell* it.

Ahh, why'd you do it, Gomie? John thought. *We taught you better.*

John stood, turning to Steve. They heard the growing blare of sirens and recognized them as police rather than ambulance or fire. Backup was on the way, and as much as John hated to leave his friends lying there in the lobby, they had a priority.

"We gotta go after the kid," John said.

Steve nodded in silence, and they headed back to the elevator.

"We need to find out what the fuck is at the root of this, Steve. We can't keep letting people get killed."

The little "2" above the doors lit up, accompanied by a soft *ding*, and then went dark again. John was helpless but to watch in his mind's eye as Gomez died, over and over. The two rode upward, reloading their guns. The "3" lit up and still the elevator rose.

* * *

Out in the hall, Nick Black screamed continuously, unable to move as she drew ever closer. The stench of decay rose as it baked off the rotted woman. He put up no resistance as it leaned his head back and sank its teeth into his throat. He didn't really feel it as his flesh tore, and the blood spilled out in copious amounts, drenching the front of his uniform and forming a puddle at his feet.

All he knew was he could no longer scream because he could no longer breathe. She took a step back as if to admire her work, his throat and a chunk of larynx falling from her mouth and onto the floor. Blood smeared what remained of her lips crimson and ran in rivulets off her chin.

As Officer Black succumbed to death, he had one clear, final thought. He remembered how he'd left the headlights on in the car, and he needed to get them turned off before the battery was all used up, and then everything faded to gray. He slowly slipped into the abyss, the smell of a million roses flooding his nose. Thoughts of his car battery ceased, and he was gone.

* * *

Officer Bill Tamir paced back and forth on the other side of the door in the grips of hysteria. He had known Nicky Black since the two of them were fifteen. They had graduated high school together, entered the academy together, and graduated from there together, too.

He mumbled to himself, a softly spoken and senseless ramble. "Nicky, Nicky, Nicky, ah shit, Nicky." It had started in his head around the same time the screaming in the hall had been brutally cut off. There was a sudden, fierce pounding on the door that made him jump.

The fucker on the other side of that door killed your friend, a small, strong voice inside him said. Grief slowly boiled up into anger and fear turned it into rage. He cocked his gun, stormed to the door, and flung it open with every intention of killing whatever was on the other side of it. What he saw standing there drained all his courage.

"Ooh, shit." In the far recesses of his mind, Bill was dimly aware he had just pissed his pants.

The monster's face was covered in *Nicky's blood, and it* growled deeply, like the hounds of Hell. His gun fell from his shaking hand as the monster attacked, swatting him with all its might, breaking his jaw in two different places. He spun a half-turn with the force of the blow and fell to the ground.

The pain was enormous, and it managed to sap some of the paralyzing terror from his slowly collapsing mind, and his survival instincts at last kicked in. He rolled over onto his back, determined to fight. The she-monster loomed over him, grinning, and all he did was die.

* * *

AJ could hear the cop being killed in the front room. He looked around frantically, trying to find something to defend them with.

"What do we do?" Clover screamed. She had already tried the window. It had opened easily, but as it slid on the track, letting in a blast of cold night air, she realized it didn't matter if it opened or not; it lead to five stories of nothing. This had not presented a problem for Logan, but she had a strong feeling that if she tried the window the only two possible outcomes were quadriplegia and death. They were trapped. It was fight or die.

In the other room, the screaming ended with a thick, strangled gargle.

There was a long moment of unnerving calm and quiet, not even gunshots from the lobby could be heard. When the abomination in the hall threw itself against the bedroom door it sounded like a bomb.

"Fuck!" AJ said, his whole body flinching so hard it was closer to a tenth of a second long seizure. Another bang against the door, followed by a crack in the wood shooting out from the deadbolt.

"Get in the bathroom," AJ said. There was nothing to be used as a weapon in the room they were in, and his hope was that tis would at least provide another door between them. Clover grabbed his arm and drug him along with her, through the bathroom door, pushing him up against the sink, then closed and locked the bathroom door behind them.

A bang, and another one, and following the third there came the sound of the bedroom door knocked off its hinges. A moment later, he heard the thing that should not be shouting his last name, a name that had been pretty much dead to him for as long as he could remember.

"Munroe!" The scream was followed by a light tapping, a tapping on the bathroom door.

Nevermore, AJ thought.

Clover looked around frantically and spotted a

wooden-handled plunger behind the toilet. She picked it up and began pulling at the red rubber cup. The light tapping grew to the frantic pounding of the criminally insane. The door shook wildly, and a long crack ran down its middle.

Déjà fucking vu, AJ thought.

"Come off!" Clover yelled, still working the cup off the plunger.

AJ looked around. There was nothing, fucking *nothing,* then he reached forward and swept the little dish of rose-shaped soaps off the top of the toilet tank. He took the lid of the tank in his hands, the ceramic heavy and cold in his grasp.

"Got it!" Clover said, yanking the cup off the plunger handle and tossing the cup into the tub. She choked up on the handle and raised it, like she had the baseball bat at the gas station the night they met.

The door imploded. Another corpse, a woman, stood in the hall. AJ charged her, using the tank lid as a kind of shield and battering ram, knocking the dead woman backward, aware of Clover following close behind him. The three of them were now in the large master suite. The dead woman lunged at AJ, and he once more held the tank lid up, bashing it against her face and keeping her from tearing out his throat.

Clover circled a few steps to the side and swung the plunger handle. There was a hollow *knock* as she connected, but still the dead woman pressed toward AJ. He braced his feet and shoved back against the weight and fury of her. Clover swung again, and again, the hollow *knock* now with a little squelching around the edges, like stomping in mud.

The dead woman's advance faltered as she turned toward Clover, and AJ lifted the tank lid above his head, bringing it down as hard as he could, the impact traveling all the way up his arms.

The blow drove the dead woman to her knees, and Clover changed her grip on the plunger handle, one hand gripping it about halfway up, the other hand braced against the end of it. She took a step forward, let out a small scream of effort, and jammed the plunger handle through the cracked dome of the dead woman's skull.

The dead woman's rotting hands came up, slapping at the handle as she howled.

The tortured screams of the corpse filled his ears and seemed to echo there, as if they had been there before. It was as if he were hearing them from long ago, perhaps hundreds of years ago. He didn't like the way they sounded but couldn't deny they sounded as if they belonged.

"Fuck...*you*!" Clover shoved the plunger handle in even further, losing her grip on it when the dead woman fell backward onto the floor, convulsing.

AJ stood above her, slamming the toilet tank lid into the other side of her skull, crushing it and, finally, the kicking stopped.

AJ dropped the tank lid, now cracked up the middle, and stepped back, panting, sweat running down his temple.

A small grin spread across his face as he turned, and saw the same little smile playing across her lips. His first thought was, *My God, are we actually enjoying this?*

"You're a goddamn natural," AJ said with a tired laugh.

"Let's get out of here," she said, yanking the plunger handle out of the skull. She took his hand and led him toward the front room. AJ took the lead when they got to the living room and, seeing what had happened to Officer Bill Tamir, stopped short.

"Don't look at this. You don't need to see it," she whispered into his ear. She squeezed his hand but stopped him, pulling him back.

"I gotta get his gun," he said.

It was on the floor about a foot from the officer's head which, in turn, lay about a foot from the body in a pool of tacky, already coagulating blood. He knelt to pick up the firearm.

* * *

Lubbock stared fixedly at the small "5" above the elevator door. Finally, it lit up, and the doors opened. The two of them stepped out of the elevator cautiously. It was quiet.

Almost too quiet, the B-movie buff in John quipped. Then the fire alarm went off. Steve jumped. He turned to him and let out a long breath, shaking a little with laughter and the adrenaline pumping in his blood.

They rounded a corner and stopped. There was a body on the ground, a cop. He knew it must be Nick Black, the one he'd stationed in the hall. John's heart sank as they neared the corpse. He tried not to notice Nick's throat had been ripped out as he passed. Steve nearly stepped on a tattered bit of meat as he skirted around the body.

As John stepped into the room, he saw both AJ and Clover. AJ kneeled to pick up a gun and, when he heard the two cops come through the door, he reacted.

How can he be that fast? John asked himself as AJ's arm became a soft blur and snatched up the gun, cocked it, and leveled it at Steve's head, all the while looking John directly in the eyes. John would replay this later and wonder about it.

They were frozen there. AJ's breathing was heavy and erratic. The gun quivered in the kid's hand, and the tendons and veins stood out in his arm.

Steve stood still, hands open, palm out.

"Kid...put the gun down," John said, trying to soothe him. "It's us, the good guys, remember?"

Clover gently closed her hand around the barrel of the gun, turning it toward the floor. John noticed with a touch of awe at her poise that she had pushed one of her own fingers in behind the trigger, so if AJ flinched in reaction the gun wouldn't—*couldn't*—go off.

"Jesus, man, I'm sorry—" AJ's apology was interrupted as someone else charged through the door. Everyone jumped and turned to see Logan as he entered.

"Ah, Mr. Perish, I presume?" John asked. The cop in him wanted to immediately start peppering the guy with questions, regardless of what Jin's letter said, but then he took a closer look at the man, at the pale and somehow ashen color of his face. Any question he might have had dried up when Logan came all the way into the hotel room, quietly closing the door behind him.

"What the fuck, John?" Steve whispered.

AJ stared at Logan's arm and reached out to Clover, clutching her sleeve.

There was a severed head stuck to his forearm, the teeth buried in the flesh. The head itself was splattered with blood and Logan's arm was a slick, red glove from his elbow all the way to his fingertips. The head still bore a few wisps of hair, but the nose looked, from where he stood, to have mostly rotted away. Logan's blood ran down off his arm and out of the tattered neck hole of the head onto the floor.

"I got two of 'em in the stairs," Logan said.

The room was silent but for the splattering of blood on the carpet, a small pool of it already forming next to Logan's boot.

"Can someone help get this off me?" Logan asked.

No one spoke. Finally, Clover cleared her throat and stepped forward, still carrying the plunger handle.

"Brace it against the door," Clover said after looking it over.

Logan held his arm up and leaned it against the door. Clover leaned in again, her face wrinkling in disgust.

"Will this make you...one of them?" AJ asked.

Logan shook his head.

"Are you ready?" Clover asked.

Logan nodded, and she stepped in closer to him, working the end of the plunger handle into the space between mouth and arm, wriggled it around, and adjusted it until she had the angle and leverage she wanted.

She looked up at him. "Count of three?"

Logan nodded. "Sure. Count of—"

Clover stepped forward and slammed the heel of her palm against the plunger handle.

"Fuck!" Logan let out a guttural bark of pain as AJ, and John flinched.

There was a crack like breaking ice, and several teeth flew out of the head, ticking off the wall, one off

Clover's forehead. The jaw now hung loose like a busted drawer. She'd popped the mandible right out of joint and dislocated its sockets, held in place only by decaying skin and muscle.

She dropped the plunger handle to the floor and, carefully, as though defusing a bomb, placed her hands around the head. Only AJ noticed the slightest of tremor in her hands. She jiggled it back and forth a little, and then pulled it off in a rush of blood and a few more falling teeth.

"Let's get a towel on that," Steve said and went toward the bathroom.

Clover looked at the bloody, rotting, severed head in her hands, and then a dark smile crossed her face, and she held the head aloft, looking up into its eyes, some of Logan's blood running down her forearm or in between her fingers and down the back of her hand.

"Alas, poor Yorick," she said in a deep voice, affecting an English accent.

"Jesus Christ," John said with a snort of laughter. She smiled again and, to AJ, it looked like she was going to start screaming, but she swallowed it, whatever it was: the horror, the grief, the exhaustion, the terrible acid trip reality that had become their waking life.

She dropped the skull into a small, metal trashcan next to a writing desk near the door with an echoing *clang*, then turned to Logan.

"Thank you," Logan said, taking a towel from Steve. Clover took the towel from Logan, and he slowly started to take off his trench coat.

He looked like shit, but he was alive, for now.

CHAPTER

SEVEN

AJ came out of the hotel feeling responsible for the twelve dead people he counted inside. John Lubbock led their small party out, bulldozing a path through the crowd. AJ couldn't turn his head in any direction without seeing a cop, reporter, hotel employee, fireman, or paramedic.

The sky was black with clouds, and the rain still poured, adding to the chaos. Everywhere were lights, flashing off police cruisers and ambulances and the fire truck that arrived. News vans from three different networks and two major papers were on the scene.

Cameramen shone hot lights in his eyes and reporters screamed questions and stabbed at his face with microphones bearing station logos as uniformed officers tried to fend them off. The lightning became a part of the mob, forming a pulsing, savage backdrop. AJ felt like the fabled cow about thirty seconds before being skeletonized by the school of piranha. He looked around for

Logan but saw no sign.

"Get in the car," John shouted above the commotion. The door was closed behind AJ and Clover, and the car crept through the mass of people. Although physically and mentally exhausted, the frenetic energy of the scene got AJ going, and he felt unnaturally hyper. It reminded him of his brief high school experiments with speed. In the bulletproof rear window, he caught his reflection and didn't know what to make of the smile he saw there.

* * *

AJ looked up at the detective across the conference table, remembering what Steve'd looked like staring down the barrel of a gun when he and John came busting through the hotel room door. In that moment, it had been as automatic as breathing, or as though his hands were being guided...and he'd almost pulled the trigger.

Chief Don Harris came in and sat next to John, who was next to Terrance. Steve sat next to Clover, with AJ next to her, the two of them holding hands under the table.

"We got a leak somewhere," John said. "It's the only way they coulda found us."

"There's still another side to all this, John," Harris said. "We don't have any idea what these...these things are, let alone what they might be capable of."

"What, you mean like telepathy?" John asked. "Let me put an APB out on Miss Cleo."

"Harris is right, though," Terrance said. "If we accept this is happening, we have to leave room for whatever else might come up."

Harris turned to AJ. "Now, what about this book?"

AJ shrugged. "All I know is that we need it as soon as we can get it."

"First thing tomorrow, John'll drive to your parents' house, followed by a couple squad cars," Harris said.

"Okay, just make sure that once I get there, they stay out of sight. I'm not up to explaining this to my mom."

They went over a few more specifics before ending the meeting. By the time they all left to go to safe house, it was around eight o'clock in the evening. John Lubbock and Steve were sent home. John protested again but was once more overruled. AJ and Clover were accompanied by Terrance and four other officers. The five of them followed their two charges into the hotel to guard them from whatever might happen.

* * *

The voice that answered the phone sounded fuzzy around the edges.

"H'lo?"

"Mom?" Clover asked, wondering how many pills she'd popped since the evening news.

"Clover? Izzat—"

In the background, her father asked who was on the phone.

Her mother cleared her throat. "It's your *daughter*," she said, perhaps thinking Clover wouldn't be able to hear, perhaps too stoned to care. Her father interrupted again.

"Where in the hell has the child been?"

The child isn't deaf, you know. Clover rubbed her eyes, wishing she'd waited until the morning to call.

"Dear?" Her mother came back on the line, sounding a bit more alert than before. "Are you all right?"

"Mom, I'm fine. It's just—"

"We tried to call you after all this terrible mess, and we couldn't get a hold of you, and Angie didn't know where you were, and she talked about some *boy*—"

The familiar hysterics trembled in her mother's voice.

"Mom—"

"And then! And then we see you on the *news* at that *hotel* where all the people were killed, but they won't say who did it, and then you were with that...that *boy*! Holding his hand! How long have you known—"

"Mother!" Clover heard her mother gasp, and then say something, and the next thing she knew, she was talking to her father. Or, rather, he was yelling at her. Her mother's drugged sobs filled the background.

Clover rubbed her eyes again. *Welcome to Introductions in Dysfunction! An American Classic!*

"Just what have you gotten yourself into, girl?"

"Dad—"

"Don't you Dad me! First, you're out in the middle of the night with some boy at a gas station, and then you drop out of touch? Now, your mother sees you on the television! What am I to think, girl? Are you on the dope or—"

"No!" *On the dope?* He had to be kidding, right?

"Is it the boy from the gas station? I just knew he would get you into something you shouldn't—"

"You don't even know him! This is *not* his fault!"

Well, *technically* she supposed it was, being as he was the one who carried a trail of zombies with him wherever he went, but she didn't blame it on him. It wasn't like either of them had known what was coming.

"And now sass talk! I'm getting worried about you, girl. Worried that—"

"You're only worried because you can't control me anymore!" Clover hissed into the phone.

"I'm worried because you're a stupid, confused little girl who has forgotten exactly who it is she's speaking to!"

Her mother wailed in the background.

Clover resisted the urge to tell him to go fuck himself or to slam the phone down. Instead, she set it gently in its cradle, breaking the connection.

"Clover," a voice said from behind her, the only voice she wanted to hear. She turned around and faced him, concern in his warm, gray eyes.

"You all right?" AJ asked.

Hot tears suddenly spilled, and he came to her, held her. She hugged him tightly, and they sat on the bed. She stared at the phone through her tears, remembering not just the most recent conversation, but all the ones preceding it.

"You gonna be okay?" AJ asked, whispering the question into her ear.

"Yeah, it's just—" she said, breaking off, not knowing what else to say. She looked at her watch. It was now 10:30 P.M. on Sunday. In the morning, they would head upstate to AJ's parents' house to get the book.

"Will you sit here with me for a while?" Clover asked, looking into his eyes.

"As long as you want me here," he said, and they resituated themselves, leaning against the headboard with the pillows propped behind their backs, her hand in his. The two of them sat like that for quite some time, not really talking, just being with each other. Eventually, AJ slipped off to sleep and, sometime in the night, awoke long enough to actually lie on the bed.

She hadn't been able to fall back asleep.

As she lay there in the darkness, she found herself wondering about a lot of things, questioning her beliefs.

She believed in a god, though certainly not the cruel hypocrite she had been raised on. She knew the living dead didn't mean that there was no God...but what *did* it mean? Who was in control and just stood aside, watching terrible things like this happen? Perhaps even causing them to happen? Maybe something, but...maybe nothing.

It was unsettling to have to lie there in the dark, on the brink of a battle she didn't understand, questioning things she had seen as unchangeable, cast in stone. All she could do was get through tonight, she supposed, and hold on until the blessed sun could take the world back from this long, wretched night.

She rolled over in her bed and waited.

* * *

AJ lay there, not sure what time it was and not really caring. He was in the dazed stage between sleeping and waking, his eyes half-open, and he was very aware of an arm that certainly wasn't his was draped across his chest. A slow smile crept across his face, and the warm body next to him nuzzled in a little closer.

He turned his head slightly and looked at her. Only a puff of blonde hair was visible under the mass of blankets they were buried in. She rolled over and opened her eyes. They were not the beautiful, green eyes he was used to but, instead, a dead sort of black. The heat seeped out of the bed, and he could no longer feel the gentle thrumming of a pulse in her arm across his chest. Her skin wasn't soft and fair but dead and peeling. It wasn't Clover. It was her corpse. AJ stared, a scream building in his chest.

Then the corpse lunged forward, sinking her teeth into his throat.

AJ sat upright in bed. He looked around the room frantically. Empty, as was the bed. He was alone.

"Ah, fuck," he said in a voice still drunk with sleep. He plopped back down onto the pillow, staring at the ceiling.

His half-opened eyes registered the door opening, and Clover walked in.

God, she's beautiful, he thought and on the heels of that, *I love her.* His eyes drifted closed, and the next thing he knew, her soft, warm lips were pressed to his. He came fully awake and kissed her back. Finally, she drew back and looked at him, smiling.

"It's time."

And there they were, an hour later, three cars in succession. There was a police cruiser out in front of Clover's blue Mazda , and John's undercover car behind them. Logan had shown up as they were preparing to leave, saying he had a lot to talk to AJ about. The strange, white-haired man seemed to have a knack of coming and going when time was short and time to question was even shorter.

AJ had looked at John, who was visibly struggling with himself, staring Logan down with those X-Ray Cop Eyes but, ultimately, said nothing. AJ again wondered what, exactly, had been in that letter, and who it had been from. Logan sat in the back of Clover's car, AJ in front, her behind the wheel, and they set out on the drive. John hadn't liked the idea of Logan riding with them alone, but ultimately gave in when Clover had pointed out there wasn't time to argue.

"The Bible is right about a couple things," Logan began. "In the beginning, there was light. All forces of life and death are controlled by separate entities, each the opposite of the other, but part of the same whole. The Being that controls the light—birth, life, and creation— is called Jha'ask. The other Being controls death, the destruction of the soul, and the Beyond. It is called Enopac."

"Should I be hearing all this?" Clover asked.

"Yes. You're a part of this, too," Logan said.

"What about God?" Clover asked. She stared at his calm face in the rearview mirror.

"There isn't *God* in the sense you're talking about. The Biblical God, Father, Son, Holy Ghost, they're just variations. Every religion has one. Jehovah, Allah, Ra, Ganesh, whatever. You see, these Beings are the essence of *every* god, of *every* religion. Enopac generally represents the Devil, although isn't really evil."

"Occupational hazard of controlling the Beyond," AJ said. It wasn't that he didn't believe Logan, he had no reason not to. Sure, it was a far different idea than he was used to, having been raised vaguely Baptist, but it all rang true to him, as if it was something he'd always known but had forgotten. He just wasn't at the stage where he could comfortably admit this to himself, and he'd always used sarcasm as a defense mechanism.

"Something like that," Logan answered with a trace of smile.

"But there *is* something after we, well, after we die?" AJ asked.

"Of course. The majority of a soul's existence is in the Beyond. Life on any level is a waystation of sorts. The concepts of Heaven and Hell are also correct. That's the one other factor basic religion got right. Limbo, too, or Purgatory, whatever you want to call it. Down there, they call it the Grindhouse. How you behave during life dictates what you receive after it.

"Now, as I was saying, these two Beings have been at peace with each other and with themselves since time out of mind, before there even *was* time. The two of them exist in a perfect balance. Then the 1300s rolled around, and another Being became a problem."

"Other what?" Somewhere deep inside, AJ knew the answer to this question, too.

"Another Being, another Entity. This one is called Daed Sixxez. He is the Lord of the Nexus, of the process of decay and agents of chaos. He gained power over bodies without souls…corpses, essentially. The longer the body is without a soul, the weaker it becomes. It breaks down. But the shorter the time, the stronger the physical being is, and easier for him to control."

"So, when does a soul leave a body?" Clover asked.

"Directly after the death of the body." There was a

short but somehow eerie silence that settled within the car, like a shroud upon dead skin.

"So, how…how'd he—it—become a problem?" AJ asked, unable to control the quaver in his voice. It was not a sign of fear, but rather of eagerness to learn.

"He figured out how to use His power. Until then, He had simply lain dormant, in awe of those other two parts, Enopac and Jha'ask. He was dumbfounded by what He saw, the things He knew, and the power They had, the power He lacked. And, eventually, it drove Him completely insane."

AJ felt a shudder rack his entire body, his entire *being*, with the thought that one of these three Supreme Entities was a fucking lunatic.

"He found his power, limited as it was, and experimented with it," Logan went on. "Finally, in the year 1348, He gathered an army of the dead in England, and very well could have taken over the planet."

"Holy shit," Clover muttered. "The Black Death."

"That's how it was covered up, yes," Logan said.

"There was only one man who stepped up to stop—"

"Why couldn't the Beings, His cosmic brothers or whatever, stop him?" AJ interrupted.

"They cannot. This was a matter out of Their control. They deal with souls before birth, during life, and after death. Walking dead don't fit into that equation. Again, one man rose to confront Him. This man was only a thief, but his heart was pure, good. *He* was good. And he saved us all."

AJ looked back curiously at Logan. There had been something in his voice… "How'd he do it?"

"Ripped out Daed's Core," Logan said as if it were obvious.

AJ turned around fully in his seat to look into Logan's eyes, instead staring at his own reflection in those ever-present sunglasses. "What?"

"Each Entity has a life source within them when they take physical form, something that lets them *be*. It's called the Core, and it's located in the center of the chest, where your solar plexus is."

"But this thief guy, how'd he know that?"

"I told him," Logan said simply. "Same as I'm telling you."

"This is too much." AJ faced forward again but, still, it felt like the truth.

Clover was silent.

"You *know* it's true," Logan said to both of them. This part of their lives had been determined so long ago that time itself was a joke. It was fate. It was destiny.

Then AJ asked, "Okay, *Methuselah*, how old are you, anyway?"

"Old," Logan said. "Put it this way, if the Crucifixion of Christ had *actually* happened, I could have been there. I was—"

"Wait, wait, wait!" Clover said. "Did you just say the Crucifixion never happened?"

"Oh, people were crucified all the time," Logan said. "But the one on which *all* Christianity is based on?"

"Yeah?" Clover gripped the steering wheel so tight her arms shook.

"Complete bullshit. Not just that, but all of it."

"Hoooooly shit," Clover said. "My parents would lose their minds if they heard this."

"No, they wouldn't," Logan said. "They'd never believe me. I have *proof* their religion is bullshit, but it wouldn't matter. To people like them, it never does."

There was a long note of silence in the car, and Logan continued.

"I was given all the knowledge of these things, of the Enopac and Jha'ask and all the rest of it—when I was created, looking almost the same as I do now. Back then, my hair was black, though."

AJ could think of nothing at all to say. What do you ask the guy who is giving you the secrets of the universe?

Logan kept talking, "I was given the job of helping The Next."

AJ found his voice again. "This first guy, what was his name?"

"His name was Corbin Munroe," Logan said and paused. "And you know, you two look a bit alike. Same nose."

Thoughts raced through AJ's head. He could hear his name, his birth name, his *real name*, being called out by dead voices over and over again, echoing across centuries and throughout the generations. He tried to speak, but nothing came out. His throat felt lined with sandpaper. He cleared it and tried again.

"What about the book?"

"The book was given to Corbin after he defeated Daed Sixxez, and he was named Guardian. By accepting this book, these responsibilities, he forever cast the fate of his family. The book was passed down from father to son, mother to daughter, whomever was the direct bloodline…few were called upon to protect it, to serve the Purpose, but most were not. Their sole Purpose was to have a child and pass the knowledge on."

"So, why does He keep coming back? If His Core or whatever was taken out?" Clover asked. Her face had taken on an odd, grayish color, like old cheese. With white knuckles, she still held the steering wheel in a death grip.

"Daed Sixxez can't be killed that way, just sent back into the Nexus in a kind of hibernation. Once the Core is removed, He returns there in a comatose state, waiting for it to regenerate itself."

"So, what happens if He gets the book?" AJ was almost afraid to hear the answer.

"He'll read it. He'll learn how to use His powers in ways He never thought imaginable. Worst of all, He'll learn how to develop them, make them stronger, almost equal to that of Enopac or Jha'ask. And then..." Logan said and stopped, his words drifting off and, again, silence settled into the car, and for much longer this time.

AJ sat watching the scenery go by and realizing he had been let in on the innermost secrets of life. In less than fifteen minutes time, he had been told what mankind had been trying to figure out and prove since the beginning. He knew now in his head, and more importantly, in his heart, the things he had been told were true.

This was his Purpose, what he was destined to do. Something that had been handed down from his ancestors in a way that was bigger than genetics or history. He turned and looked at Logan.

"What happens if I fail?"

"If you fail, if Dead Sixxez isn't stopped, Perdition will be visited upon the Earth, and death will rain down like a plague. The dead will rise and walk in numbers far greater than those of the living. Everyone will be put to death and resurrected as part of the army. The sun will go out, and the sky will turn as red as the blood that stains the earth."

AJ got a cigarette out of his pack, but his hand shook too much for him to light it.

"But you have no reason to think you'll fail," Logan said. "None in your family ever have."

AJ heard him speak, and understood what he said, but it was as if Logan had spoken from somewhere far away. The world swam briefly and took on a strange, dreamlike quality.

Suddenly, the car was too small, too small by far. He had never suffered from claustrophobia before, but he was now in the grips of it. A hot sweat broke out all over his body, and he knew he was going to puke.

"Pull over," he said but his voice was so weak at first no one had heard. He spoke up again, feeling his stomach turn. "Clover, stop the car."

She turned and looked at him, doing a double take. "Oh, shit! Are you okay?"

I must look like the living dead, he thought.

Hysterical laughter rose in him, but another wave of nausea knocked it down. The car slowed and pulled to the side of the road. AJ was dimly aware John had turned his flashers on behind them and also pulled over, as did the cruiser ahead of them.

AJ opened the door and got out, stumbling but maintaining his balance. He heard the soft *ding of the* car and heard the computer voice advise that *a door is ajar.*

Lubbock stopped his car and got out, pushing his hat back on his head and scratching his brow.

AJ staggered off the road toward a grove of bushes. Everything he had eaten in the last day came up in a warm rush as he reached the other side of the shrubbery. He grimaced at the sight of the technicolor puddle and spat over and over, trying to rid his mouth of the foul taste. He stood there a moment later with his hands on his knees until he was sure his period of regurgitation had passed. When he turned, Clover stood in front of him, smiling.

"Looks like the fate of mankind rests on the shoulders of a guy who can't even keep down his Lucky Charms." AJ managed a small grin. Clover stared for a second, and then broke into laughter.

"Now, now...that's not a very heroic thing to say."

He felt a little better, but even as he thought the improvement might only be a temporary one, the nausea started to creep back.

John and Logan stood next to Clover's car, the detective taking the opportunity to light a cigar, waiting for the kids to return.

"So. Mr. *Perish,* is it?" John asked. They'd met at the hotel, but only briefly. There just hadn't been time then for John to really get a read on the guy, something he was sure Perish had made sure of.

"You can call me Logan."

"I would typically introduce myself here, but it seems you already know who I am, that right?"

Logan turned, and they watched the two kids as they made their way back to the road, hand in hand.

"Jin spoke highly of you," Logan said. "I trust you read his letter?"

"I did," John said. "Burned it after."

"Good," Logan said. "And your verdict?"

John heaved a long sigh, staring down at the smoldering tip of his cigar.

"If that shit-show at the hotel hadn't happened yesterday? Might be a different story. Then again, it might not. I seen some things these last few days I have no sane explanation for. People that should have been—who *were dead*—getting up and walking around. Choked me, one of them. A woman who had slit her wrists and bled out in her bathtub hours before she was ever on that autopsy table. This is *after* she tried to choke out our boy, of course."

John sighed and took his hat off with one hand and ran the other across his head, his short hair rasping against his calloused palm. He placed the hat back on his head and took another couple puffs on his cigar.

They paused in their conversation for a moment, to the sounds of AJ, again vomiting in the bushes.

"If this was *anything* else," John continued. "If it were *any other case* in the world that ran along the normal course of things, you'd have been cuffed to a table in a small room with no windows and a big pane a' two-way glass set into the wall, and you and me, we would have had ourselves a long conversation. Again, *if* it were like any other case."

"But it isn't," Logan said, his voice almost a whisper.

"No," John said. "It isn't. Neither was Jin's last case. Do you know anything about it? Todd Bowden?"

"I don't know much about *Mr.* Bowden," Logan reached up as he spoke, the tip of his finger gently running across the bottom end of the scar that started at his hairline and ended at his cheekbone. "I met his wife once, though."

"No shit?"

Logan nodded. "It was, well, a while ago. Long before she was Tereza Bowden. I'm here to help, Detective. That's all I want you to know, and it's all I want to do. I've been in this particular line of work a very long time, and it seems lately that things are getting worse. We needed Jin, same as we need AJ, same as we need you. I know that, when things got bad at the end there, for Jin, when you started seeing things you couldn't explain, I know you stepped back."

"I—"

Logan held up a hand. "You were ordered to, I know that, and more, Jin knows that. But you felt a sense of relief at those orders; at least a part of you did. The things you saw were at war with everything you'd learned to expect from this world, and that's understandable. Forgivable, even. So, is climbing into a bottle to try and forget those things, and to try and erase the guilt you feel for turning your back on your friend, orders or no.

"If it helps to know this, there isn't a single thing you could have done to help him, at the time. These two kids, though, you can help them, but not by interfering with me. No doubt you've already had someone run that name Perish, and my description, through your computers. You might have even pulled one of my prints before we left the hotel."

"Thought about it," John said. "I really did."

"You won't find anything. All you'll do is waste time, and time is the thing we can afford to waste the least. We're on the same side here, yes?"

John stared into the distance for another long moment.

He turned to Logan, hand extended.

"I'm happy to have the help," John said as Logan took his hand,

A moment later, AJ reappeared, walking back toward the car, wiping his mouth with the back of one hand while Clover held the other.

"He gonna be all right?" John asked.

"Oh, yeah," Logan said. "Happens every time."

John looked at him and grinned. He turned and walked back to his car.

About an hour later, as they neared their destination, John flashed his lights again, and all three vehicles pulled to the side of the road. He got out and walked up to the passenger side of Clover's car. AJ unrolled the window, and John motioned for one of the detectives in the squad car to join him.

"Okay, kid. You said your parents got a lot of hedges and shit out front?" John asked.

"Yeah. I figure if the two of you park there, it shouldn't be a problem. You can't really see the road from inside the yard."

They all drove on.

"Take a right here," AJ directed. Clover flicked on her blinker.

"That's your house?" she asked. It was a huge, three-story Victorian home set in the middle of a two-acre plot. "Damn."

The car rolled to a stop in the driveway. Only then could they see the picture window in the living room was smashed. Splatters of what could only be blood stained the white siding below it. The front door looked as if it had been hit by a hurricane, the screen barely hanging on by a hinge.

"My parents." AJ bolted for the house, paying no attention to the screams behind him: one Clover, yelling for John, and one was Logan, yelling for him to stop.

He ripped the screen door off the last hinge, flinging it into the rose bed next to the stoop, and rushed in the house.

"Mom! Dad!" AJ heard the radio on in the kitchen and headed toward it. He stopped in the doorway. His mother stood at the counter with her back to him, and she appeared to be chopping up vegetables.

"Mom?" he asked in a small voice. It was all he could muster. She didn't turn, didn't speak. "Ma?" he asked, this time a little louder.

Then something happened. The room changed, and the temperature plummeted. The lights overhead flickered, and then exploded.

"What the fuck?" AJ shielded himself from the shower of glass and fluorescent bulbs.

His mother turned around, and her throat was gone. It had been ripped out, leaving a gaping hole the size of a softball in her neck. Blood covered the front of her shirt and pants.

Then her eyes changed. They turned from their normal shade of light hazel to a cold, dead black AJ knew all too well. And then she spoke. It wasn't her soft, kind voice he heard. It was the voice of a madman, much lower and brimming with insanity.

"Mommy's not home right now," the voice said, and she charged at him with a knife raised. AJ backed up into the wall, screaming, beginning to cry.

Two shots were fired. John stood in the doorway, his gun trained on AJ's dead mother, having pulled the trigger mere moments before she—*it*—could run a knife through her son. AJ sank to the floor and put his head on his knees.

He had no idea how long he sat against the wall. There was no time, there was only pain. He barely registered a few muffled screams and another series of gunshots as they rang out in another part of the house.

All was quiet, and he cried harder than he could ever remember. He didn't want to cry, he fucking *hated* to cry, but he couldn't help it.

Sepia-toned floods of childhood trips to the park and snowball fights collapsed all over him. Bittersweet recollections of a thousand beautiful things paraded through his heart with nihilistic indifference, smashing and tearing it, even breaking it in a few places. He squeezed his eyes shut and saw her years ago, walking him to school while they sang "Hey Jude," and the hot tears pushed through his eyes, and then he heard his name.

"AJ? Come in here." It was Logan.

AJ sat a moment longer, not knowing if he could summon the strength or the courage to get up.

Then John Lubbock was kneeling beside him. "Kid…we found your father. He's still alive, but…"

"What?" AJ looked up.

"He's upstairs," John said and stood, holding out a hand. AJ let himself be helped to his feet. The tears still wet on his cheeks as he walked upstairs, scrubbing fiercely at his eyes with his arm as he went.

His father was in AJ's old room, propped against the wall with a blanket over his midsection. He had been eviscerated. There was a suspicious, quivering lump next to him on the floor, a shape under the blood-soaked blanket.

He was dying but wasn't dead yet. His eyes came to life when he saw his son. The circle of strangers around him parted as AJ kneeled beside him.

His father's breathing was fast and shallow.

"Came. For. It," he said in gasps.

"For what?" It had been the book. The fucking book.

"Hid. F-from. Them."

"I'm so sorry," AJ said softly, tears once more rolling freely down his face.

"Not. Your. F-fault. F-f-fate."

"Wh-where is it, Dad?" AJ asked, not noticing the others had left the room in respect for a father's last moments with his son.

"D…don't you…know?" His father's voice was getting weaker, but he smiled.

"I'm sorry, Dad," AJ whispered to his father, whose eyes were still open but didn't look as if they were seeing anything they could comprehend.

"I'll find. You. Again. On. Other…side."

AJ grimaced as his father coughed up a torrent of blood, then grinned through it, cursing his son with fuel for a thousand nightmares. Then his eyes closed, and his father died.

AJ kissed him once on the forehead and covered him with the blanket.

Clover leaned over to Logan. "Is his dad going to… you know. Change," she asked, her voice a whisper.

Logan shook his head. "Daed's presence is gone for now. John drove him out."

AJ went to the window and kneeled, pulling up the loose floorboard that had always been there. Hidden within it was a secret drawer, enough to keep a small boy amused for a long time. His father had enjoyed it as a child before him. AJ reached into the drawer and pulled out the massive volume of text that had brought so much ruin down on all of them.

As he touched the book, a potent energy slowly filled him. He held the book in awe. It was a full six inches thick and was bound in old leather the color of half-dried blood. A symbol of inlaid ancient silver was on the cover, not shiny and decorative but looking like some decrepit warning from another time. This same, tired alloy ran up the spine of the book, out along its edges, and formed the lock on it as well.

While he held it, the sorrow seemed to leak out of him. The book felt a little heavier for a moment, as if it had soaked up his pain by replacing it with a feeling of raw power. AJ looked around his childhood room for what would be the last time and went outside to join the others. When he stepped out of the house onto the front lawn, they formed a rough semi-circle around him, and he looked at each of them in turn.

There was Clover, beautiful Clover, with her green eyes filled with tears and concern. There was John, endlessly chewing one of his foul cigars and looking somehow as if he'd just woken up. Logan was, well... Logan. The guy's emotions were impossible to read. There was Steve, looking exhausted and avoiding any real eye contact, and Terrance, head bowed, hands clasped in front of him as though in prayer.

There were two other uniformed cops AJ didn't know, but they were obviously new to the whole living dead thing. Their faces held only slightly more color than one of the corpses they'd been fighting.

"I've got the book," he said simply, holding it out with one hand for all of them to see. The book didn't seem to weigh that much anymore.

"I was afraid they might have—" Logan began, an actual detectable note of relief leaking through his tightly sealed walls.

"Yeah? Well, they didn't," AJ snapped. "They got my mom and my dad. My life. But they didn't get this fucking book." He sat down on the step, his voice trailing off at the end. "How did they know?"

"Daed's powers have grown," Logan said. "He must've known it was here."

"Or it could still be a leak," John said flatly, but he sounded like he didn't much believe it anymore.

AJ looked up into the detective's eyes. "If it's a leak, I'll kill whoever it was."

Clover joined him on the step. She leaned her head against his shoulder, and he thought he might cry again.

* * *

Logan sat in the backseat of Clover's car with her behind the wheel again.

Daed's powers had increased, all right. He had heard His thick, damaged voice when it came out of Gina Lancaster's mouth. Until AJ had come out of the house with the book, Logan had been sure it had been taken, that they were too late. But now that they had it, he was positive Daed would be stopped again, that they would succeed. AJ turned around in his seat.

"How do I kill him?"

"I told you. You have to get His Core."

"No, I don't want to put Him to *sleep*. I want to *destroy* Him."

"I don't know if you can." Logan had heard that same, cold edge that was in AJ's voice in the voices of those before him. It meant that whatever innocence was left in the boy had finally finished dying. But, to Logan, it also meant another Munroe was finally able to accept what he was and what he had to do.

Logan's thoughts again turned to his enemy, the being he had sought after and helped defeat through all seven levels of existence, and wondered if Daed Sixxez, the mad God of the Dead, *could* be completely destroyed.

The only way for *anything* to be completely blocked from one level was to have died on it, as far as he knew. If Daed was able to speak through AJ's mother, what else could He do? Had He known where the book was, or was one of their own somehow working against them? And if so, who could it possibly be?

He just didn't know.

* * *

Clover took one hand off the wheel and held one of AJ's. She hated seeing him this way but, under the circumstances, there wasn't much anyone could do to help him. She could be with him, though, be there for him. Both his parents were gone, carried away by some great violence she didn't understand. Internally, she shuddered as she thought of what AJ had told her, about his mother charging him with a knife, her throat mostly gone.

You've still got me, she thought at him and squeezed his hand. This time, he squeezed back.

* * *

Somewhere beneath the city, a pair of black, apocalyptic eyes opened, the vision of Munroe fading. His mind thumped with pain from still being partly in the mother's head when the pig had shot her. But the headache was already going the way of the vision. Daed's mind slowly bubbled with anger, thinking of the pig He'd gotten to. He had been sure of success, but the cop had failed.

There were words to be had with this particular officer, oh, yes. No one failed Daed Sixxez and lived. Until, of course, He killed them. Then they became soldiers and slaves. He pushed gleeful thoughts of torture aside but wouldn't forget them. Right now, His main concern was that little boy and the book.

Daed knew it was *possible* for Him to be defeated again, but He thought His time for victory on this level was coming around. If He could get His hands on the book, the circle would close, and the dead would clog the streets. The world would become a sadistic perversion of what it was, and he would rule it all.

The Dark Lord of the Nexus sat and thought, to plot. His mind turned, twisting and squirming like a clot of blackened worms, and He had an idea.

* * *

Lubbock drove in silence. The only other person in the car with him was Peters, one of the uniformed boys Chief Harris had sent along. He had been too shaken up to drive, so Terrance was behind the wheel of the other patrol car.

They had to figure out what was next. They finally had this book. He had seen it. John sensed the complete power it held, hidden, and awaiting release. He hoped Logan knew what he was doing because he was out of ideas. He had become a cop for a number of reasons, and he was damn good at his job, this job he loved.

But this was a little out of his jurisdiction, so to speak. He was used to dealing the lowest forms of life ever to be spat from a womb but nothing like this. With this sort of thing, there were no guidelines, no rules. No set precedent that could give him an angle on how to go about approaching it.

Not even everything he had seen during the Bowden investigation had prepared him for this. Most of that had been deep rumor and hearsay, the kind of stuff you would dismiss as bullshit conspiracy and drunk-talk if only you hadn't heard the same thing so many times.

John Lubbock's thoughts turned to the kid. He felt terrible for him. His life was going to be permanently changed if he managed to get through this alive. John supposed he himself would just go back to being a cop, doing normal cop things, assuming he wasn't going to be forced out like Jin had been.

He would take his vacation first, he decided. All of it at once. He'd been accumulating a lot of it over the years, and he started planning on going away to somewhere warm and bright where the dead stayed dead, and the living brought him margaritas on the beach.

But AJ? His life was basically ruined. Maybe something would come of him and the girl, and he hoped so. God knew the kid deserved it.

* * *

John, Logan, Clover, and AJ sat around a shitty kitchen table in a small safe house that Steve had suggested. The house had been seized a year back during a massive drug-bust from a white-power militia group that financed itself by running guns and meth and had been used—after intense fumigation and cleaning—as meeting places for undercover narco buys and stings or as a place for a witness to lay low before a trial.

The book sat in the middle of the table, but all eyes were on Logan.

"So, I have to read it or what?" AJ looked at the unreal thickness of the book. It was bigger than any he'd ever seen.

"You'll want to read it all eventually, the parts unlocked to you, anyway, but most of it won't help you now. Two days ago, it might have made a bigger difference, but the main thing is we have it, and he doesn't. But you have to confront Him and stop Him before He gets too strong."

"Won't He just kill me?" AJ asked. He saw Clover flinch and, under the table, she wrapped her feet around his ankle.

"He can't. You have something else He wants."

"Other than that?" Clover pointed at the one, true bible in the center of the table. Logan shook his head and looked up into AJ's eyes.

"Your soul," Logan said, and it was AJ's turn to flinch. "The only way to ensure His success is to consume your being, your life essence. He'd have no one to stop Him in the future, your family line would be eradicated."

"So, basically, He doesn't want me to have kids?"

"No. As long as your *soul* exists, it will find a body to host it. Reproduction is just the most convenient method of passing on a Purpose.

"I have held council with Enopac and Jha'ask, through their intermediary, a man by the name of Cain Dulouz. At least, he takes the shape of a man. He told me Daed is more powerful than ever before, but He is also more vulnerable. The possibility of success has clouded His mind since the dawn of His time, and now that it seems the closest, the final confrontation will be different than any other. You are going to be the first Munroe He will try to consume."

"So, you've never done this before?" AJ asked.

"In a sense," Logan replied.

"In a sense? This asshole is going to try and eat my soul, and that's all you can say? Well, I guess, *in a sense*, we're fucked."

"The only person who can stop you from succeeding is you," Logan said, his voice still calm and level.

"You sound like a fucking guidance counselor! Don't lay that bullshit on me!"

"It's been laid on you!" Logan said, finally becoming riled. "It was laid on you hundreds of years ago, and that's all there is! It might not be fair, or right, but…it…*is*."

AJ stood up so fast his chair was knocked to the floor. He slammed both hands on the table as he stood. "I'm afraid!"

"Good. Get used to it because you're going to be fucking *terrified* before all this is done." Logan's voice had become calm again, almost indifferent. The tension in the air grew thick. It was a living, sweating thing. The two of them stared at each other across the table, Logan sitting, and AJ standing. One was a man of unknown age, a man without a childhood, a wanderer through the worlds. The other was a twenty-two-year-old kid on the brink of his own destiny, and the fate of mankind as he knew it was suspended over his head like an executioner's finely honed blade.

"But what if I fail?" AJ asked again, quietly.

"Then success wasn't meant to be yours in the first place," Logan said.

AJ picked up his chair and sat back down, lighting a cigarette as Logan spoke.

"Each life has a Purpose, one thing that must be done. If you fail, then your Purpose was not to succeed. If you confront Daed, the hands of fate will do the rest."

"Then I don't have a choice?" AJ asked.

"You have a choice. You always have a choice. You just need to make the right one."

AJ let all that sink in. He took a deep drag from his cigarette and spoke. "How do I find him?"

"When the time of confrontation nears, the Entities will come to you in a dream—or send their emissary—as it always has been and shall always be. They will show you the way, and soon."

John got up from the table and went to sit on the

couch. He poured a cup of coffee. Not knowing what else to do, AJ picked up the giant, ancient book and went to the bedroom. He sat against the headboard with the book in his lap. He didn't open it to the middle, he opened the cover and was going to check the front to see if it had a table of contents or a foreword or something, but pages turned with it.

The book opened itself, and he read:

The universe has been looked upon by two Beings since before the dawn of time, in as such that they created it. One is Life, Jha'ask. The other is Death, Enopac. Neither is good or evil, although they created both.

These Beings are creators of all things with and without a soul.

Each soul is assigned a Purpose that must be filled before it leaves the living body. The Purpose of one may seem more significant than that of another, but each Purpose is a vital part of the eventual whole, the One.

When the amalgamation of Purposes is complete, life as it is will become obsolete. All Beings will reach a level of perfect balance between body and mind and soul, and all shall become an Entity all their own.

This is the plan, the gift of Jha'ask and Enopac bestowing upon us the ability to become what they are, albeit on a different level.

When the One is reached, all pain and evil and suffering shall cease, and all shall know a level of pure happiness as of yet incomprehensible to any conscious mind.

We must realize there is a good and an evil, but only because it was created by the Entities. Evil serves a purpose, it is a part of the Balance, and without it there would be no good. Although all live under the roof of free will, all must realize everything happens for a reason, and the reason is the reaching of the One. No single man, woman, child, bird, beast, insect, or fish may reach the One without the combined efforts of every other man, woman, child, bird, beast, insect, and fish that has ever lived, is living, or will someday live.

It is a truth that not every Purpose can be filled before the soul exits the body. If the body dies before the Purpose is reached, that soul is altered, changed anew, and assigned a different body. In time, the One shall be reached, and all souls shall be evolved into their perfect state.

AJ looked up from the book and let everything sort itself out a little in his head. More pages turned on their own volition and, when they stopped, he read on.

There is one who serves against the Purpose, against the One. He is at a level of evil far beyond the imagination of mortal man, evil at a level that was unintended and is a danger to the Balance.

He has always been there, the Dark Lord of the Nexus, the Servant of the Random. He seeks death instead of life, ugliness instead of beauty, destruction instead of creation, nothingness instead of the One.

This third Entity has yet to realize the broad, sickening scope of his powers, and only this text may show Him the path. But it is necessary to have such potentially dangerous pages, for the book would be incomplete without them. This text shall be the charge and sole responsibility for whomever the Entities deem worthy the role of Guardian. None but the Protector need to know of this text's existence, and no other but the Protector need worry about its safekeeping from Daed Sixxez, the empty god.

Only one Purpose is outlined and laid out before the soul

it is assigned to, and that is the Purpose of the Protector. At all costs and at all risk to loss of life or love must the Protector keep the pages within from Daed Sixxez and all other servants of the Random. For if this book should fall into His keeping, should the knowledge within be conveyed to Him, the One shall never be reached, and all that has been fought over and suffered for will be destroyed and made obscene.

AJ closed the book. He set it next to him on the bed and leaned back, closed his eyes for a moment, and absorbed what he'd read. When he opened them again, Clover stood in the doorway.

"Hi," she said simply and sat down on the edge of the bed. "You all right?"

"I'm better."

"Do you want me to leave?" she asked.

"No, that's the last thing I want right now, to be alone."

She moved to him, sitting next to him on the bed. She held his hand and looked into his eyes as they filled with tears.

"They're gone."

Clover seemed to be at a loss for words. It's hard enough to comfort someone after they lose a person they love, but under such malign circumstances, it seemed next to impossible. What could she say?

Instead of speaking, she put one arm around him, held his hand with the other, and leaned her head on his shoulders, hugging him as close as possible. It was perhaps the best thing she could have done.

CHAPTER EIGHT

Terrance had arrived for his shift of guard duty after AJ had retired to his room with the book. On any normal case, having to pull a shit guard detail would have pissed him off...but this one was different.

In normal police work, there were a lot of gray areas. He knew it was a shitty world when you were down, and you had to do what you needed to survive. A lot of good people had to do bad things to get by, but the bad things were often rotten pieces in a larger, nobler puzzle. Sometimes, it was hard to tell the bad people from the good. But this, this was as clear cut as you could want. Both sides were as clearly defined as high noon and midnight.

Time passed slowly for him, uneventfully. Everyone else was asleep. The two kids were in one room, Logan in another. John was asleep soundly in the tiny third room, the one in between AJ and the door. Terrance looked around. He knew the history of the place and was glad to see all that racist bullshit had been removed.

Didn't leave much else, he thought. The walls were bare, and the few pieces of remaining furniture just on the other side were barely in good repair. He sat alone in the silence on a threadbare couch, slowly whittling away the minutes until his replacement was due.

Finally, there was a light tap on the door. Terrance flinched at the sound. He'd expected to be able to see the approaching lights on Steve's car coming down the long, dirt road. He stood and moved across the room, quick and silent as a cat, his hand already on the butt of his gun.

Terrance peered through the peephole and saw Steve Nielsen standing on the front stoop, staring off to his left. He exhaled a shaky breath. He took his hand off his gun and unlocked and opened the door.

"Hey, man," Terrance said as Steve walked past him and sat on the couch without so much as looking at him. Steve motioned for him to sit down next on the couch, still without speaking.

Terrance was getting a bad vibe. He almost dropped one hand back to the butt of his gun. He stopped himself and forced out a laugh. Had he really almost drawn his gun on Steve?

Terrance sat down. "Anything wrong?"

Steve looked at him with empty, black eyes. "Not yet," he said in a low and deranged voice Logan and AJ would have recognized. Terrance tried to look away and found he couldn't.

"Wh-wha…" Terrance tried to speak and was unable. His eyes ached, and he was lost in the double black holes in Steve's head. The eyes were huge. They… were…everything.

The pain moved through Terrance's skull, creeping like an intelligent cancer and spreading even faster. Steve started to speak but not in a language Terrance could understand. The red-haired detective turned traitor put a hand on each of Terrance's cheeks and spoke faster and faster in a low voice so as not to disturb the others.

Terrance's brain itched as if there were bugs crawling on it. He couldn't stop looking into Steve's eyes, Gina Lancaster's eyes, Daed Sixxez's eyes. Steve stopped talking, and the voice coming from his mouth now echoed inside Terrance's skull. It told him what was happening and what he must do. Daed Sixxez had gotten inside his head.

* * *

Clover lay awake in the darkness, the soft, pleasant ache still between her legs. A syrupy smile crossed her face as she thought of it, how wonderful it had been. AJ lay next to her in the bed, gone to the world and sleeping better than he had in a long time. She nuzzled in a little closer to him, knowing she was going to have to get up and use the bathroom and not wanting to. It was so warm and perfect in the bed they shared.

Clover ran her hand lightly across his chest, which was narrow but strong. A perfect, thin patch of dark hair grew there, and she scratched her fingers gently through it.

She was so glad she had come in to check on him when she had. At first, she was nervous about it. She didn't want to invade his privacy if he wanted to be alone.

He had cried, which was sweet and broke her heart a little. They talked, and talking progressed to touching.

Her nipples hardened now as they had when he touched them. She heard his soft, nonsense murmurs and love sounds in her ears, felt the warm push of air across her neck as his breathing grew a little heavier.

Clover had been with other guys, but it had never been anything like this. It had been long and slow and hot and delicious, the way she'd always thought making love would be.

She looked at him lying there asleep, sprawled on his back, snoring ever-so-slightly. *He deserves his rest*, she thought, and almost giggled in the darkness, considering waking him up for another go after she peed.

From the front room, she heard a knock, and her entire body stiffened. As if sensing her duress, AJ stirred in his sleep. The temperature of the room seemed to drop, and she shivered. Then she heard the words of Terrance Wills and, from his tone, she knew it was all right. She relaxed again and lounged in bed a little longer, thinking of the sounds they had made when they came, how his whole body seemed to flex against hers before relaxing completely.

Her bladder finally won—it was what awakened her—and Clover got out of bed and pulled her jeans on over her dark blue panties. She was too cold to look for her bra or her top, but she saw AJ's plain, white T-shirt on the floor next to the bed, so she slipped it on and walked out of the room.

She glanced into the front room as she crossed the hall to the bathroom. Detectives Nielsen and Wills sat on the couch, talking about something. It was an intense conversation from the look of it.

When she was done, she looked in the mirror. The

shirt was baggy on AJ and huge on her. She pulled the neck hole to one side and saw a small, purple hickey on her collarbone. She smiled to herself and opened the door.

* * *

Logan sat on his bed, still fully clothed. This was wrong. It *had* been right, this house, this place, but it was wrong now. He could feel it in the air. He heard a knock on the door from the front room and listened until he heard Terrance open up and greet his relief.

Logan took in and released several long, low breaths, hoping to calm himself, telling himself he felt this way because the time was drawing closer.

No. Something was *wrong*.

He stood and crossed the room to his coat, which hung over the back of a shitty wooden chair with uneven legs, the only thing he had taken off. He dug through the pockets of his coat, his stomach sinking before he even found what he was looking for. There was no need to find the artifact for which he quested. He could see the light it cast, so bright it was almost white, blazing, the full light of noonday sun contained within the pocket of his coat.

"AJ!" Logan screamed. He grabbed his shotgun, and that was when he heard windows being smashed all over the house.

* * *

Out of the corner of eyes that had once been his own, Terrance saw Clover come out of the bathroom and go back into the bedroom. He thought she had looked up at them but wasn't sure. He had tried desperately to warn her, to warn all of them. To scream or even blink.

Terrance knew now what had to be done, what he would be forced to do. He didn't want to do these things. All he really wanted was to regain control of his body again, enough to draw his gun and put a fucking slug into the head of this bastard.

Nothing had been explained to him, but when Daed Sixxez hijacked his body and entered his head, Terrance knew. He shared Daed's thoughts as much as the Other controlled his. He had, all at once, known Steve had been promised things: wealth and power and scores of slave girls to bend to his will. They were false promises, all of them, but it had been enough to take a hold in the man's brain, his fucking *soul*, and turn him against them.

Terrance also knew Steve had to betray them of his own free will before Sixxez could completely gain control over him. Steve had freely given them up at the Fireside Hotel, which led to the death of several innocent people, some of them cops.

And Terrance knew that if he got the chance, he would kill Steve Nielsen.

You won't get the chance, laughed the god in his head.

Somewhere in the house, as though far away, Terrance heard Logan scream the kid's name.

The front door was not so much kicked in as it simply exploded, knocked clean off its hinges and slamming to the floor. The walking dead flooded into the house after it. The windows in the front room—one looking out into the porch and a larger one looking to the side yard—shattered.

NO! he screamed in the only place he could: his head. *Give me back my body!*

The only answer was sick laughter. Terrance's head was turned for him, the tendons in his neck creaking. Though the windows were barred, the glass lay in a thousand glittering pieces on the floor.

There were bars on the windows, but those bars were already covered with the decaying hands of the creepers, pulling on them, smashing themselves against the place where the bars were joined to the house, the floor trembling against the onslaught of their combined efforts and mass. He watched as Steve made his way back out through the front door, the creepers parting to let him pass, untouched.

He heard John scream and fire his gun once, twice, again.

The creepers shambled past him, still coming in through the open front door. There was a screaming of metal on metal as the bars on one of the front windows came loose, and he heard that same sound in another room of the house.

* * *

AJ was jolted awake by Logan screaming his name. He reached out for Clover, finding her side of the bed empty, the sheets already cool. He then saw her, standing in the door to their room, looking out. Glass exploded in the front room. She screamed and slammed the door, locking it.

AJ rolled out of bed and pulled his pants on. Gunfire rang out in the room next door, the sound of it slamming into his ears and seeming to suck the air out of the house, leaving behind a high-pitched whine that would be a steady backdrop in his head for the next two days.

"What—" AJ began, but the small window next to the bed blew inward, cutting him off. He covered his eyes with his left arm, feeling little pieces and bits of glass bounce off him.

Arms came in through the window, between the bars, groping for the book that sat on the little stand next to the bed.

"No! Bastard!" Clover stepped forward, catching the heavy brass lamp as it fell off the bedside table. She raised it high and brought it down with a grunt on one of the arms questing between the bars. The *crunch* of the bones breaking was lost in another round of gunshots.

She slammed the base of the lamp down again, and AJ could see yellowed bones busting through slack, gray flesh, and there was not a drop of blood that flowed. He grabbed the book off the nightstand in one arm and tucked it to his chest, then pulled Clover back from another hand coming in through the window. They were on the bars now, those hands, so many hands, and he could see from the little bit of wiggle the bars already had they wouldn't hold for long.

"Come on!" AJ said, grabbing Clover by the hand and leading them toward the door. He flung it open, and he went cold.

* * *

Logan opened his door and heard three shots come from John's room. He heard a scream and a crash from

AJ's. Terrance stood in the middle of the front room, his mouth a frozen rictus of pain and terror, his body locked at the joints and quivering as though an electric current were passing through it. Dead men streamed around him.

Logan brought his modified shotgun up and fired, then shifted his aim, fired again, again, again, skull after skull exploding in a spray of bones reduced to shrapnel and buckshot tearing through them.

He sensed more than heard the door to AJ's room open. He fired again, and again, blowing one man apart at the chest. John's door was kicked open from within, and John backed out of it, firing his gun.

"They're coming in through the window!" John screamed.

Logan fired again, knowing his magazine must be nearing empty, and then turned to AJ.

"Use it!" Logan screamed.

"What?"

"The book! Use the book!" Logan dropped one magazine out of the shotgun and slammed another one home even before the first had hit the floor. He racked the shotgun and fired again.

"I don't know how!" AJ screamed over the noise.

***

Use the book? AJ looked down at the book in his hands, aware now of the heat coming from it. The heat seemed to flow from the massive volume and into his fingers, right into the center of him.

"The bars!" Clover yelled, tugging his arm. He

turned and saw the pre-manufactured cage being pulled off the side of the house. A creeper crawled through the window, but a gun went off outside, and its head exploded. Steve appeared and yanked the body out of the window.

"We're clear this way! Come on!" Steve said, turning and firing his gun twice more into the night. He turned back to the window, hand outstretched.

"Watch the glass!" he warned Clover as she stuffed her feet into her shoes and went toward him. She took his hand, and he helped her out of the window and onto the lawn.

"Come on!" Steve shouted, hand outstretched again.

AJ started toward the window and stopped, still shoeless and shirtless, looking at the jagged pieces of busted window littered across the stained green carpet of their room.

"Now! Come on!" Steve yelled, Clover's voice joining his.

He quickly glanced at the doorway. Logan and John still pumped round after round into the coming wave of the undead but were making their way towards his room.

"Go, kid!" Lubbock shouted over his shoulder.

"Come on, give it to me! Give me the book!" Steve screamed.

AJ held it out and saw a flicker in Steve's eyes, not one of light but of darkness. Steve dove halfway through the open window, arms outstretched, reaching for the book, his stomach slamming into the bottom sill. AJ took a stumbling step backwards just in time.

"What the fuck?" AJ said.

Steve braced his hands against the windowsill, shards of glass sinking into his palms—one of them actually popping out the back of his left hand—and pushed himself back outside again. AJ saw the last three inches of a shard of glass jutting out of his stomach, his clean, white shirt already soaked through with blood. Ignoring the glass in his hands, Steve drew his gun and pointed it at AJ's head.

* * *

Clover stared with sick fascination at the shard of glass coming out of Steve's stomach, and she could feel the air around her turn cold. He drew his gun with bleeding hands and aimed it back through the window. She charged forward, lowering her shoulder as she had done on the lacrosse field as a seventh grader when she meant to *really* check a bitch, slamming into him as he pulled the trigger, the bullet blowing a hole in the wall behind AJ's head, an inch—maybe two—to the left.

* * *

The book was hot in AJ's hand now, and he felt the wind of the bullet passing by his face just as he registered the fact that Steve shot at him and Clover had likely saved his life. He looked down, and the book was *steaming*, a clean, pure steam that held its own inner light.

"AJ!" Logan screamed again from the doorway.

AJ ignored him, staring down at the seal on the front of the book, which was almost too bright to look at.

"I don't know what to do," he said to himself, and then felt a kind of calm descend over him. He turned toward the door and raised the book over his head as he went, the seal on the cover facing out into the hall.

"HELP ME!" AJ screamed, and a beam of that pure, white light shot out of the front of the book, blowing the dead men it touched completely to dust.

Another dead man came toward John, and he didn't have time to get his gun around. AJ turned the book and screamed again, a wordless exultation to the universe, the veins on his arms and in his neck standing out in stark relief as the light burst forth from the book again.

But there were more of them, and more behind those.

He pivoted, screamed again, and focused his mind, his body, and his entire *being* on the book. Another beam of light shot out, wider and brighter than the others had been, and not in a single short blast like before, but as a solid thing, almost physical. Logan shot two more on his left as John reloaded his gun.

John's door was pulled off its hinges, and AJ turned to see another wave of them crowded into his room, all trying to get through the door at once. He focused again, and the light shot out, filling John's room and leaving nothing but dust when he was finished sweeping it left to right.

Terrance stumbled toward them, untouched by the mass of creepers, bleeding from his eyes and ears. He had his gun drawn, leveled at AJ's head, his eyes flickering back and forth from his natural hazel to the darkest black over and over like a strobe light, his finger wrapped around the trigger.

* * *

Steve lashed out and locked one steel clamp of a hand around Clover's wrist, grinding the bones together. AJ shouts were lost in the noise of gunshots and death. She screamed again as Steve drew her toward him. Clover drew her knee up as hard as she could into his balls.

Steve's face paled a shade, and he vomited a steaming clot onto himself. Hot bile splashed onto the bare dirt of the back yard and across her shoes, but his grasp didn't falter.

Then the house lit up with a white light. It came flooding out of the windows, lighting the darkened yard up like it was the middle of the day. It was the last thing she saw before Steve Nielsen's fist crashed into her face, breaking her nose. His fist came down again, mashing her lips against her teeth and knocking her unconscious.

* * *

Terrance staggered toward AJ. A small jet of blood squirted out of Terrance's left ear, and he pointed the gun at the kid he was supposed to protect.

"Help me, John!" Terrence screamed. "I can't stop! I'm sorry, but I can't. Please, just fucking *KILL ME!*"

Terrance pulled the trigger right as John shoved himself in front of AJ, knocking him almost to the floor.

John heard the crash of a .38 and hot pain tore through his left shoulder; his whole arm went numb.

Terrance continued his advance, his eyes flickering like a TV with bad reception. Hazel then black. Black then hazel. The flow of blood doubled from his nose and ears when he adjusted his aim, and once more AJ found himself staring down the barrel of a gun.

"GET OUT OF MY HEAD!" Terrance screamed.

Blood poured from his ears and nose. One thick, red tear ran from the corner of one eye, and Terrance put his police issued .38 in his mouth and pulled the trigger. His body remained standing for an entire second, then collapsed onto AJ, the dead weight of the man pinning him to the ground, soaking him with blood.

AJ shut his eyes against the sting of the other man's blood and struggled to roll the corpse off him.

"Goddamn it, Logan, help me!"

Logan fired his gun twice more, and the last two creepers dropped to the ground. He swiveled and grabbed Terrance by the belt and, with one hand, threw him across the room. AJ jumped to his feet, the book still in his hands.

"Where is she?" he asked. "Clover? *Clover!*"

He started toward the front door, stepping on a hot shell casing, and burning the sole of his foot, picking his way through shattered corpses and piles of dust, the result of his handiwork. Logan followed them, and they reached the front door together, AJ a step ahead of him.

All he could see were taillights in the distance, lighting up the rooster tail of dust from the dirt road as they receded.

"NO!"

Logan ran past him, slamming another magazine into his shotgun as he ran. He climbed on his bike and drove his foot down to start it but, instead of the roar AJ had expected, there was a sputter, and a cough, and then nothing. AJ saw tangled wires coming from the engine of the bike, and the four flat tires John's car sat on.

The taillights crested a slight hill, and then dropped out of sight when it reached the other side.

AJ's legs gave out beneath him, and he collapsed into the dirt, the book lying forgotten at his side.

She was gone.

CHAPTER NINE

Daed Sixxez physically recoiled when Terrance Wills took his own life. An explosion of pain rocked through Daed's head, but His pure, absolute rage pushed it away. He put His hands upon His face, an expression beneath them a mask of grotesque fury.

"So... Fucking... CLOSE!" he screamed, digging fingernails into pale flesh the color of dirty snow. He raked trenches in the flesh, opening wounds, which oozed a black, viscous ichor.

But what was done was done. It was time to focus on what He had. The girl.

* * *

AJ sat slumped against the wall, waiting for the ambulance to come. He was pale and looked extremely ill. The gash on his forehead was still bleeding. The look of utter loss and defeat was painted sadly across his face. AJ laid his hands across it, fingertips on his forehead.

AJ knew then why his hand had been guided to Steve when it had held the gun, and he would have given anything to be able to go back and pull that trigger. In the distance, he could hear the slow warble of an ambulance, and he turned his thoughts from Clover to John. He'd been shot at point-blank range with a .38 in the shoulder. Lubbock had been coherent enough to tell them he couldn't feel his arm, couldn't move it, and did they think he might die.

AJ slammed his fists against the ground. "Fuck!" He looked at Logan, who retrieved the book from the dust of the front yard where AJ had dropped it and hadn't put it down since. He did, however, seem vaguely uncomfortable holding it. He could smoke the fucking thing for all AJ cared.

There was blood everywhere. His own, John's, and a whole lot of Terrance's.

AJ leaned his abused head in his hands. It felt like it would never stop hurting. There he sat, until the ambulance came, his tears quietly mixing with his blood, wishing he had listened and pulled the trigger when fate had asked.

* * *

They sat in the waiting room, doing just that. AJ had no idea what time it was and wouldn't have cared, anyway. The stitches in his forehead itched under the bandage, and his head still hurt despite the Vicodin.

They knew John was alive, but that was all. No one

had come to update them on the fact or to tell them of his condition. AJ looked down at his hands and scratched dried blood off the backs of them, off his knuckles. His pants and shirt were stiff with it, and it felt awful against his skin.

Was she alive or dead?

He felt a sick rolling in his body and was afraid that the next time he saw her, maybe it would be like the nightmare he had. Her hair would be robbed of its shine by death, her perfect smile a homicidal smirk. He thought of her deep green eyes turned to black.

Stop! he yelled inside his head. Thinking about it wouldn't help anything. She would be okay. She had to be. He stopped the immediate doubt from surfacing as best he could.

Logan tapped his leg and motioned toward the door. AJ looked up, and John's doctor entered the waiting room. They went to him.

"How is he?" AJ asked.

"He's alive," the doctor replied. "The bullet clipped his collarbone on the left side, otherwise it might have just gone straight through. Instead…well, he's also suffered some nerve and tendon trauma." The doctor checked his chart again. "He may also lose some or all use of his left arm, but only time will tell us that."

"Can we see him?" AJ asked.

"Not tonight. He needs his rest. There were some complications in removing the bullet, and some fragments of bone, and he had to be heavily sedated. I'm not sure you could wake him up even if I allowed a visit."

"Then when?" AJ shuddered as he thought of bone fragments.

"Why don't you two go get some rest? Come back tomorrow, and we'll make sure you get to see your friend."

They thanked him and turned to leave. Outside they were met by a police car, and they got in. AJ had seen enough police cars to last him the rest of his life. He knew the cops were doing everything they could for him, but that wasn't the point.

He felt like, for the remainder of his days, he would be reminded of this monstrous reality that surrounded him, seeming to permeate and poison everything he once knew. Every time he saw a cop or an ambulance or even a goddamn hotel room, he would revisit the pain and carnage that had fallen out of time and landed on his shoulders, doing everything it could to break them.

AJ sat silently in the back of the cruiser as it weaved through the city streets. Were they headed to another safe house? A hotel? Back to the station? He thought to ask but simply didn't give enough of a shit so, instead, he rode in silence. All he knew was that when he got *wherever* they were going, Clover wouldn't be there. She was in the hands of some horrible amalgamation of evil and flesh.

All this hit him out of nowhere, but he accepted it. He had always been a big believer in karma and fate. But what had she done to deserve this? She had been thrust into the thick of it along with him. He knew he would spend the rest of his life with her, if he ever got her back. His one true love had been snatched away from him and stolen in the night, and there was not a thing he could do about it. Yet.

He thought all these things, unable to stop himself, and it slowly carved away at his insides, hollowing out a special place for those particular sorrows. John Lubbock was there, and he might never use his left arm again. His parents were there, and all they had done was take in a helpless, orphaned child. Clover was there simply because she seemed to be nowhere else.

These thoughts were small, bitter knives, and when they cut, it hurt in a way he never thought possible. AJ was far older now than he had been only one short week ago. And how old would he be when this was all over? Assuming the world wasn't choked and beaten to death by every collective nightmare it held, what was all this doing to him? He felt like he was slowly losing his mind, a person at a time.

Would it be possible for him to lead a normal life?

Just give her back to me, he prayed. *Just give her back.* He turned in his seat and looked at Logan, and before he could stop himself, the question popped out of AJ's mouth.

"Do you think Clover's alive?"

Logan flinched at the mention of her name. "I can't possibly answer that question, AJ. This is not a situation I've ever been in."

"Couldn't you *hold council* or whatever it is you do? Talk to Them?"

"I could try, but I can't guarantee it'll work. And if it does, you must be prepared for the fact you may not like what I tell you."

AJ nodded and swallowed hard. "I have to know, one way or another."

"You love her."

"More than anything." AJ took another drag. "Have you ever, you know...loved anyone?"

"Love is not my Purpose," Logan said.

"But that's not what I asked." There was a long silence, and AJ was about to abandon hope of an answer when Logan finally spoke up.

"I did once. As much as something like me can, I suppose I loved her."

"Who was she?" AJ asked as another question popped into his head. "*When* was she?"

"Annette was her name. In New Orleans, early 1900s. Not this New Orleans, though. One a little higher up."

AJ let that last bit go. "What happened?"

"She aged and died. I didn't. Then I was called again. I wonder sometimes...but it's irrelevant. Love isn't in my Purpose."

"So, what would you do if this all ends? With me, I mean. If I succeed?"

"If Daed Sixxez were banished from this level?" Logan seemed to be asking the question to himself, as if he had never considered it before. "I'd just go on, I suppose. The Entities would show me where. There's always work for my kind."

"What's all this about levels? You've mentioned that a couple of times."

"There isn't one world, one existence. Everything that has ever happened or will ever happen in your world is on one level. There are six others."

"Are they like this one?" AJ asked with a childlike sense of awe in his voice.

"Some of them." The words hung in the air, and the conversation faded. Silence settled once more in the car and remained unbroken until they reached their destination, a motel with a mostly empty parking lot and a sign missing enough letters AJ was unable to decipher the name of it.

Another cozy night at the Give a Fuck Motel, he thought, trying to puzzle out the actual name while the officer driving them went to the office to get the keys.

* * *

Clover opened her eyes. One of them, anyway. The other was swollen shut. Her head felt like a rotting tooth. Wave after wave of pain kicked her into consciousness. Her lips had been split open, and some of her hair had been pulled out.

Clover found herself in a large, round room, with walls made of old, ugly brick. The lighting was dim, a sickly green luminance with an undeterminable origin.

She couldn't move her arms. They were outstretched as if she had been crucified. She turned her head left and right and understood why she couldn't move them. Hell, she couldn't even see them from below her elbow. They were encased in a dark gray substance that seemed organic, although what it could be she had no idea. It slowly moved around her arms and legs, the sensation against her skin was like putting your arms in a barrel packed tightly with huge, sedated worms.

It was warm, but not in a pleasant way. The heat emanating from it was ill, feverish. From her arms it grew out on either side, spreading up and down the curve of the greasy stone. Along the floor, it ran back to her feet and held her legs up to the knees.

She struggled against it to free herself, feeling the grip on her arms and legs tighten. It twisted as it

clenched, wrenching her left arm painfully. She immediately stopped her struggle, but the pain didn't stop in
her arms or in her legs, and it felt like her arm was being
ripped off or at least broken off and—

Only when her body slumped back into unconsciousness did the pressure on her arms relent.

It was dark, but a soft darkness, penetrated only by
the small candle flickering on the table. Her eye wasn't
swollen, and she didn't have a bald patch where hair had
been pulled out. Her arms were still outstretched, not
out but up. It was all right, though, she put them there. In
her hands were AJ's, her eyes were closed, and he kissed
her deeply.

They had been under the covers at first, lying there
naked in each other's arms, and he warmed her up by
holding her and just by being there. She said something
about him being like an oven, and he smiled and kissed
her on the forehead. It had made her feel like a little kid.

Her mom had always kissed her on the forehead,
but this was different, this was more. He looked into her
eyes, and he thought to her. She heard it in her head as
clear as if he'd spoken it.

I love you. Can you hear me?

She smiled her answer and took her arms from
around his back and put them around his neck and rolled
onto her back, bringing him on top of her. She looked
up at him, and he filled the world. He was all there was
and all that mattered was that he was there with her.

It was slow for a long time, an excruciatingly pleasant eternity, then it was faster and there was bliss there
was love, and oh, God, it was never like this before.
She never thought it could be, and it seemed to go on

forever, to go on and on until she thought the pleasure would softly kill her. His whole body flexed on top of hers, in hers, and she did the same, and it was pure, and it was perfect.

AJ took her hands in his and stretched them up above her head. Well, not really above her head, more out to the sides and... What was she thinking? He wasn't on top of her, he was in front of her, standing in front of her, his greasy hands cupping her chin. His hands were cold, his nails ragged and digging into her skin. And when he kissed her, it wasn't love, it was hate, it was pain and fear. It wasn't AJ, not all, it was Him, she—

She opened her eyes with a scream and saw Him walking slowly toward her from the tunnel on the other side of the chamber. The light, that dead, green light was His, He commanded it. It followed Him, obeyed Him, hid His face from every angle, casting shadows where there shouldn't be, like the shadow on her heart.

The scream died in her throat, having barely made it out at all.

Then it laughed, this cancerous silhouette laughed as it continued toward her. He spoke, and she recognized it. It was insanity. It was Gina Lancaster and Terrance Wills and Steve Nielsen, and it was *Him*.

"Rise and shine," He said and let out a small, lunatic cackle. That was when her bladder let go, she had no warning and no choice, just a warm stain spreading down the legs of her pants. Her stomach was a block of ice, her tears hot and stinging and just as sudden. She was racked with violent shivers as the air grew cold.

"Not feeling talkative, dear heart?" He asked her and laughed again. It was the sound of brain damage. He took a few final steps closer, now no more than a foot from her. She was face to face with the physical form of a nightmare god.

His hair was long, hanging down to the middle of His back in greasy strands. His skin was an imperfect white. Not pale, but *white*, as if He were covered in dirty clown makeup. His lips were dead and gray and smeared broadly in a hideous grin. His body was covered in scars, as twisted and disgusting as the thing that wore them. She gasped in spite of herself as He took another step closer, and she got her first good look into His eyes.

She had looked into Steve Nielsen's eyes when he was possessed, but what she had seen in his was a fraction of the real thing. They weren't black, or empty or insane, it was as if they were just…gone. Two empty portals leading to an unthinkable world of landscapes bound in human flesh, the misery-filled skies looking down upon a pulsating tumor, the dead sun vomiting its desperate green light forever.

She realized she was being slowly hypnotized and found it difficult to break the eye lock. She closed her eyes, feeling her mind wanting to crack. It held, but Clover knew it wouldn't if she had to look into those eyes much more.

"Wh-what are you?" she finally choked out in a voice hushed with terror.

"You already know. That white-haired fuck told you all about me." Then He spoke in a Logan's voice, "Daed Sixxez, Lord of the Nexus, and He's completely insane." At this last part He threw His head back and laughed. Her body seemed to soak up the sound, much the same way it soaked up radiation from an X-ray or UV rays from the sun. It made her eye swell a little more and her heart pound a little harder. You could get cancer from hearing that laugh, she would swear on it.

He stopped laughing as suddenly as He had started, His face serious. She watched a spider crawl out of His nose and into His mouth.

"I'll have his soul. The soul of The Next, the end of life, control of a world filled with walking dead."

"You can't win," she said, knowing it was a bad idea but unable to stop herself.

"Listen to me, you little bitch!" His voice filled with rage. He drew closer, so close she could smell Him, could see the pores of His skin. To add to her own private horror, she realized now there was something beneath it, writhing and itching to get out, something more horrible than any mind could imagine was zipped up inside, waiting.

"The time has come. This circle is about to close, and when that little shit shows up I'll consume his life force. I'll eat him up and suck the marrow from his bones!" An almost dreamy look stole across His makeshift face. "I'll make his ribs into a footstool. And you…" He brushed her hair back and ran His finger across her face, down her neck and to her left nipple, which He slowly rubbed between His thumb and forefinger. "I'll make you my mistress. How's that sound?"

"Go to Hell!"

"I don't need to. I can bring it to us." He laughed again and leaned forward, sticking His rattlesnake tongue out and licking it across the side of her face. It felt like sandpaper coated with mucus. She could still feel the path that finger had traced down onto her breast, as if it had left a trail of hot slime in its wake. She knew if He wanted her, He would take her.

She closed her eyes against the rising nausea this brought forth. Her stomach seemed to turn on an almost *cellular* level, as though every last molecule in her body were about to vomit. *Hurry, AJ, I need you.*

CHAPTER
TEN

Hurry, AJ, I need you.

AJ sat up straight and looked around the room, wide-eyed. He shook his head to clear it. He had heard Clover's voice. Except that wasn't quite right, was it? He hadn't really *heard* anything. It was almost as if he had thought it. Those words, *her words*, had suddenly been in his mind, and he had *sensed* her, damn it. He now knew she was alive, there was no doubt about that. But for how long?

AJ could feel the time running out as an almost physical thing, like blood running from an opened vein. He felt small and helpless, like a child. Of course, as a child, he'd never awakened in an unfamiliar room that looked like it had been furnished from a yard sale in the seventies and stank of cigarettes, bad crank, and straight up human funk. He looked up as Logan came out of the bathroom.

"You all right?" Logan asked, taking a closer look

at him.

"Yeah, why?"

"You look like you saw a ghost." Logan stared a moment longer, raising an eyebrow ever so slightly.

AJ opened his mouth to tell Logan of what he'd heard, that he was *certain* Clover was alive, but snapped it shut again, darting his eyes to the cop in the room. He had been perfectly nice and helpful...but they didn't know *him*.

Logan nodded his head almost imperceptibly, and then turned to the cop, who sat at the small, stained table. "Can we go now?"

The officer nodded and stood. AJ got off the bed and found his shoes. The three of them left the motel room and got back into the police car and headed to the hospital.

* * *

John adjusted his bed so he was more or less sitting up, reclined. He flipped through all nine channels at his disposal, still hopelessly searching for something that wasn't on. There was a church channel. Skip. A Spanish channel. Skip. A rerun of *Three's Company*. Barf. Channel after channel broadcasting crap flipped by, then renewed the cycle again with *Teletubbies*.

John clicked off the TV. If he'd had his gun, he might have shot it in disgust, put the fucker out of its misery. He groped for the little buzzer that rang at the nurses' station just down the hall. He could hear it faintly as it went off, then dropped the control indifferently beside him on the bed. A minute or so later a young, pretty brunette walked in.

Real classy-lookin' dame, John thought. It wasn't the first thing to cross his mind, but it was one of them.

"Yes, Mr. Lubbock?"

"Call me John, will ya?"

"Of course, John. Now what did you need?"

"Could I get something to eat?" John asked.

"Well, the lunch is served in another hour—"

"Ah, come on. I'm dyin' here." He gave her his most endearing puppy dog grin and, to his delight, it initiated a small but sincere smile from her, and the intensity of their eye contact was bumped up a notch. It was almost as if she just noticed he was there.

"Welllll...okay. I'll go downstairs and see what I can find. Any special cravings?"

"How 'bout a doughnut?" John said, the words popping out before he could stop them or say anything else.

Are you fuckin' kidding me? John thought, wishing now for his stitches to bust so he could roll over and bleed to death. *A fuckin' doughnut, you fat fuck?*

"I'll see what I can do, but I'm not promising anything." She smiled at him again, and his pulse quickened.

"Thank you, uh..."

"Sherri." She stuck her hand out to shake, and he took it, then in a flash of boldness that was totally unlike him, he kissed it. "Thank you, Sherri."

She blushed and took her hand back. "Well, it's good to see you have some of your energy back." She laughed and turned to go. John watched, admiring the way she swung her hips. The door shut behind her, and the moment was over.

John blinked twice, and then looked down at his hand. He tried to clench it into a fist. A dull, throbbing pain began in his shoulder and spread down to his tingling fingertips. He was able to close it a little bit at least. Not much more than a twitch, really, but he had to be positive in a situation like this, right?

Sure, he was worried about his arm. But he was more worried about last night. He had blacked out shortly after being shot and had no idea what happened. Again, he tried to stay positive, to believe the best possible scenario until he was told something else: Terrance came back to normal, then he and Logan shot Steve full of so many holes he whistled when his body fell lifelessly to the ground. Yeah.

John continued to think these things over until his door opened again, and Sherri poked her head in.

"Good news, John."

"What? My stocks are up?"

She giggled, and he fell for her all over again.

"No…I got you some doughnuts. And you have visitors," she replied and swung the door open, stepping inside and letting AJ and Logan in.

"John, how ya doin'?" AJ asked.

"I'll let you all catch up," Sherri said and set a plate containing two glazed and a sprinkled doughnut down on John's bed tray.

"Thank you, Sherri, you're the best!"

She looked back at him and smiled as she left.

"What did the doctors say?" AJ asked, trying not to glance down at the bandaged, lifeless limb.

"They said it's possible I could lose the use of it, but

that it's unlikely. I'm lucky. Nowhere near the damage that coulda been done, and I guess the bullet missed some major artery by about an inch, otherwise I likely woulda bled to death."

"Jesus Christ," AJ said.

"Kid, I'll be fine. I'll have to do physical therapy and all that happy shit, but doc thinks I'll gain a hundred percent use back. Best case scenario," John said. "Now, shut the door, will you?"

Logan closed the door, and then stood, leaning against it, to keep out any surprise visitors.

John ran his good hand over his face. "I'm so goddamned sorry, kid. We're gonna get her back, you understand me?"

AJ nodded, not quite trusting himself to speak unless he had to. His eyes burned and the world around him blurred...but only for a moment.

"Is she okay?" John asked quietly, not quite looking at AJ.

"She's alive, but they have her. *He* has her."

"How do you know?"

AJ shook his head, frowning. "I... Fuck man. I just know. I heard her in my head this morning." He shot a quick look to Logan, raising one eyebrow as Logan had done at the motel, hoping Logan would make the connection. Logan nodded, and AJ turned back to John. "I have a feeling she's okay, but she won't be for long."

"Did they get the book?" John asked, looking back and forth between the two of them.

"No," Logan said, pulling his trench coat back to reveal an ancient leather satchel hanging against his left hip, the strap slung diagonally across his body. The bag was taut on its strap with the weight of the book. He pulled out a makeshift bag, which had started life as a hotel sheet, three of the book corners pushing out of the cloth. It looked to John like some alien cocoon, and it gave him the chills.

"That's something, though, right?" John asked, looking back and forth between AJ and Logan. "Didn't you say as long as we got this book, we're good to go, yeah?"

"It's something, yeah," AJ said with a sigh.

"It's *everything*," Logan said.

"So, what do we do now?" John took a doughnut off the tray as an excuse to look away. AJ shrugged, chewing his thumbnail, and looking at Logan for an answer.

"The only thing we can do," Logan said. "Wait for The Calling."

AJ and John shared a look, neither knowing what Logan was talking about.

"What's *The Calling?*" AJ asked, adding a sportscaster inflection to his voice.

John caught what may have been laughter rising on Logan's face, just for an instant, before the man's age and experience crushed it.

"It's like having a dream while you're awake, like a vision."

"And..." AJ prompted.

"And you will speak with the Entities, with Jha'ask and Enopac. They will tell you the time for confrontation has come."

"Then what?"

"You...*confront* Him," Logan said in perfect deadpan. John wasn't sure, but it might have been an attempt at humor. It reminded him of someone finding a particularly interesting tool after having lost it for a long time. It was a little rusty, but you had to try it out a little at a time, making sure it still worked.

"But how do I find him? Do they show me?"

"No. You'll just know, like you do with Clover."

AJ felt more to the bone straight up exhausted than he could ever remember being. He crossed the room and sat heavily in a chair with a sigh and a slump.

"You all right?" John asked him. All at once, the kid didn't look so good.

AJ shrugged. "This is all so fucking strange, man. Every time I think I know its asshole from its elbow, it grows another arm or something, you know? It feels like I'm suffocating."

"Listen, kid," Lubbock began, setting his doughnut back on the tray. "You're handling this better than anyone could expect to. Besides, it'll be over soon enough, I s'pose."

"I hope so, John. I really do." AJ ran his hands through his hair and looked at the floor.

* * *

The pain, the pain, oh, God, the pain, was the only thought running through Steve's head. He had entered a new realm of physical, psychological, and spiritual agony since returning to Daed Sixxez without the book.

Daed stood back, examining Steve where he hung on the wall, like someone studying their own painting. He could keep someone alive and in pain for a very long time; He had developed a talent for it.

Daed had started by pulling his eyes out. He had held the first one out in front of him and forced Steve to watch as He popped it between cold, pale fingers. He pulled out Steve's teeth. And his tongue. Then off came his toenails, his fingernails, and his cock. He had beat him, cut him, and burnt him. The body now only vaguely resembled that of a human being.

Daed had gone about doing all this one thing at a time, slowly and methodically. And he enjoyed all of it, every minute, relished every scream.

He could hardly wait to hear Munroe scream that same way, it would be sweetest music to His ears, each drop of crimson blood would be the twisted liquid joy only one such as Daed Sixxez could feel.

When He was done with the boy, He would do something with the girl. He had big plans for her. After the circle closed and His powers were complete, He would make her a slave, a mistress. He licked His lips as He thought of all the things He would do to her and what He would make her do to Him. Images of sick, nasty sex ran through His head as He took a solid grip on one of Steve's ears. He braced His other hand against the side of the man's head and pulled.

Inhuman, primal screams issued from the bloody, toothless hole that was the mouth as the wet, meaty, tearing sound of the ear being separated from the head began. More blood ran out of the body, dripping and splattering the gore-streaked bricks of the grimy floor. If the holes of Steve's missing eyes had still been capable of sight, perhaps they would have seen Daed's grin of sadistic glee spreading wider.

The ear landed with a plop, sending up tiny splashes

of blood. The focus came back to Daed's black eyes. The grin wasn't as wide anymore, but it was still there. He licked the blood off His fingers and turned away from the ruined form on the wall, leaving it to twitch and shudder in the dark. He walked away, unknowingly stepping on Steve's other eyeball and popping it as He went.

He had things to do now, things that must be done in order to prepare for the confrontation ever-so-close at hand. Over the last few nights, the moon had risen into the sky like a soul leaving a body. It was a fat, white orb and perfect but for one thing: it was not yet full. In two days' time, the moon would be complete; a wide, open eye to watch as He claimed His throne and brought the end to man.

When it rose in forty-eight hours, it would be a killing moon, a harvest moon, and it would be red like the blood He had licked off His fingers, the blood that was now trickling down His lower lip. Daed wiped absently at the rivulet, smearing it across His chin.

In two days, His circle would close forever, one way or another. He knew this was His last chance to control this level, this ring of life. He would either be triumphant and rule or be defeated and banned from this realm forever.

This seemed a little odd to Him. He didn't know it was possible to kill a god and didn't know how it could be done. If only He'd gotten that fucking book…

No matter. He would be victorious. He could smell it in the air, the smell of victory was the heavy stink of rotting flesh and bodies bloated with gas and time. He could taste it like the salty, coppery-red taste on His tongue.

He knew it, and he knew He had to prepare. There would be no more attacks on the boy. No more undead minions would be sent out into the night, Munroe was too strong for them now, and his powers would only increase as the confrontation drew nearer. Daed would rest, conserve every last ounce of his Hellish strength, for win or lose, Daed knew the battle would be the biggest of His long and strange existence.

* * *

Clover stood where she had stood since she had first awakened from one nightmare into another. She had no idea how long she had been there, there was no time. There was fear, there was pain, and there was Him. She had managed some sleep, from pure exhaustion, but had been awakened by screams that held more suffering than she ever thought possible.

Clover had no way of knowing for sure that it was Steve Nielsen screaming, but she thought that it was. She wasn't too sure how she felt about it, either. He had willingly betrayed them, had stolen her away into the night and delivered her unto the threshold of madness. This warranted a punishment, but she didn't think Charles Manson or Hitler or even Dick Cheney deserved to go through the things that could make a man scream like that.

However, she didn't feel remorse either. Clover was numb to it all, like her arms had become after being outstretched for so long. The numbness ended in her shoulders, but a deep, dull ache spread throughout them and down into her back. She couldn't feel her legs from below the knee, but above, they were two knotted and weakening pillars of fire.

"Have a nice rest, my sweet?"

She looked up and saw Daed Sixxez approaching her. "Can I sit down or something?" she asked, not expecting much or making eye contact.

"But, of course, my dear, all you need but do is ask." Daed gave His hand a lazy wave, the gray matter that encased her grew warmer, the feverish heat uncomfortable on her skin. It moved, shifting and turning, making dreadful skittering-whisper noise—the sound of thousands of spiders teeming across a mausoleum floor—as it reshaped itself, and Clover found herself sitting in a terrible throne. Her wrists were secured to the arms of it, her legs to the base.

"Now then, how's that?" Daed asked, leaning a little closer. She watched lice hopping gleefully in the matted clump of His hair and saw the dried smear of blood on His chin.

"B-better." The sight of Him seemed to freeze out and kill everything inside her that was once good or kind or beautiful. And as disgusting and vile a creature that He was, she was terrified to learn it was getting steadily harder and harder to look away from Him, to break the stare that was almost involuntary in its beginnings.

It seemed He was slowly taking her mind for ransom, holding it against her will just as He was holding her body. Finally, she was able to break the eye contact and look down again, this time at her lap. Before she did, she saw a smile form on His lips, a demented grin on the face of all evils. He moved to her side and bent in close, whispering in her ear, the smell of death riding His words as if they were a pale horse.

"Fight it, my sweet. It's so much more fun when you fight it." He reached out with one blood-slicked finger, circling it into her ear, then dragging it down her neck and once more to her left nipple. Her skin threatened to crawl right off in defense of the touch, and a sudden throb of agony pulsed inside her left breast, growing, and then fading, finally fading, when He moved His finger away.

"You're wrong," she whispered.

"Really?" he asked, His voice playful like a child.

"Soon you'll be dead, too."

He laughed at her.

"You're afraid—" she began.

"Afraid? Of a boy?" The playful note drained from His inflections, replaced with something angry, something deadly.

"You're terrified of the very thought of him! You—"

"Silence!" He roared in her ear, making her jump. He moved around in front of her in a single fluid motion, kneeling, and taking her head in His hands.

"I don't *have* to keep you alive." His black eyes bored twin pits in her soul, and, staring into them, her brain itched. It threatened to give way, to let Him completely in before she again looked to her knees, shaking hard.

Clover had never feared for her life before, had never been put in a situation where she thought it was likely she would die. She decided in the interest of self-preservation it would be best just to keep silent and not antagonize Him until AJ showed up.

God, she wished it would be soon. She wanted to see him more than anything, and prayed she would live, too, no matter what followed. The only thing that would make her happier would be to watch him rip the sinister, sneering head off this monster shaped like a man.

CHAPTER ELEVEN

Logan rode in silence in the back of the police cruiser. They were headed to one final motel, one final resting place along the way. Outside the window the city rolled past them, unaware and uncaring of their problems. Logan wasn't sure if Daed Sixxez could be killed.

He supposed AJ would find out. Logan had a feeling about him, had faith in AJ's victory.

The moon was getting fuller and, so far, every confrontation had taken place on the night it was at the fullest.

The cruiser pulled into a parking lot.

"You two hang here, I'll go get the key from the office," the driver said. AJ nodded and, when the cop shut the door, turned to Logan. AJ seemed as if he were about to speak, but he said nothing. Logan knew he could have coaxed it out of him but, if it was important, AJ would talk about it on his own soon enough.

The two of them sat in the car until the cop came to take them to their room. It paled in comparison to their suite at the Fireside, but it was adequate. Logan had slept in worse places.

"Well, at least there's a fridge," AJ said, the sarcasm heavy. He shut the door on the foot-high refrigerator that would have trouble holding a six pack of long necks.

"I can live with it if you can." Logan sat down on one of the single beds.

"I've slept in worse places," AJ said as he lit a cigarette and propped a pillow against the headboard. "Like my apartment," he added, blowing out a stream of smoke.

Enopac and Jha'ask saw all this. This and everything else, they watched, constantly watched.

He is younger than all the rest, Jha'ask observed.

He is a brave boy, Enopac replied. The two Entities watched as the day in AJ's world went by. For him time passed, for them it was of no consequence.

When darkness comes, we must hold council with him, Jha'ask said. Enopac silently agreed.

And the girl?

Not until we must.

* * *

"John," Sherri said. His eyes popped open, and he sat straight up in bed, pulling his IV out and scaring the hell out of her in the process.

"Ah, Christ." John lay back down on his sweat-soaked pillow.

"Are you all right?" Sherri asked, placing the IV back

in and placing a few extra strips of medical tape across it just in case.

"I am now." John was wide awake with pain and an adrenaline rush from the dream. Dream? Gruesome fucking nightmare.

"Well, I heard you scream from the hall—"

"You heard me scream?"

"Must have been some nightmare." Sherri laid a cool, comforting hand on his sweaty forehead. It helped ease away the shakes.

"Must have," John agreed, not wanting to talk about it.

"Do you need anything else? Something for the pain?"

John looked up at her and saw worry sketched across her pretty face, and more than just the professional kind her job required. "I'll be fine," he said. Their eyes stayed locked a little longer, and there were a thousand things he could tell her.

She stood abruptly and straightened her white uniform, seeming a bit confused as to where she might be. "Well, I've got to get back to my rounds."

"Yeah, there's probably some TV I could catch up on," John said, feeling better in making her laugh.

"I'll be back in an hour or so, but you buzz me if you need anything before then," she said, drifting toward the door.

"Will do." John raised his good arm in a small wave, and she was gone. He realized what was happening. Something which had not happened to him since he had worked with Anna Derkins from Narcotics.

Had it really been four years? John contemplated it a

bit longer and decided it had been. Hell, maybe this time
he would get lucky, and find a woman who could stand
him for more than six months at a time. Much stranger
shit had been happening lately, and he was tired of being
alone.

***

AJ lay in his bed, sound asleep. A deep dreamless
sleep.

Until now.

First it was black, all black, endless dark that stretched
beyond the corners of time. Very slowly, the light came.
It began as a pinpoint a thousand miles away, lethargically
spreading and bringing beauty to a once dead landscape,
like slowly breathing life into a lifeless body.

Two figures stepped out of the light and into view,
identical save the robes they wore. Jha'ask wore one the
color of cream and Enopac wore one a dark maroon.
Both had hoods, and as they drew closer, Jha'ask reached
up with one slender, graceful limb and pulled it back,
revealing a perfectly featureless head and face. No hair,
no eyes, ears, or mouth. There was a small protrusion
where the nose might have been, but that was all.

Enopac didn't remove the hood.

AJ Munroe, Jha'ask thought, and AJ received it tele-
pathically. He found he had no need to speak, merely to
think.

I'm here, AJ thought.

Tomorrow, you must seek out the empty god and destroy Him.

I'm afraid.

As well you should be, child. He has the power to end every-

thing that has already begun.

Where is he?

We shall guide you tomorrow, and you must not hesitate when the time comes.

I want to end it. Not for a hundred years or a thousand, but forever. How can I do this?

Enopac took a step forward and communicated for the first time. *You must first offer him your soul,* Enopac began, then explained.

* * *

AJ looked at his watch. It was only two in the afternoon. He had been awake since about eight this morning, filled with a nervous energy and a cold fear. He wanted to get it over, all of it. But, at the same time, each tick of the second hand sounded like death, and each one was a little louder than the last.

He was still confident Clover was alive, although he hadn't experienced a second mental connection with her. In the back of his mind, there was a pressing realization he tried to ignore.

Even if he won, if *he* saw the sun come up tomorrow, that didn't mean Clover would. And what an evil twist of fate that would be, the final punchline to a drawn-out and maddening cosmic joke that he seemed to be on the losing end of.

"When do you think it will happen?" AJ asked, sitting down on the corner of his bed, and then standing right back up again and stuffing his hands in his pockets.

"Just before sunset," Logan said. "That's when it always happens."

AJ checked his watch again, wanting to tear his hair out because only one minute had passed since the last time he did so.

Sunset. Four and a half more hours to go, hours that would pass with agonizing slowness. He checked his watch again and lit a cigarette. He stared at the glowing end of it, making a resolution.

I'll quit smoking tomorrow, he thought. *If I die tonight, it won't matter, but I'll be damned if I live through this and die of fucking cancer.*

* * *

Daed Sixxez sat in His throne, drumming His fingers against the armrest. Soon the sun would set upon this world one last time. With the coming of the blood moon, a new era would begin. Each passing minute brought more confidence to the empty god waiting beneath the city, confident He would not only defeat the boy, but the boy would actually give in.

He had seen it in a vision, early this morning. AJ would offer life and soul, Daed would take it without a struggle, would drink the lifeblood from Munroe's scrawny child's wrist as the girl watched from beyond, screaming and crying. Daed had never had a vision that did not come true.

He looked over at Clover, who was slumped in her chair, asleep. Daed cackled wildly and ran His eyes hungrily over her body, anticipating. She woke, as if even in sleep made uneasy by His stare. She turned red when she saw Him looking at her and quickly looked away. Daed smiled a lunatic smile and went to her, bending down to her face.

"Don't worry, dear heart. It'll all be over soon."

"I'm not the one with something to worry about."

"You feel it, too, don't you?" he mused. "You know that his soul will be mine."

"You'll be dead by dawn," Clover spat.

"You're wrong. You know it and you can feel it. And I know it. I saw it all in a dream." He paused for a second, His eyes like black holes in the sky. "And you're the key, my dear. He's going to give himself up to save you." He walked away, laughing that horrible laugh.

Clover felt her heart sink. She loved AJ, she knew that, and she knew he loved her. But was his love strong enough to condemn the world? Surely not. It would be conceited of her to think that. Besides, she wouldn't let him. She would rather die first.

But still the black thoughts lingered. They stuck in her mind now that Daed had voiced what she had been denying, after He gave voice to the very thing she feared.

All I can do is wait, she thought, and so she did.

* * *

John Lubbock sat in his hospital bed, hating it and tired of being there. It was the cop in him. He chuckled to himself at that, as if there was anything in there *but* cop. A little heart maybe, but that was all. He didn't paint or play an instrument or want to learn how to crochet a fucking afghan.

He was *police*, and there was nothing more he wanted to do than go with AJ and Logan. The television set flickered from the perch in the corner, casting shadows in the dimmed light of his room. The sun set slowly in the west, burning away the blue of the sky and replacing it with the strangest sunset John had ever seen.

As he lay there watching, the clouds twisted and warped around themselves, making shapes he'd never seen in the sky before. A cumulonimbus became an angry, red skull, glowing with doom. It faded as quickly as it formed, drifting off to the right and becoming a burning corpse.

He watched this creep show in the sky, thinking of AJ's visit an hour and a half ago. The kid had been understandably preoccupied. John closed his eyes against the evil in the sky, wishing he could reach the curtains to draw them.

John thought back to a couple hours ago, and the tiny knock on the door, so small he wasn't sure he'd even heard it until the door cracked open, and AJ came in. He had been antsy and paranoid. He jumped at every sound, turned his head to inspect shifting peripheral shadows.

"You all right, kid?" John had asked.

"Yes. No...well, as good as can be expected I guess."

"It's tonight, isn't it?" John didn't need to ask to know.

"Yeah. To tell you the truth, I don't know how I even feel about it. I'm numb. Mostly numb."

"You'll be fine, kid. Don't worry—"

"I can't *not* worry," AJ interrupted. "Not with her there, and I could die tonight. I'm just not sure if I'm ready to leave this world for another."

The two silently regarded each other, thinking of everything they had been through and seen.

"Hell, I don't have the words, John, not like I want.

But I came to say goodbye and to thank you."

"AJ—"

"No, let me say what I need to. I plan on going to wherever He is and stopping Him, killing Him. I want to destroy Him. But if I can't, I wanted to thank you." AJ looked out the window, where it was still the middle of the afternoon. He collected himself and looked back at the detective "You've been in this as long as I have, John. And not a lot of people would have done that, I think. Most people would lose their shit if they got choked by a corpse in a city morgue, but you didn't. You helped me."

John held his good arm wide. AJ hugged the barrel-chested man carefully, trying not to hurt him. John whacked him a good one on the back with his uninjured hand, and AJ stood back up, wiping at his eyes.

"Just know that if I don't come back—"

"Kid, if you don't come back, it won't matter what I know, because I got a feeling if that happens, it's game over for the rest of us."

AJ's face had visibly paled.

"No pressure, huh?" John asked, succeeding in making the kid smile a little. "I'll see you tomorrow, either in this world or the other," John said.

AJ nodded and backed up a step.

"I suppose. I-I gotta get going, John. It's close, real close." AJ had then turned and walked out.

And here we are, John now thought, stealing another look out the window, where the light was being slowly sucked from the sky. John wondered if he would ever see the kid again.

* * *

Across town, AJ looked at the bloody sky, watching the clouds.

"Do you see that?" AJ pointed as a skull turned to a body that changed to a rat.

Logan looked out the window and nodded.

"Does it mean anything?"

Logan shrugged. Sometimes his indifference was infuriating. AJ tried to take his eyes off the sky. Slowly, he felt different. The nervous energy crept out. So did the worry, and the excitement, and the fear. The only thing he felt was the need to move. He paced back and forth like a caged animal.

"Are you sure we don't need the book?" AJ asked.

They had stopped and put it in a safety deposit box Logan had opened days before, adding both AJ's and Clover's name to the list of people to be given access to it in his absence while he was there.

"Everything you need to know, you've been shown."

"What about, remember? At the house? How it… vaporized those motherfuckers?"

"It doesn't work on Daed," Logan said. "It's been tried, believe me."

"I need some air," AJ muttered, just loud enough for Logan to hear. The hunter stood and holstered his guns, pulled on his trench coat, and followed.

Just outside the door to their room, AJ stood perfectly still, his head slightly cocked to the side as if he was listening to something no one else could hear. He looked across the parking lot in the fading daylight, taking a tentative step forward. He looked up at the slowly ascending crimson orb.

Bad moon a-risin', AJ thought and looked left, then right. He paused for a second before continuing. It was an odd feeling, like he sat in the passenger seat of his body after twenty-two years behind the wheel. He wondered if he would be able to stop walking if he tried. But he didn't try. If anything, he walked a little faster. With each step, he felt a power within him surge and grow.

His entire being was fully awake and finely tuned. The colors of the world were more vivid, and though it was dark, he found he could see perfectly. He heard everything from the sound of Logan's soft, even breathing fifteen feet behind him, to a car being started six blocks away.

AJ had no idea where he was going or where he had been, he was navigating entirely on instinct. If he felt he needed to turn one way or another he did, and the traffic lights turned with him as if in confirmation. The sense of power and vitality grew steadily stronger. He came to an intersection and hooked a right without hesitation, crossing the street without even bothering to look for traffic.

As he stepped off the curb, the light turned green. After reaching the other side, he cut across a vacant lot and went down an alley. Finally, he stopped. He felt no need to move any particular direction. He looked around. This couldn't be it, could it? An alley? Then he looked down to see he stood right in front of a manhole cover. He bent and stuck his fingers through the grated metal and lifted.

Logan watched, amazed, as AJ pulled the sixty-pound circle of steel off the ground and flung it to his left with one hand, making it look simple.

AJ descended the slick metal rungs of the ladder. He looked up at Logan and started, as if seeing him for the first time. "You coming?"

Logan nodded, and AJ disappeared underground.

Although the tunnel was completely devoid of light, AJ could still see just fine. Not that there was much to look at.

AJ stopped in his tracks, his body trembling, and his testicles trying to crawl back home as the coffin chorus of laughter washed through the tunnel.

Him, was all AJ thought, and resumed his pace as the laughter fading out to nothing. It was silent but for the soft echo of their footsteps. They walked for what seemed like an eternity before they finally saw a pinpoint of light at the end of the tunnel, and it simultaneously filled AJ with dread and joy. Then there was something else.

"Logan?" AJ whispered in the darkness.

"I feel it, too."

The two slowed to a stop, and AJ looked around. "What's that shit on the walls?" he asked, noticing it for the first time. A gray substance was there, coating the entire mouth of the tunnel, lumping here and there, lazily swirling like a wall of smoke.

"Keep moving," Logan said. AJ started walking again, slower now, his eyes not on the light in the distance but the walls. It was like an acid trip, seeing shapes and sensing a pattern he couldn't quite catch. AJ saw movement in his peripheral vision, and he snapped his head to the right before it sank back into the turning nothingness. A groping, gray hand stuck out for a second then melted back into the wall.

AJ turned, wide-eyed, to the left. A crude face protruded and receded, a silent scream on its lips.

"Get away from the wall!" Logan shouted, checking AJ out of the way as a spike shot out, eight feet long, and stuck itself through Logan's side, then sunk back.

"Fuck!" Logan looked down at the new wound as blood spurted out. A feverish hand came out of the wall and grabbed AJ by the biceps, pulling him closer. He managed to break free, but two more shot out, one grabbing his shirt and another clutching his leg.

He was jerked into the gray matter and tried to scream when it covered his mouth. A head popped out of the wall and sank needle-like teeth into his shoulder. Logan appeared, yanking him away, shredding the hands that held him. The torn remains hit the ground and were absorbed back up into the ever-moving wallpaper of decay.

Another spike shot from behind them and punched through Logan's trench coat, barely missing his other side.

"We may have a serious fucking problem here," Logan said, one hand pressed against his wound to stop the bleeding. AJ pulled the Zippo from his pocket and flicked it open, advancing toward the wall and spinning the wheel. A flame dutifully arose. AJ pressed the lighter into the wall.

At first, it looked as though the lighter went out. Then there was a soft *phwump*, and the flames spread, coating the tunnel with fire and a stink that could be matched by nothing else. A scream arose from nowhere, from everywhere, and a flaming hand shot out of the wall and pressed against AJ's ribs, melting his shirt to his skin.

He screamed and staggered back as the sizzling of his flesh continued. He stripped off his shirt, tearing off a large portion of the blister that had instantly formed in the perfect shape of a hand.

That'll make a hell of a story, he thought wildly and stared down at the suppurating mess.

"What the hell is that stuff?" AJ yelled over the crackling of the fire and the heavy stench of putrid, rotten meat pounding up his nose, making his eyes water.

"Decay!" Logan yelled back, steadying AJ on his feet, both ducking away from a chunk of it, flaming and falling from the ceiling. "Human decay! He still has power over their remains." The decay had been a thin coating and burned quickly. The fire dwindled, eating itself out of existence.

"Go!" Logan shouted. "I'm wounded. Leave me but stop him. For all your fathers, stop him for good!" Logan began slowly walking back the way they had come, waving AJ forward.

CHAPTER TWELVE

Daed had been listening closely, listening with his mind as Logan got stabbed in the side. He'd heard the fire, too. He'd felt it. As the decay went up in a funeral pyre, Daed screamed. His body smoked all over right along with the decay, a piece of his hair had burst into flame before he could pull back into himself and out of the flames. He now stared at the tunnel, its round walls and ceiling a half circle of fire. He stared through the center of it and could sense him.

Then AJ Munroe, The Next, stepped out of the ring of fire the tunnel had become and into His chamber.

"Daed!" he screamed and strode forward.

Sixxez stood and looked into AJ's eyes for the first time. They were the eyes of all his ancestors, each one that Daed had faced, each one that had stopped Him, again and again, snatching what was rightfully His away from Him at the last instant.

But tonight, Daed thought, *that ends.*

Clover looked up when she heard the screams in the tunnel, and she watched the fire grow before dying. Then AJ was there, his shirt was gone and there was a hell of a burn on his side that looked like a hand. He was bleeding from a wound on his shoulder, but he was there. At the sight of him, she struggled in her restraints. They automatically tightened to the point of pain.

"AJ," she screamed, the tears freely running down her dirty cheeks, cutting clean paths through the grime. He looked over, seeing her for the first time, and despite everything that had happened and was about to, he smiled at her. She could live another hundred years and never forget he stopped to smile at her.

That was when Daed Sixxez struck, charging forward, lifting AJ off the ground, and slamming him back down.

AJ had time to look at Clover before the breath was knocked out of him, and he found himself staring up at the ceiling through blurring eyes. He saw Daed in time to see His fist roping down and meeting his left eye. The pain exploded, and more punches rained down. AJ lifted his leg and hooked it around Daed's arm.

Power coursed through him like a current, and he knocked the god off him. Both stood, circling each other in the middle of the room. In unison, they lunged forward and locked up, hands on each other's shoulders, both trying to get an edge. The foreign strength seemed to consume AJ, and the two of them were equally matched.

Daed dug His fingers into the bite wound on AJ's shoulder, His sharpened fingernails cutting though the other shoulder as well. AJ's fingers punched through

Daed's spongy flesh, and thick, green-black blood oozed out.

"Enough!" Daed screamed, and they both pushed back, drawing apart. "You move closer, and she dies." Sixxez pointed toward Clover as her chair shifted, growing a hundred different spikes and barbs that were pointed at all her vital organs.

"Oh, shit," she said.

I've won! It's happening just as I foresaw! Daed thought, the success after all these centuries of failure reeling in His head. AJ froze where he was at. Daed grinned at the hatred in his eyes.

"If you harm her, I'll tear your fucking head off," AJ said, in a simple, matter-of-fact tone. Daed believed it was true, too. The little shit thought it was, at least.

"That may be, but that wouldn't help her any, would it?" he asked through a jeering, mocking smile.

AJ stared back. "You can't win."

"I already have, boy."

"You *know* I can kill you. You're just delaying the fact."

"That's neither here nor there," Daed said, waving it away as though it were a minor detail they were discussing, and not an end to his millennia of existence. "I have a deal to offer you."

Do you remember? Enopac asked in AJ's head.

I do, AJ thought, and looked from Clover to Daed. "What kind of deal?"

"One that will benefit all of us," Sixxez began. "It will allow you two lovebirds to be together and live a long and meaningful life. It will allow me to rule the world."

"I'm not sure I follow," AJ said.

"Don't do it!" Clover shouted. "Kill him!" AJ ignored her for the first and last time in his life.

"Give me your soul, your life force, and I'll leave, I'll rip out my own Core in front of you if you want. Back to the Nexus for another hundred years. When I return, you two will be dead and gone, and even if you breed, your life force will not be passed on. The responsibility of your clan shall be lifted from your shoulders." Daed grinned.

AJ looked at Clover, back to Daed. "If I refuse?"

"I promise you she won't live to see the sun again, no matter what else happens."

AJ fell quiet, putting on his poker face and pretending to contemplate. The battle was finally over, except for the formalities.

"I'll do it," AJ said.

"NO!" Clover screamed. She slumped as much as her bindings would allow and cried.

A black, macabre joy leapt up inside Daed Sixxez at AJ's agreement. From far away, Jha'ask and Enopac watched, everything else in existence slowing to a stop, as though the two Entities had giant pause button, not just on AJ's world, but *all* worlds, on *all* planes of existence, causing a delay no one would ever notice.

It is almost time, Enopac said.

Sixxez pulled a long dagger from his side. "You'll have to cut yourself, offer it to me. I will drink your blood, and your soul will come with it."

AJ took a small step back as Daed's skin bulged in places. It was as if there were bugs and worms and everything nasty crawling around beneath the surface of His skin. His true form strained to be born into His kingdom.

AJ took the knife. "How much of a cut?"

"Just enough for it to bleed," Sixxez said, and AJ was revolted as he watched Him lick His lips, a long, forked tongue flicking in and out. AJ looked into the god's black, empty eyes, something terrible in them beginning to spin. AJ cut open his palm and held out his arm as his own softly glowing blood dripped onto the floor.

THE CIRCLE IS CLOSED! I'VE WON! I'VE FINALLY WON! Daed screamed in His head with a maniacal joy. Sixxez took hold of AJ's wrist, admiring the iridescent, red streams before plastering His mouth to AJ's palm, tasting the blood.

AJ felt cold and empty, little by little the otherworldly strength he'd been filled with drained away.

Daed also weakened, His god power being diluted with the blood of a mortal.

AJ stared into Daed's eyes, waiting, growing colder. He turned and looked at Clover, who stared through her tears.

"I love you," AJ said and tightened his grip on the knife he still held.

He looked back into Daed's eyes, watching as they flickered, watching them turn from the dead, empty black of all pain and all loss to the light gray color he saw in his own eyes every time he looked into the mirror. He knew his eyes would flicker the same way but, instead, gray to black.

Clover could feel the bonds of her throne loosen. She was able to move her wrists and kicked one of her legs free.

AJ plunged the knife into Daed Sixxez's stomach. Daed screamed, His mouth painted red with AJ's blood.

Both stared down at the wound in Daed's belly, watching a surge of green-black gore come splashing out. AJ had time to think he'd failed, the timing was off, and he'd waited too long or not long enough, when the sludge ran a little thinner, and a little redder.

Daed watched in horror, His hands going to His stomach and trying to hold it in, screaming, all the while screaming, until AJ shoved his hand into Daed Sixxez's mouth.

AJ grabbed a fistful of greasy, black hair and pulled Daed's head back, leaning over Him and shoving his hand in deeper.

Clover retched, having nothing in her stomach to vomit, when she realized she could see the shape of AJ's hand as it stretched out the strange flesh of Daed's throat. She watched as the fist-shape flexed and relaxed, then she turned to the left and retched again, coughing up a bitter stream of stomach bile.

As she leaned, her right arm pulled free of the restraint. Her chair shook, beginning to fall apart, and she tried to stand before she was dropped on her ass. She stumbled and fell over as it was, her legs half numb and tingling with pins and needles. She lay there and watched as AJ's arm disappeared into Daed's mouth at the elbow.

AJ clenched his teeth against the pain as Daed bit down like a rabid pit bull, breaking the skin of his biceps. In theory, he knew what he was looking for, he flexed his fingers out, and then he felt it: a hot, quivering sphere about the size of a baseball, right in the center of what was supposed to be Daed's chest, It was the center of a dying god, a dying god who hadn't known that to consume the life force of a mortal was to become *as* a mortal, and every mortal thing must pass.

Daed hadn't known because that knowledge was in the book.

* * *

Clover stumbled to her feet, looking down at the bricks of the floor. She hadn't realized until now that the throne that had effectively been her prison cell hadn't fallen apart because Daed was weakening, but rather, because He'd wanted it to move.

The gray matter had sifted itself across the floor of the tunnel, working its way around and over AJ's feet without him noticing. She saw what was going to happen and before she had a chance to so much as scream his name, the gray matter shot up in a spike, punching through AJ's body.

The tip entered him just beneath and to the left of his belly button, traveling straight up through him, through his insides, and punching out at the back of his neck, to the right of his spine. The spike kept growing, thickening at the base, pulling him upward as it went, his arm snaking out of Daed's mouth like the world's most disgusting circus trick in reverse.

When the spike stopped growing, his dangling sneakers looked to be about three-and-a-half feet from the floor. At the base, the spike was thick enough Clover didn't think she would have been able to wrap her hands all the way around it.

At the point where it entered AJ's stomach, the spike was maybe the diameter of her wrist, if not a little thinner. It came out the back of his neck no thicker than a pencil, tapering to a sharp and perfect point. His hand, though streaked red with blood and clots of green and black gore, was empty.

Her eyes were wide in her head and, for a moment, she could see everything, could see the way Daed was slowly getting Himself back under control, how His eyes flickered back to that empty, solid black. She could see the steady stream of blood as it ran out of the hole in AJ's belly, down the spike, pooling on the floor. Her heart pounded in her ears, could hear the fucking *blood in her own veins*, and then in her head, a small, still voice:

Help us, the voice said.

Jha'ask, she thought.

You can stop this, said a second.

Enopac.

Save it, save it all, said the first. *Take his burden.*

Still, she stood as though locked into place, her heart not breaking, but *fucking broken*, soul-sick, and in so much pain she couldn't even scream, the world growing to the roar of all the oceans in her ears, and she watched the wound in Daed's stomach slowly begin to knit itself back together, though He was still stunned and finishing whatever transformation He had been angling for.

The second small, still voice was back, the voice of Enopac, the voice of all the darkness in all creation, and it appealed to something else in her, something perhaps not as noble as what the first voice had asked, but all the more effective for that.

Vengeance.

That was all it said, a quick pulse almost like an electric current in her head and in her heart, there and gone, and she looked up at AJ, his eyes wide and glazed, his chin a mask of blood, and she knew that this, *this* was how she would see him from now on, for a while at least, and maybe forever.

She would see his fragile body punctured through like meat on a skewer, his soft, kind, gray eyes milky and dull, his face covered in his own blood. She would no longer think of the moment he stood in her doorway, smiling at her, about to bring her breakfast in bed when she first thought of him.

She bolted forward and picked the knife up off the blood-slicked cavern floor. She looked up before she used it and had just enough time to stare into His eyes. They flickered black, and she waited.

Black and gray and black.

And gray.

She slashed out with the knife, cutting His throat to the strange black bone of His spine, the blade actually chipping against it.

His eyes—still gray—widened, and his lips, once dead and black, were now flushed with color. With blood, AJ's blood. His lips smiled even as they blushed from gray to pink.

Then a second mouth, this one with no lips, opened across His throat, and blood-red blood—his blood, AJ's blood—sprayed out, splattering her face and neck and chest and arms.

Daed staggered back a step and, even as His dirty, clown-like, makeup-colored skin flushed toward something resembling human life, it paled, too. Not back toward what it had been before, but something wholly new and unthinkable for Him, towards the pale color of a mortal, bleeding to death.

She swung the knife again, this time in an upward arc, slamming it into Him beneath the sternum. With a grunt of effort, she dragged it straight up. The blade went straight through the quivering mass of His Core, even as it changed and veined itself into a heart, even as it grew aorta and pumped, the blade carved through it and out the back.

Clover stared at the gaping, melting mouth, into Daed's eyes. The green ooze flooded out over the blade and over Clover's fist, running to the ground steaming. Red blood, AJ's blood, also ran out onto the floor. The two vital fluids were immiscible, self-separating into little puddles here and there, smoking. Daed howled and Clover released the handle of the knife, stepping back.

Burden, the voice in her head told her.

Vengeance, said the other.

Still Daed screamed, His eyes had doubled in size, sclera running from the corners. The gray iris muddied out to black, and then the black iris bulged a little, then something on the surface of it burst. Two finger-thick, black worms crawled out of Daed's eyes and onto his cheeks, back in through the mouth hanging wide, the lips liquefying, melting, and running down His neck.

"Oh, fuck," Clover said, gagging, and staggered back a little more, but continued to stare as the pale skin vibrated and breathed, pores opening and closing, then staying open so she could see into Him. A screen door of rotten flesh that came apart, and it wasn't flesh but maggots, millions and millions of pale maggots that hugged themselves tightly together, knitting a barely passable hide.

That moment, the shock and sadness and flat-out fucking *horror* were crushed within her, dwarfed and shunted aside as though AJ had been nothing to her, meaningless next to the feeling of raw triumph she felt, of righteous *fucking* justice having been served.

In the days ahead she would have time to examine this moment, to study it and eat herself up with guilt over it but, right then, there was nothing but a kind of pure and unfiltered joy she had never even guessed attainable. The writhing husk dropped to the floor, squirming, and melting away with the rest of His body.

His insides were not muscle nor bone but worms, black worms of all sizes, and He was still screaming and staring through the holes His eye-worms had crawled from. The whole decaying form melted slowly, giving off a poisonous-smelling steam. The liquefied remains ate through the brick floor of the chamber.

A brilliant white light began from everywhere, and grew brighter, as though an externalization of the triumph she had felt surging through her.

As she watched the light grow and get brighter, a wind from another world blew back her hair and rippled her clothes, then it was bright, so bright the light drowned out everything else. There was nothing else, only the light mattered.

Then it was gone. Clover stood there, alone, and looked down where Daed had been. There was nothing except for a black scorch that shouldn't have been noticeable with all the other grime...but the grime was gone. There was a rough circle about ten feet in diameter, the center of it the scorch, and the floor there was immaculate, cleaner than it had been the day it had been laid.

Clover started to question but stopped. Who was she going to ask a question of? The voices in her head? She had felt them as a physical thing, a presence, but that presence was unequivocally gone, leaving her feeling husked out and alone in a completely new and different way.

Instead, she turned to AJ, laying on the floor, the gray matter having crumbled, with two more holes in him that he'd never been meant to have, lying in a pool of his own blood. She kissed him on the forehead and slowly sank from her knees to the floor, lying beside him and weeping.

The triumph was gone, the shock was gone, the existential abandonment she felt at the departure of the Entities that had briefly been in her head, all of it was gone. In place of those things was only grief, and grief, and grief.

* * *

Logan still sat against the wall beneath the manhole. His stab wound had stopped bleeding as his advanced body took over, working to heal itself. Then he heard the unmistakable echo of approaching footsteps. He stood and realized a change had taken place. One so gradual it had been overlooked. He felt different than he ever had before, as if some huge and nasty weight had been eased off his chest. Forever.

Logan peered down the tunnel, his supernatural eyesight picking out a lone figure, and something in him changed, that lightness once more became a weight, and he was filled with a new understanding.

"Clover!" he called.

There was no answer. She came closer, covered in drying blood, and though her face was streaked clean in places by tears, her eyes were hard and clear.

He stood, staring, not knowing what question to ask.

"I'm sorry," he said.

She took a long, shuddering breath. "You have to help me get his body out of there," she said. "I can't carry him."

CHAPTER
THIRTEEN

Three Weeks Later

Once more, Logan made slow, rumbling progress on his Harley, down that same road of busted pavement. When the road ended, he came once more to a blue mailbox on a large, iron post. Logan turned his bike to the right and crossed a cattle-guard and once more drove up to the neat little house.

He had not exactly been in high spirits the first time he'd made this journey, not with what had been coming. That mindset had been nothing compared to the black mood he was in, had been in since carrying AJ's body out of the sewer. He had no business feeling this way, according to Cain. They'd won, after all. Not the war, true, that was still coming, but this had been a major battle, and they'd come out victorious.

It shouldn't have happened that way, Logan thought as he had countless times in the last weeks, as he had told Cain over and over. *AJ shouldn't have died.*

It was always going to be the girl, Cain reminded him.

Logan pushed these thoughts from his head as he rounded the last bend, and the neat little house came into view,

Jin was already waiting for him on the porch. Logan turned his bike up the little path connecting the driveway to the front walk, pulling his bike up to the steps of the porch. He took from his pocket that same small, square parcel, once more wrapped in plain, brown paper. The retired detective reached out for it with a shaking hand, but then hugged it tightly to his chest once it was back in his possession.

"Mr. Perish," the retired detective said by way of a greeting, nodding.

"Keep your notes handy and sharpen your knives, Jin," Logan said. "Things are getting worse."

He twisted the throttle on the bike and left, the rear wheel digging a long, black stripe of exposed soil through the lushly green and well-kept lawn, the owner of the house staring after him, the parcel cradled in his hands.

* * *

Five Months Later

Clover stood in the bathroom, staring at herself, naked from the waist up. She looked at the bulge of her stomach that once had been a flat plane. Though this still amazed her, worried her, fascinated her, broke her heart, and filled it just the same, it was not, at this moment, *why* she looked in the mirror.

She stared at her naked left breast, trying to find any kind of discoloration of the skin or anomaly of the flesh. She raised her left arm and rested it across the top of her head, testing it for lumps with her right hand the way they'd been taught in high school. She found nothing; no redness or irritation of the skin, and certainly no lumps, but this did not bring the relief she had anticipated.

She closed her eyes and, like a flash from a strobe light, she saw that horrible, grinning face; the dirty-pale and psychotically gleeful visage of a crazed god. For a moment, she felt the path of his finger across her skin like a burning trail of slime, and then it came again. A deep throbbing ache inside her breast, building to an almost unbearable crescendo of pain.

She closed her eyes and bit her lip, grunting against the pain as it built and built, and then held…held…held longer than ever before. She gripped the edge of the sink to keep from falling, and then finally, *finally*, it broke, receding like the remnants of a wave sucked back into the ocean after crashing against the beach.

No, the current absence of a lump brought no relief, only the worry it was in there, quietly but quickly metastasizing—growing, ever-growing—until it would be too late to treat. She opened her eyes, staring into them through the mirror, chewing her lip and wiping away the sweat that popped up across her brow.

Outside, she heard the dog, a rescue Malamute she'd named Nikolai, as he barked.

She put her bra and shirt back on.

Maybe with that fucking book out of the house… Clover thought, trailing off. The dog barked louder.

She left the bathroom and headed toward her bedroom, pausing to straighten a framed picture John had given her from his time in Mexico after he had gotten out of the hospital. It had been the last time they'd spoken, and likely would be, John had said.

He'd said it sitting right there at the small apartment she used to live in, one of his large, blocky hands over hers. He said this was also why he had been the only one from the department at AJ's funeral, going to which, he told her, had cost him a recent promotion.

My name's been scrubbed from the case, he'd said to her, looking a little ill when he'd said it. *So's yours, and his. It's all been redacted.*

What are they saying happened?

The official story is some bullshit about meth addicts, witnesses, everything tied up with the three of you in WITSEC.

Three of us?

John had cleared his throat and straightened his tie and rubbed the back of his head and did everything but look right at her. *Soon to be family of three now in WITSEC.*

They had not only erased AJ's name from the case but had *also erased his death*. That visit had ended with her screaming at him. Classic bit of Messenger Killing, that had been. She didn't regret it, but she also hoped she would someday see John again.

Outside, she ambled over to the large, wrought-iron gate that fenced her two acres. With the help of a forged marriage certificate and some other pertinent legal documents in those first awful two days after AJ's death, also courtesy of John, or at least some people he knew, she'd inherited the assets of AJ's adoptive parents, as well as the trust his birth parents had set up for him. She couldn't bear to step foot inside AJ's childhood home, so she'd moved a little further south where the weather was better and there weren't so many memories.

"Ms. Danning?" the man on the other side of the fence finally spoke.

"It's Lancaster actually," Clover said, and hit the button to unlock the gate. The stranger swung it open and stepped into the yard.

"I take it you've been informed on why I'm here?"

"The Book."

"Yes. I'm a Dogmatic Investigator. My name is Cain Dulouz, and—"

"I'm not sure I want to know any of that," Clover said, quietly, while staring down at her feet.

"Well, in any case, I...*we* wanted to thank you."

"Thank me?" Clover said quietly.

"Yes," Cain said. "You did an extraordinary thing."

Clover saw the father of her unborn child lying on the ground with a hole punched through him every night in her dreams, sometimes over and over. She saw him coughing blood out through his grin, his mother's throat ripped out and all the world's dead standing up to come after her, his name called out over a dead tongue a thousand times.

But she was more than the sum of her nightmares, wasn't she?

Okay, yeah, she was a girl who had saved the world once upon a time, had taken up an ancient burden she hadn't entirely understood. Unknowingly, at the time, also placing that burden on her child. Clover wrapped one hand protectively around her stomach, the other holding an old leather bag out at arm's length as if it contained something vile and nasty.

She supposed maybe it did. She hefted its immense weight for a final time. She had read a lot of that book. The parts she was supposed to, anyway. Some pages were locked to her and were meant to be read by someone else. Now, she just wanted to be rid of it. Always had, in truth.

"There something in here for you, Mr. Dulouz?" Clover wondered aloud.

The Dogmatic Investigator snorted and took a pull off a tiny silver flask, which then disappeared back into his coat. He took the burden from her as though it were nothing, and she hated him a little for it. When he opened the bag, it was filled with a soft light, and the expression on his face was one of reverence. He took the book out and inspected it, then looked at her.

"No, not for me, I just need to hang on to it a while." Cain let a small grin slip out from under the shadow cast by the brim of his Sam Spade hat and held his hand out. Like magic, there was a business card in it.

"Why are you giving this to me?" Clover asked, studying the card.

"You've taken on this burden, Ms. Lancaster. You and I both have been cursed and blessed with the knowledge that things like these exist so, if you should notice anything...out of order, you'll know how to reach me." Cain turned to go, the book back in its bag and all of it tucked safely beneath his arm, when he stopped suddenly and faced her again. "By the way, I have a message from an associate of mine. I believe you've worked with him before."

"Who? Logan?" She hadn't heard from him since...

Cain nodded. "He sai—"

"I'm not getting involved," Clover said, a little louder than she intended.

Cain smiled a thin smile and looked at her. "He just wanted me to say hello, ma'am. You need to understand something, though. You've done a great service to the universe, no one would ever say any different. You're not the only one to do that, though. Another man I'm working with, his name is Harry—"

"I'm *not* getting involved!" Clover said.

"You're *already* involved," Cain snapped, narrowing his eyes a little. He then shook his head and took another drink from his flask. "*Your* battle is over, for now, and *your* enemy was vanquished, but there are *always more of them*. There's a little girl on the east coast, Nina's her name. Less than a year from now, she's... Look, when her time comes to step up, and step up again, and again, *she's going to do it*. Right now, she's only eleven years old. That's why I gave you that card."

"I'm *done*," Clover said.

"Bad things are happening," Cain said. "There's a war coming, and it's been coming for a long time. If you want there to be a world left for that little boy in your belly to live in, for *anyone* to live in, you may have to re-think that."

Clover's eyes stung with the tears about to start running down her cheek.

Cain held his hands up, palms out. "I didn't come here to upset you, but to thank you, and to warn you, and tell you we always need people like you."

"You can't have him!" She said, her hands now around her belly, around the little life in there, all she had left of AJ.

At her feet, Nikolai bared his teeth and growled, then barked at Cain, who was already nodding, the expression of a harried messenger tasked with delivering news he knows no one wanted to hear stamped across his face.

"Why me?" she asked without knowing she was going to. She stepped forward and grabbed the sleeve of his overcoat, looking into his flat, brown eyes.

"It was *always* going to be you," Cain said softly. "What's the saying your people here use? That particular star of yours has been in alignment a looong time. Just as long as AJ's was. I'm talking hundreds of years. *Generations.* Not to say it couldn't have happened another way, but this was *always* an option. You know that, right? Take comfort in the fact you never had a lot of choice in the matter once you set upon a certain path. If A then B then C. You felt it, didn't you? The night you met him."

"Felt what?" she asked, her voice a whisper because she knew.

"The Hand of Providence," Cain said, and her body broke out in goose flesh. "The feeling of not being *moved* exactly, but that everything, *every single thing* you were doing, was right. What you were *supposed* to be doing."

She swallowed hard and wiped at her eyes and nodded. It didn't make it easier. Nothing made anything any easier.

"I know," Cain said, nodding his head as though he had heard her thought. "I know this has been harder on you than I likely can imagine, and I'm sorry."

Clover started to cry, and Nikolai whined, looking up at her.

"You know what would have happened if you

hadn't picked up that knife, and I don't know if that's any comfort to you, what you stopped from happening, but it should be. Anyway, it was a pleasure to meet you. And you're right, get that checked."

She jumped a little, thinking of moments ago, staring at herself in the mirror, left arm up, and then draped sideways across her head.

"As soon as possible, get it checked. Please." Dulouz said, then tipped his hat to Clover and gave her another, "Ma'am," then turned and left.

She lingered, watching as the other man walked away, wiping a tear off her face with the heel of her palm. She could see the outline of a car through him, and a tree as well. She watched as Cain Dulouz walked away, growing transparent, disappearing before he'd reached the end of the long drive, and wondered if he had arrived the same way.

"They *can't* have you," Clover whispered, her hands once more wrapped around herself. She looked down at the curve of her belly as she spoke but couldn't have said if she was trying to reassure her baby, or herself.

Later that night, when she finally made it to bed, Nikolai asleep at her feet, she slept soundly and without dreams for the first time since that fateful night she'd walked into a gas station and, within the first five minutes, she had seen a dead body—though it was upright and walking at the time—and, also, she had fallen in love.

ACKNOWLEDGMENTS

First and foremost; A.M. Rycroft, who took a chance where no one else would, and for that I will be forever grateful.

Lily Luchesi, who did the final edits and stitched up a couple plot holes that had been hanging around for a decade or more. She gets all my references and calls me on all my bullshit, which is simply everything you could ever ask for in an editor.

Double-A, who read it first and helped me take a string of tropes and cliches held together by the unearned confidence of a first-time novelist and turn it into an actual book.

And Arran McNicol, my brother-man from a different motherland. Your friendship, patience, and keen eye helped me turn this from a book to a good book.

Again, all of you, thank you.

ABOUT THE
AUTHOR

Elias Anderson was born in the wastelands of south-eastern Montana in the late 70s before his family moved to Colorado, where they bounced around the state for the next 21 years. He relocated again to California, then Oregon, only to settle back in Denver with his wife, son, and daughter.

He has worked as a staff writer and reporter, food critic, copy writer, and editor. He has published books, poetry, articles, essays, and short stories in hard copy and web-based publications.

Have a question for Elias? Follow him on Goodreads at (www.goodreads.com/eliasanderson) and ask away!

STAY IN THE LOOP

Subscribe to the Epic Publishing mailing list to stay up to date on new releases, author interviews, giveaways, and more. Go to www.epic-publishing.com/subscribe to get started.